*Never, Ever Land*

# *Never, Ever Land*

## John Charles Lawrence

Copyright © 2011 by John Charles Lawrence.

Library of Congress Control Number: 2011909869
ISBN:         Hardcover      978-1-4628-8863-4
              Softcover       978-1-4628-8864-1
              Ebook           978-1-4628-8865-8

All rights reserved. No part of this book may be reproduced or transmitted in any form or by any means, electronic or mechanical, including photocopying, recording, or by any information storage and retrieval system, without permission in writing from the copyright owner.

This is a work of fiction. Names, characters, places and incidents either are the product of the author's imagination or are used fictitiously, and any resemblance to any actual persons, living or dead, events, or locales is entirely coincidental.

This book was printed in the United States of America.

**Acknowledgement:**
**John would like to thank his friend and artist Robert W. Stark III for sharing his painting titled *Pink Ladies* for this book cover.**

**To order additional copies of this book, contact:**
Xlibris Corporation
1-888-795-4274
www.Xlibris.com
Orders@Xlibris.com
100724

# Contents

| | |
|---|---|
| 1st Period Story Time | 13 |
| Skategoat | 22 |
| Hello, Mr. Chips | 28 |
| Impaired Faculties | 34 |
| Asset Management | 43 |
| That Thing | 47 |
| C'est la guerre | 52 |
| Now-or-Never Land | 63 |
| Miss Fortune | 69 |
| Fetish Ball | 74 |
| Water World | 77 |
| Manhattan is Burning | 85 |
| We Wear the Masque | 98 |
| Precarious | 101 |
| Precarious 2, the sequel | 103 |
| Seersuckers | 111 |
| East Egg, NY | 121 |
| Phobaphobia | 127 |
| The Keymaster | 129 |
| Links | 134 |
| As Little a Web as This | 137 |
| Sky | 142 |

| | |
|---|---|
| Hammer Time | 146 |
| Fuse | 157 |
| My Time of Day | 159 |
| ZZ | 164 |
| Pajama Game | 170 |
| April Fools | 176 |
| Brute Neighbors.edu | 183 |
| Extinguish | 190 |
| Mountains | 193 |
| The Rest is Silence | 202 |
| The Age of Consent | 207 |
| Writer | 210 |
| No Frigate Like a Book | 214 |

# Dedication

To My Dear Mother, Ruthie
Who taught me to walk, talk, read & write.
But not necessarily in that order.

## FACTS

Almost all descriptions of artwork, architecture, documents, historical figures, dreams, secret rituals and handshakes in this novel are generally accurate. Some of the names have been changed to avoid litigation.

The Sagamore Hill School was an independent, coeducational K-12 prep school in Oyster Bay, NY, one mile from Sagamore Hill, the Roosevelt's Oyster Bay estate, and fifteen miles from Manhattan.

On August 15, 1902, in the charter for The Sagamore Hill School, Archibald Bulloch Roosevelt, son of President Theodore Roosevelt, plagiarizing John Winthrop, wrote:

> **Go and build it. So we shall be as a city on a hill, the eyes of the people upon us. The only way to avoid shipwreck is to abridge ourselves of our superfluities. We must be knit together as one. We must delight in each other. We must rejoice together, mourn together, labor and suffer together. We must love one another, so that our seed shall live. But if our hearts turn away, if we are seduced and worship our pleasures and profits, if we deal falsely in this work we have undertaken, we shall be made a story.**

When we are green, still half-created, we believe that our dreams are rights, that the world is disposed to act in our best interests, and that falling and dying are for quitters. We live on the innocent and monstrous assurance that we alone, of all the people ever born, have a special arrangement whereby we will be allowed to stay green forever. That assurance burns very bright at certain moments.

~Tobias Wolfe—*This Boy's Life*

Just because you feel it doesn't mean it's there.

~Radiohead

# 1st PERIOD
# Story-time

Blah, blah, blah. My name is Benjamin Goodspeed, dammit! I am twenty-nine years old. I take drugs. I teach high school. I am unreliable. No, that is not some typographical error. I am truly not reliable. Do not tell me at some later date that I did not tell you that. I am putting it in writing. Should I sign it too? I encourage you not to rely on me. Yes, I am serious. Do not listen to a word I say. I cannot be trusted. I do not want to be trusted. I should not be trusted. Do not send your children to my school. The kids there smoke a lot of pot. More so than me even. The D.A.R.E counselors at school explained to us that marijuana is a gateway drug. I agree with them. Marijuana brought me here, to the North Shore of Long Island. To teach your children. To woo your women. To smoke your pipes and borrow your sport coats. Do not tell me at some later date that I did not tell you that. I did. I just did.

Since coming to Long Island, my name has become inextricably linked to the name Harvard. Don't think I haven't tried to extricate it. They won't let me. People can't talk about me without mentioning where I went to school. That name Harvard—or as I prefer "Hah-vahd" spoken like a boozy Kennedy—never fails to ruin a perfectly good conversation. There is no graceful way to say that word. No subtle way to slip it in. I simply avoid saying it. I haven't said it in years. If someone asks me where I went to school I say "Massachusetts" or "a small school in New England" or even just "East Coast." But that doesn't really work, people here want more details. They don't want to know everything about you, pretty much just where you went to college. (The mystique is a mistake, by the way. Hahvahd is just as dopey as the next college.)

"How are you" is not a question here, it is a statement you make with a zippy smile and several exclamation points. How are you!!! I'm well, how are you!!! No pause for an answer. In fact most people start walking faster when they say it as if things are so good and the fall breeze so-o bracing that it would be folly to come to a stop for a conversation. Yes, I have started using words like "folly" since moving here. That part is not so bad. It makes me laugh. I can say pretty much anything I want here—because I went to that school in Cambridge. Even stupid stuff like "crikey" and "sacre bleue" and "zoinks." I am considered witty. Students and parents laugh at almost everything I say. I approach a group of juniors and ask them to stop "lollygagging" in the hallway, and they all crack up. Even the ones who are not stoned laugh, not that there are any of those. I steal lines from "The Simpsons" and they act like I am Mark Twain. It's as if we are all part of some weird Dickensian prior existence. (That part I enjoy too.) Dickens is like an alternate reality. Dickens is like taking drugs. Do not take drugs and then read Dickens. Don't say I didn't warn you. Dickens is not the only one who is. Tolstoy is. And Dostoevsky. And Conrad. And Joyce. And Margaret Thatcher. (Sorry, just checking to see if you were paying attention.) Shakespeare is not like taking drugs; Shakespeare makes you want to take drugs.

I get to introduce children to each of those guys. I get to spend my days and weeks thinking about and talking about those guys. (We do not read books written by women; as I have told you, this is a place of old, old ways, older than you and me.) The school pays me money for this. (I spend the money on drugs.) I go weeks walking around thinking that I am, in fact, Henry David Thoreau, a sojourner in this civilized life. I subsist on beans and bread. But I do not count out the beans I eat; the school has people who do that for me. Baking bread becomes a ritual and eating a sacrament. I wander into a room filled with eleventh graders and announce, "Public opinion is a weak tyrant. Compared with our own private opinion." One girl nods her head in agreement and apologizes to me. The sea of C-minuses in the back of the room sit up straight; the girls daintily arrange their hands in their laps. That was not the reaction I was after. (Although the truth was that I, myself, didn't know what I was after.) Far be it from me to play the Puritan. Quickly I recover face by spreading my feet apart, taking two bow-legged steps into the room and drawing six-shooters from their holsters that I shoot into the sky Yosemite Sam-style, complete with sound effects. (I may also have Yosemite-Sammed, "What a ma-roon! What an Eskimo Pie head!") I retreat to the sound of laughter and a room full of 17-year-old boys playing with guns.

At a rainy soccer game when a gaggle of mothers gander our team's goalie, who had not faced a shot all day, doing somersaults and cartwheels while singing the theme song to "Fame," I say, "the mass of men lead lives of quiet desperation." They grin and peer up at me as if I just handed them a warm cup of cocoa. They lean the tiniest bit in my direction as if huddling around a heat source. While that was not my goal before then, it so often became my goal afterward. (These are the women I would come to call "the naughty mommies," but I am getting ahead of myself.)

I raid thrift shops and dress in musty, Jazz-era three-piece suits with oldfangled lapels and silk ties hand-painted with scenes from dog tracks and aviaries. I call people "old sport." But no one notices. They're too busy with their exclamation points. They don't even consider me eccentric. Why would anyone let me do that? I am not qualified to teach your children. I am a child myself for Christ's sake.

I live above the boathouse on the estate of Oliver Wendell Dalrymple, known to all by a variety of monikers—the Big Cheese, the Cheese Man, Mayor McCheese—which he earned during his ice hockey career at Williams College. He was a goaltender of limited excellence. With much glee, his wife, Jamie T. Dalrymple, likened his stature in goal to a slice of Swiss cheese. Having accumulated a net worth of two billion dollars since those days, most of his peers ceased using those names. Jamie T. never would. Having lived within eyeshot of his home for two weeks, I had heard the myths, but never met the man.

Jamie T. had her own fortune. She was known to me as "Brickhouse" due to her burlesque gardening and her . . . uh . . . physique. Of all of the stars in the North Shore sky, Brickhouse was, without any doubt, a lodestar.

We are not reading Dickens today; it is just the second day of school. So I take drugs before leaving the house. No, I am not going to tell you what I took, that would be untoward, unseemly. Let's see if you can guess what I took. Let's see if you can guess who we are reading today.

> In the kindling light of dawn, silent ghosts of grey flannel fog closed off Locust Valley from Long Island Sound and the whole rest of the world. Fog sat like a lid on the hills and made the valley a simmering pot. Leftover August heat shimmered over the water like jet fuel.
> 
> I woke to the sound of gunfire.
> 
> Amid waving cattails and sea-grass, Mayor McCheese waded stirrup-deep into the great wet barnyard of Long Island Sound. Another gunshot, along with a light breeze, eased him out of muddy fog into murky focus. He straddled a snuff-colored polo pony. He was bursting at every seam with importance. The snout of his rifle exhaled a thin, blue wisp of smoke.

An unsuccessful swat at a mosquito smudged his stubbled face with grease. A soggy cigar, which served as a type of ballast, disintegrated in his left hand. The shadow of a taller man wavered in the wrinkled sea. He looked the way I felt after another long night of insomnia. Behind him, along with his best days, perched a second rifle, a small transistor radio and a box of Cubans. Stuck between stations, the radio broadcasted rolling surf.

The rifles seemed out of place. Could he be hunting out of season and through this fog? Shooting skeet two hundred yards from where his children slept? Was he using a gun to fish? He stared out to sea at *something*. He made me feel a good deal sharper and more alert, but exactly what drove that diesel engine I did not know. I was too tired to know the truth.

[Cue the bass beat.]

At the other end of the property, the world was unzipping itself. Powder blue sunshine peaked through the bodice formed by two grand oak trees. Sprinklers whispered suggestively and sprayed the air with silver. Poolside, Brickhouse languidly unbuttoned and stripped off her blouse and slipped out of her shorts. Rising, she unveiled a petite, ember-red bikini embroidered with bumblebees. The careless tussle of Godiva chocolate hair, the Café au Lait tint of her naked arms and legs, the unsatisfied lips puckered into a whistle rendered me silent, cotton-mouthed, blinking into the sun.

Her face was lean, angular and handsome. From fifty paces I could see the prismatic surface of the swimming pool expressed in her eyes. Those great unblinking things. Eyes that were a kind of Freemasonry. I watched her thoughts floating next to mine. Discretely, with a classical grace, she reached behind herself, plucked the bottom of her suit from her heart-shaped derrière and snapped it back into its proper place.

This was how I spent my days here, stuck between the charming and the pitiable, the stylish and the sad, money and love. I felt as though I had set a telescope in the center of the room and looked first through the small end out one window and then through the large end in the other direction. Was I viewing my future and my past? The inevitable and the evitable? Were these the two roads that diverge in my yellow wood?

[Note to self: smoke less marijuana, starting tomorrow.]

Abort Fitzgerald impersonation. Repeat: abort. Or was that Steinbeck? I mix those two up. You might do better to wait until the day is over to write its history. Besides, it is one thing to see the Dalrymples in the distance and something else to have them close up against you.

From the top step of my boathouse bungalow, I could trace the shape of the main road to my school from a ribbon of dirt and dust that hovered above the trees in the wake of over-sized military-like vehicles underburdened by the frantic to-ing and fro-ing of haute housewives and their towheaded tots. You could also hear a rumble. I imagined the ribbon to be a trail of smoke rising from a track of fire or a lit fuse. I imagined myself to be the one who lit that fuse. Like a cartoon bloodhound I chased the path of its flame every morning.

From the sea to the school's doorstep was a cinematic land of grand and spacious lawns whose gates were kept ajar by hugely friendly trees and yawning wealth. Hawks cast lazy shadows over everything. Bees hummed, birds sang, wind sighed. From the sky all you could see were dense woods broken only by the occasional dirt road, graveled path, horse corral and burning garden. From the top floor of the school's main building, you could see the ocean. My students could pick out the masts of family schooners. Some could point to their estates.

This place was as much a work of fiction as any of the novels we dissect. I feel the need to tell you that. The stories I tell? They're fiction too. I longed to be in this place; I longed to be with these people. At twenty-nine you can still craft a fantasy from hallucination, misinterpretation and wishful thinking. Craft a fantasy and believe in it. Tales that begin tall become towering. Fibs, fuck-ups, even small fabrications lead to elaborate fictions, which spread and grow the way a virus spreads and grows. Lies, half-truths and critical omissions become the modus operandi of self preservation. I was no longer simply embellishing a tale in the telling the way a six-year-old does, but was manufacturing something whole. Then I did not know what was beginning and many of the emotions I did not know I possessed until I expressed them.

So I began to tell myself that none of this happened, that I had invented all of it. That this place even did not exist. That I had not, in fact, woke this morning, or last, and that my father and the others were not dead. My siblings and I were gripped by a force outside of ourselves. Grief scattered us. Please understand that I did not believe this fantasy. You must understand. I knew what I was doing: telling you a tale. I told you before not to trust me. I knew what I was doing. I was an inventor. I invented. I had to invent and use that invention to get hold of myself. In that way, it worked. I was able to create something my heart could desire.

Once I had established a fantasy about my father being alive, I was able to break it down and argue with myself, and then accept the fact that he was dead.

I must also state here that the faster things happened, the slower they happened, the passage and rhythm of time changed, and when I remember back to what happened then, each event is a frozen incident. In my recollection, there was a long interval between my first and my last days at The Sagamore Hill School. And in that time the dust cloud over the road seemed to hover indefinitely. Yet it could not have been more than a matter of months.

Just as surely as I chased that blazing fuse each day, each day I watched it writhe and snake and ravel itself right up to its climax on the front steps of the school into the spherical explosive dubbed *Headmaster*. With long, creaking, Italian leather feet and broad, flat hands as big and as hard as textbooks, he kaboomed greetings accompanied by withering handshakes, handshakes that said, "Today we run faster, we stretch our arms farther!!!" (Yes, he must be the author, the framer, the fondling father of this world of three exclamation points.) With the polished ease and arrogance of a pharaoh, he steered children toward the front door.

When I reached the school's front steps, my mind was static. My steps were the steps of a person at the bottom of the sea. The people around me moved like underwater swimmers.

Dr. Finn Fenstermacher was immense—tall, distant and grammatical.[1] While most middle-aged men gained weight resentfully, Finn gained every pound with pride, wearing it the way a general wears stars. His hair was a puff of white smoke. He smelled of Wintergreen Lifesavers and saddle soap. His complexion was cracked with purple capillaries. His eyes were the color of twelve-year-old Scotch. All at once I liked him. I would clench his hand

---

[1] **The kids called him "Fensterfucker." (In time I would too.) He was said to be inordinately fond of adolescent boys.**

with everything I had, and smile as jovially as I knew how. In Finn's universe, life is a zero sum game where *he* wins because *you* lose. End. Of. Story. "Suck it up" and "shake it off" were phrases he muttered under his breath constantly. Details were not his forté. He regarded the faculty with a mixture of curiosity and befuddlement; he was not of their ilk. He was indifferent to the day-to-day goings-on of the school. The only rules he adhered to—beyond the dictums of the King's English—were that groups of men or boys were to be referred to as "gentlemen" and individual males as "sir," similarly women and girls were referred to as "ladies," and individual females as "dear" or "ma'am" depending upon their age. (These phrases were also quite useful when you couldn't remember someone's name.) He was the court of first and last appeal here—the arbiter of all things—and he knew it. We saw him first thing every morning and then not again until the next morning.

As I climbed the steps I called out "Sir! Good morning!" My voice was too loud. I may have been shouting, although I could still only manage one exclamation point. The sun glinted off his bow tie. He glanced at the gold watch on the underside of his wrist.

"Well!!!" His voice was an ex cathedra basso, resonant and patriarchal. He could do a lot with one word. This one and the silence that lulled around it parannoyed me further.

He sported a bespoke blazer the color of a putting green. I joshed, "Hey, did you win the Masters?"

"Not yet," he replied looking past me while brushing his hand through that puff of white smoke as if he were trying to clear away a fog. He would have been better off carrying a net and holding a trident. Like all of the men in my life, he was not fond of dialogue.

**"Teenage girls are the canaries in the coalmine."**

~Antonya Nelson

"Mr. Goodspeed, look what happened to me during our soccer game yesterday," her voice had a trace of apology in it. It tapped the glass of the bell jar of sleep that had covered me seated comfortably in my classroom. Only nursing mothers, assassins and high school English teachers could sleep through the vaudeville that played before the curtain of each school day.

Thrust before me was a tender panorama of glowing, knee-socked flesh—a naked seaside of calf and thigh—an argyle tangle of thorns, balanced on my desk as if it were a ballet barre. Withholding one pleat of her micro mini, Palmer Jones flaunted the fresh wound at the peak of her thigh. I clutched behind the fig leaf of the morning roll.

"Chloë calls them 'strawberries,'" she continued, her voice as clear as dew.

This is the "Once upon a time" of the Sagamore Hill School story. What do you say to something like that? I would have introduced Palmer differently, maybe mentioned her eyes first—implying windows and souls—and probably would not have worked my way down to that other window. Not right away at least. At 8:00 a.m. Yet this is the initial state of your protagonist's . . . uh . . . affairs. (Boy, I wish I had a thesaurus; that's not the word I want.)

Palmer cast a curvaceous shadow. She had arrived unannounced as far too many of these otherwise polite people tend to do. A simple knock on the door would suffice.

Palmer was eighteen with the bobbed black hair, powder-pale skin and seemingly fairy tale, talk-to-the-animals good nature of Snow White. She even wore a red bow in her hair. And when she lingered in the hallway, freshmen gathered around her like dwarves. Snow White, however, was just her surface; her soul was more Harriet the Spy. She was always scribbling stealthily in her notepad and nodding her head knowingly, to whom I couldn't tell, about what I didn't know.

Palmer's bump-and-grind was just part of the morning song-and-dance.

In the backstage quiet of the hallway lingered the rows of gangly lockers and pigeon-grey boys, the petty kisses and stolen fights over what Heather said about Claire concerning a lie Christian told according to a note from Melissa1 to Melissa2 in Latin class, the sacred in-between, of yesterday and tomorrow, the first syllables of today, the he-saids and the she-saids, the "he likes her's" versus the "she likes him's," the hook ups and break ups, Likes and Loves, the Pretty People and the Satanists, the Eew's and Ahh's, the OMG's, the skirted and the neck-tied, the Et Ceteras and the Ellipses, stars forming, stars fizzling out, the improv-ed and the scripted, falsehood and facsimile, story-tellers, plagiarists, pranksters and propagandists, cramming, copying, caffeining, vaudevillians, well-lighted fools, walking shadows, a petty pace. The warble of a clarinet, the rat-a-tat of a drum, a sophomore stage-whispering, "Commence!"

"Coach Fink calls them strawberries," Palmer echoed herself as if Chloë's word didn't possess enough authority.

I was familiar with strawberries.

"Every silver lining has a dark cloud," I mumbled, keeping my eyes above her waist.

Palmer tittered while biting her lower lip. Her lips were berry-bright and swollen from constant biting. She jangled her bracelet, which was charmed with soccer balls and martini glasses. She smelled like silver. Tiffany silver.

"I swear, Mr. Goodspeed, where do you come up with these *sayings*?" (I had said "pointless suffering is pointless" last week. This was not particle physics.) I hazarded another look south. She continued to expose herself. That was an awfully long leg.

"It's a gift, I guess," I shrugged.

"Like, *totally*." She shared one sparkle of her smile. I resisted it.

Palmer's face, like all beautiful faces, tricked you into thinking she was other than what she was, somehow smarter, more interesting, kinder, better in every way. Instinctively Palmer knew this, and she wielded her misbegotten power like a pimp. Her smile was her own work of fiction that she shared with all of the boys and each, in turn, confused it with affection. Each felt that he was its lone source, he the author of her smile's candy luster. In that way Palmer played the role of a Siren singing an entire school to shipwreck.

I couldn't think of anything to say. I smiled, all lips, no teeth. The light kaleidoscoped over her shoulder. A nausea of color.

"It still *burns*," she trilled fingering her strawberry thigh.

Like, totally.

While I did see red, I was no longer looking in her direction. Turning away I saw myself in the mirror the sun had made of the window. The outside of me provided so little information about the inside. I saw a moody young man in a hand-me-down coat and tie, legs crossed, sitting in profile. I made a church steeple with my fingers and contemplated it. I straightened my tie. Thin bare shoulders appeared behind me. Already I longed for the end of the day.

The morning bell was as subtle as a car alarm. And everyone ignored it as they would a car alarm.

"We creamed those dykes from Brearley," Palmer continued.

It was way too early for me to be teacher-ly, but I was grateful for the opportunity to change the subject.

"Palmer, please, the customary term is *lesbians*. You creamed the lesbians from Brearley. Only dykes can use the term dykes."

She didn't even smile. She blushed all the way down to the pink bow on her silk cami.

The bell rang again. Palmer dissolved out of focus.

# Skategoat

I hail from Hackensack, New Jersey, AKA: Hackysack. (We were a leather footbag whose very purpose was to be kicked around.) Hackysack is like looking in a mirror, like hearing my voice on a tape recorder; it didn't make me happy, but that's the way it was.

Only for Frick, my five-year-old nephew, would I leave the land of a thousand colors to return to the blues and grays of Hackysack. Through greasy rain on a gritty night I navigated over bridges and through tunnels to get to him. I paid tolls; I waited in line. I utilized cars, trains, busses and taxis. My past is as streaky and smeared as the windows. For the last hour the windshield alternately fogged, wiped clean and smeared again to a 2-4-2 beat.

In the sepia light of dusk, the wind sang spiteful songs through chain-link fences; it stripped off the few leaves that hid one yard from another. The cold drew houses closer together. Power lines flew in lazy arcs. Black birds scribbled in the sky. The whole town, no longer softened by greenery, seemed shrunken and pinched. My gloom would deepen the closer I got, would grow until it matched that of my childhood home.

The house was as insubstantial as a shadow, the shape and color of despair. A ramshackle porch ran along its width, propping up the roof with a series of raw four-by-fours. The windows were glowing blue squares, one for every working television. Our gardens grew cement; the yard was balding, the trees had scurvy. Everything worth stealing had been stolen. In the course of a decade away from here, I had entertained many delusions about who I was and where I came from, but here was the bare stalk of it.

Just then a valium I had taken an hour earlier bloomed like a little yellow crocus through the snow of my mind. A silly crocus, tricked into arriving before springtime. I vowed to go in cheerfully and chat openly with everyone about everything. Trips home don't have to be such a big deal. We can agree to agree. We can face the future together.

I spied blue camouflage pajamas seated by a window when I pulled into the driveway. When Frick saw me, he dashed out of sight. I paused to pay the taxi driver and prepare myself.

Wearing rubber galoshes that swallowed his legs to the knees—he would have been better off trying to sprint in snowshoes—Frick bolted out the door with gun held high. His hair shined silver in the streetlight. He exaggerated the look of a sniper poking his head out of a bank.

"You'll never take me out alive!" he cried.

As always, I was packing a loaded index finger and prepared to bust some caps. Also as per usual, Frick had left himself exposed, out in the open, with no one covering him. A rookie mistake. I used the passenger-side door as a shield and rose quickly to pop him once in the right thigh. I wasn't trying to kill him; I just wanted to bring him down. Teach him a lesson. He fell in a heap, but recovered enough to drag himself behind a brick light post, his right leg stiff at his side, his right hand covering the bullet hole.

Standing upright, I shouted at Frick from behind the cover of the car door. "How many times have I told you not to come out in the open without somebody covering you?" (We had spent hours discussing the finer points of bank robbery.)

"Don't try that reverse psychiatry on me," Frick shouted back. When he spoke excitedly about anything, his eyes—brown, watery, sleepy under long lashes—would lighten and darken, alternating between the color of chocolate milk and milk chocolate.

That broke my concentration. I stepped out from behind the door, still shouting, "No really, Frick, *how many times*? Get Grammy to cover you if you have to."

"Whatever! Come and get me, copper," Frick called out. He maintained a devilish grin and sudden laugh. His grin didn't imply that he might be up to something; it stated very frankly that he was always up to something.

"No, time out."

"Time out? Babytalk, babytalk, it's a wonder you can walk."

"Stop. I'm not going to shoot you again."

"Don't make me your skategoat."

"I'm serious, Frick."

"Suit yourself."

Frick rolled out from cover onto his stomach, held his right hand high with his left and squeezed off one round into the center of my chest, while growling, "Eat Kevlar-piercing lead, punk!"

What the . . . ? The bullet left me peg-legged, staggering, gasping for breath, clutching at my chest, crashing to the ground.

Rubber tires crunched through gravel as the taxi retreated. Frick waited until my pants were good and soaked before he stepped out to check the pulse in my neck. When his search for vital signs was suitably unsuccessful, Frick spiked his gloves to the ground and started singing, "For he's a jolly good fellow. For he's a jolly good fellow . . ."

He was not referring to me. I walked away, unimpressed. Who taught him that Kevlar-piercing bullshit?

Standing barefoot in the doorway, in a tattered nightgown, open at the neck, stood Frick's mother, my sister Mary Elizabeth (not to be confused with my sisters Mary Ellen or Mary Margaret). The screen door gave the metal door frame three quick smacks. A heavy raft of clouds crossed her face.

My sister was a Russian novel that nobody wanted to read.

"Did you just shoot my fucking five-year-old?"

We weren't big on greetings. Her arms were crossed; this was a rhetorical question. Frick's mother cursed fluently like a bitter, middle-aged divorced woman with three kids, which she was. But, still, she wouldn't let a sentence pass without adding shit, fuck, asshole, . . . *something*. Jesus Christ, it was fucking annoying.

"No, *he* shot *me*."

"Two wrongs don't make a fuckin' right."

"Huh?"

"You know a child is killed by an asshole with a handgun once every seven minutes in the United States."

"Thank you, Oprah."

"Let's see if I have this straight. Frick is a fuckin' bank robber who has to shoot his way out of the bank. And you're the rogue police officer?"

"You can be the bank robber next time if you like."

"Why not let Frick be the fuckin' cop?"

"This is your solution?" You can never guess the qualities loss will bring out in a person. A line appeared between her eyebrows like an exclamation point.

Through a frosted window I could see Frick commando-crawling across the driveway to the front door. His right arm had somehow become incapacitated along with his right leg. Experience told me talk was not going to change her.

"Two reasons Frick can't be the cop. One, that would mean I have to shoot my way into the bank, which makes no sense, and two, if you play the game right, the odds are stacked in the bank robber's favor. Frick knows this; he just gets excited and fucks up." (Hell, everyone swore more often in this house.)

"Oh-h gre-eat. And this is what you're teaching him?"

"There is not a single note of gratitude in your voice." I seemed to have forgotten all of the reasonable responses to this.

"Why can't you teach him something useful, like chess?"

"Chess is corny," Frick snorted, inside now, steam rising off of him. I held my hands in the air, palms out to make sure Elizabeth knew *I did not tell him to say that*. (I am always speaking in italics when she is around.)

"Besides, there are no good sound effects for chess," Frick shrugged. I couldn't stifle a smile.

When Frick ran down the hall to the bathroom, Elizabeth said to me, "This isn't funny. He *needs* you."

"No, *I* need *him*."

"How many times do I have to tell you . . . ?" Silence was a trait inconsistent with her general nature. What she is about to tell me for the fiftieth time I intuited years ago.

On a masculinity scale of one to ten with Arnold Schwarzenegger as Conan the Barbarian at 10 and Pee Wee Herman at 1, Frick's father stood firmly at 2, right next to Alan Alda. His worst habit was bad luck. Referring to me as either "Harvard boy" or "Junior" did not help his case.

So it was left to me, with my toker's cough, $120,000 of debt and general unemployability, to be his next best male role model.

Elizabeth was a CPA, and she studied us accordingly. She knew all of our assets and liabilities. She kept them on a spreadsheet in her head. She was constantly cataloguing them and offering unwelcome quarterly reports, reports that were filled with equal parts wishful thinking and scorn. Among other things she was: handicapped by a trusting disposition, reliably fanatical on most any subject and very much interested in material things, in purchasing whatever was expensive and ugly. All of my previous encounters with her left me with no desire for more. I felt I had erected a clearly defined spite fence between us ages before; it was just like her to ignore it.

Then, there was the matter of brain chemistry. To say my sister was bi-polar was an understatement. She was tri-polar. Or multi-polar. Or just polar. Really, I couldn't even visit all of her poles, although some were part of mandatory family excursions. I preferred the term "manic" anyway; it's closer to "maniac." The image of her scantily dressed and muttering to herself haunted us, haunted every single one of us. Her oeuvre of poles defined us. They were the leitmotif in home movies. At family gatherings my siblings studied one another trying to decipher who else in this genetic game of Russian roulette had a bullet destined for their chamber?

> **"Once we've seen it, then we can never unsee it."**
> ~Meg Wolitzer

The first day the Port Authority officially declared my father "missing," we gathered at our home in Hackysack. Frick spent the entire day repeating one phrase. I bumped into him in the hallway and he called out, "No way, Jose" before changing directions and ducking into his room. His tone left no room for discussion. Later in the day his mother asked him, "Would you like some lunch, Frick?"

"No way, Jose."

"Do you want to come to the store with us?"

"No way, Jose."

"Frick, it's time for bed."

"No way, Jose."

"Lights out, Frick."

"No way, Jose."

The second day he had less fight in him, so I think he just repeated the first phrase that came to him.

"Frick, would you like a snack?"

"Sticky buns."

"Frick, would you like to play Monopoly?"

"Sticky buns."

"It's 5:00; you need to change out of your pajamas."

"Sticky buns."

I couldn't have said it better myself. On the third day, when there was no hope left for survivors, Frick lost the power of speech altogether. With blue moons under his eyes, he wandered the halls of my father's house, dragging a three-foot-tall, rubber Godzilla by the tail. Whenever the monster's feet hit the ground, it made a loud stomping noise, akin to the sound of Godzilla trampling through Tokyo. When Frick twisted the tail by banging it against a door or wall, Godzilla let out a tremendous roar, sparks fired from its maw, his eyes burned red, and smoke flared from his nostrils.

Between meals we retreated to our respective bedrooms to watch our private televisions and doze. Throughout the day, a ten-ton mythical creature roamed the halls overpowering everything in its path. The noise was loud enough to keep you awake, but not loud enough to make you ask him to stop.

Stomp!

Stomp!

"Roar!" Sparks. Fire. Smoke.

Stomp!

Stomp!

"Roar!" Sparks. Fire. Smoke.

Godzilla roared all day long. And he left buildings toppled, people trampled, Tokyo decimated and fuming with black smoke. And it felt about right.

# Hello, Mr. Chips

She wore lambskin jodhpurs, knee-high black leather riding boots and carried a horsewhip. She balanced on her toes at her locker, clicking her heels together. The doorway of my classroom provided a picture frame as she kicked out of her boots, stepped into her skirt, wriggled it into place and peeled her pants down and off.

Just like that, like a warm breath on cold eyeglasses, she blew into my life.

She stepped out of the frame.

A pause.

A white blouse appeared on two fingers as if it were a laboratory specimen and then fell to the floor. A bouquet of red roses and a gold trophy landed next to the blouse. The trophy struck the metal locker door, which rang like a concierge's bell. One crystalline chime. Perfectly pitched. Fading off in ripples.

I removed my Clark Kent's and polished them with my shirt-tail. I did my best to look like Mr. Chips.

She was the thirteen-year-old girl wonder of the Twelfth Grade and the daughter of the eight-fingered Woodshop teacher, he the school's foremost authority on "jury duty" and napping.

Our eyes met, mouths broke into smiles. She strode toward me as if we were old friends.

"Oh . . ." She went, "you're Benjamin Goodspeed. I've heard a lot about you." So I go, "You're Wendy Love. Don't believe everything you hear." And she was like, "I'm in your English class." Then I was all, "As I hear things, you *are* my English class." And she was all, "Don't believe everything you hear." So I said, "It comes in handy around here doesn't it. i.e., English. The language." And she said, "To wit: Quite." Her voice was shivery. She tucked her hair behind her ears. I could feel her breath on my shoulder.

She was a pixie stik. One sock on, one sock off. She looked like she could fit anywhere, slip through narrow spaces, hide easily. Her clothing was similarly slight.

"So, a quick flogging before practice?" I said nodding at the switch now clutched officiously in her fist which punched her hip. She smiled, one ladylike arm reaching behind her back to hold the wrist of the other, legs crossed at her ankles. I watched the sun cast a wavering square of light around the black silhouette of a ballerina onto the chalkboard.

A ballerina with a whip in her hand.

"Thursdays are my only days for riding, what with high school, college, soccer and all," She had thin, almost translucent skin, like the flesh of a flower. Her backpack was a stuffed panda bear whose arms and legs wrapped her in a hug. She balanced on her toes as she spoke to me, aspiring to my height.

"College?"

"I take English, History, Spanish and Latin with the Twelfth Grade, Vector Mechanics and Matrix Algebra at the university down the road."

I produced a faux yawn and stretch. "What, no string theory?"

She gave me a steady, blasé look. I could hear ping-pong balls bouncing in another room. Little stars twinkled inside the darkness of her pupils. She made a little cross with her fingers, which referred either to me or string theory.

She smelled like cinnamon. Cinnamon dusting a soft cloud of cream in a cup of cappuccino. I stood for a moment feeling the pink-eyed, unshaven air around me and dreaming of the joint I would smoke during my walk through the woods to soccer practice. (The secret to getting high at school was establishing myself as a smoker who rolled his own cigarettes.)

Now might be a good time to discuss boundaries, but, as I said I have soccer practice, then student council . . . then papers to grade, always papers to grade.

> **"We'd rather have the iceberg than the ship."**
> ~Elizabeth Bishop

She bared both feet with two quick hops to the right. This left her slightly winded, shirt un-tucked.

"It's Love, by the way."

I leaned closer to her. "Excuse me?"

"It's Love."

"What is?"

"Me. I am. Or it is. My name. I mean, it's what they call me. Love. Nobody calls me Wendy."

The stories I'd heard came back to me. The kindest said of her, "she ought to be painted." The less kind said other things.

In the fluorescence of the classroom, which rendered most grotesque, Love was a DaVinci sketch, all sinew and symmetry. Every line a curve. Even dry clothes sticking to her like wet paint.

The windows framed a dozen foamy shaving cream clouds. The curtains whipped and snapped in the breeze.

"Do you mind if I ask, Mr. Goodspeed? Where did you come from?"

"You mean like birds and bees where did I come from?"

"Uh, no. I'm thirteen, not retarded."

"Right, sorry." I offered her an apple from my desk. She looked at it inquisitively. "Too cliché?"

She nodded affirmation.

"I'm from New Jersey." I said, which made her wince.

"Well then, my condolences. You're the first person I have met from there." She lied politely. "They call subs 'hoagies' in Hoboken. I read that somewhere."

"Subs?"

"Sandwiches. We call them 'wedges.'"

"Wedges are a type of shoe."

"I bet you listen to Bruce Springsteen?"

"Not if I can help it."

"My dad says that Bruce Springsteen is under-rated because Bob Dylan is over-rated."

"Can't they both be over-rated?"

"I know, and can a guy called 'the boss' even be *under-rated*?"

"Not in Jersey."

"See!"

"See what?"

"GMTA."

"?"

"Great minds think alike. You can't underrate someone you also refer to as the boss."

"Oh, right, got it, *boss*."

"Do you ever feel like you were born in the wrong place?"

"Daily."

"I feel like I was born in the wrong era, at the wrong time."

"Sometimes I think I was born into the wrong species."

"Or the wrong family." Her left hip was slung out with her copy of *The Scarlet Letter* balanced on it as if it were a child.

"You know, if you had been born in 1640, you would have been burned at the stake." The instant I said it, I wished I hadn't.

She hesitated and squinted one eye as she looked at me as if she were taking aim or holding back a tear. Finally she shot back, "But of course, seems like a better way to go." Her words came out in wispy clouds.

"Not for me," I responded while bent over my duffel bag, rummaging, "I can't stand smoke."

"Who can, really?"

"Yeah, I guess you're right." I said out of the side of my mouth, feeling chastened, as the other side of my mouth puckered around a previously-rolled cigarette, which was 50 percent Humboldt County's finest. Looking crossed-eye at it, "Sorry, doctor's orders."

"As if," she mimicked out of the corner of her mouth while gnawing reflectively on a cuticle.

Shaking out a match, I let one stream of smoke curl out of my mouth and rasped, "Nail biting is a bad habit."

"Oh really."

Love's world was not so different from mine. Her world was "The Island," part Dr Moreau, part *Lord of the Flies*. AKA: the valley of ashes, a Lilliput between the white palaces of the North Shore and the clapboard cottages of the South. Towns called Hicksville, Plainview, Mutton and Weed. Glittery girls with angry fumes of hair, and confusing, asymmetric clothing. The Jordache look. Glossy boys with whiny Honda Civic mutations, which they nicknamed in chrome script on dramatically tinted windshields ("Ice, Ice Babie," "Desperado"). For them, Walt Whitman was a shopping mall, Fitzgerald a name they couldn't place. The Island was "almost." The Island was "coulda." The Island was Betamax. Eight-tracks. K-cars. Food processors. Aluminum siding. Paved front yards. Cinder blocks. A rusted map of the past. Rust-colored. Rust-flavored. All directions were given in reference to the train station or the prison. While the North Shore of Long Island suffered from abnormally high self esteem, The Island had no esteem of any kind.

"Have you ever been deeply in love?" She inquired, apropos of nothing, but showing painstaking interest.

I sneezed at this. The voice in her eyes was deep and throaty.

I thought I heard an alarm bell ring.

"With a person?" My cigarette bobbed on my lip with the pronunciation of each syllable.

She squinted at me and puckered her lips. Waiting. "Does chocolate count? . . . Dogs? . . . Movie stars? . . . Sleep?" She refused to yield even a slight smile. She closed her right eye as she continued to squint, as if she were peering through a loupe; she was appraising me. (Does she know that her bulb is brighter than mine?) (When I was 13, I was 13, humping furniture and whatnot.)

She made me afraid of being clumsy or dull. I was actually worried about getting this question wrong. What do I possibly say to this?

The alarm continued to sound.

"Uh, Mr. Goodspeed, it is customary to evacuate the building when the fire alarm goes off."

I heard it clearly now, the fire alarm. Floodlights strobed the hallway. The alarm sounded more like an air raid siren.

"Fire drill, schmire drill," I said feeling my face flush. I opened the window to the fire escape. "Short cut, more doctor's orders."

"Yippee!" Love sang, clapping her palms with fingers splayed.

Green forests rolled in dyslexic waves from the school to the shore a mile away. Teddy Roosevelt once gazed out on these wooded slopes in his mornings on horseback. The Sagamore Hill School comprised a Romanesque, limestone and mortar manor complete with a moat. It looked like the kind of castle found only in storybooks. The castle served as the Upper School; servants quarters served as the Lower School. Pastures acted as playing fields, carved out of the trees a half mile from the main building. The school was founded by people with biblical names and prehistoric wealth. This was Archie Roosevelt's city on a hill.

Students and teachers were grazing in the fields and parking lots. (How long had they been out here?) I was them too, looking up and wondering. The fire marshals' police scanners and walkie-talkies crackled with coded messages. The fire alarm faded in the wind as we descended the black wrought iron staircase. Cooks, dishwashers, kitchen help, janitors, business managers, mistresses, trophy wives, spouses, infants, secretaries, helicopter parents, librarians, P.E. teachers, visitors, the kindergarten hamsters—*every body* fled the building.

Love puckered her lips, turned an invisible key and then threw it over her shoulder. This was not a drill.

# Impaired Faculties

Pussy was the first parent I met. That's what she said, unsolicited, I kid you not, "I'm Pussy Señor. My daughter Fern is in your English class."

So I said, "Nice to meet you, Mrs. Señor . . ."

And she said, "*Please, call me Pussy.*"

I tried again. "Right, o-kay."

"*Pussy,*" she replied.

Ri-i-ight. O-kaaay. No, I won't be calling you—or anyone else for that matter—Pussy. Not in public anyway.

"Fern is a great girl," I volunteered. At that point I'd experienced one half-day of classes. I had no idea who Fern was.

"*Pussy, please.*" You don't hear that often. And you seldom hear a woman italicize those words. I resigned myself to avoiding sentences that required any form of direct address.

Exactly two hours later, I sat shotgun as Pussy auto-piloted a McLaren convertible, her "station car,"[2] the color of a cloudless sky. The top down; the windows up. The trees were black; the sky was violet. Scenery scrolled by the windows. The streets were lined with yellow sequins. We were doing fifty; it felt like eighty. She was driving me home after cocktails at the headmaster's house.

Mrs. Robin "Pussy" Señor is fire. The flame of her red locks blazed around her face like the corona of a sun. Her body was as taut as a wooden match stick.[3] Her tongue was pierced with a diamond stud that flashed and flickered as she spoke to me. Both Pussy and Brickhouse officered the school's board of directors. Both frequented Knickerbocker

---

[2] For most a station car was a junker you were not afraid to leave overnight at the Long Island Railroad station. The Dalrymple's, for example, used a 1973 Ford Country Squire station wagon, which had snow tires permanently stuck on the rear wheels that caused it to make a high pitched whistling sound on dry pavement.

[3] And, yes, needless to say, she was lit.

and The Breakers, each a lifelong member. Both wintered at Chamonix and summered in Corsica, weekended in Alta or Nantucket. The similarities ended there; the rivalry didn't.

Brickhouse's money was old; Pussy's was ancient. Except for a season of belly-dancing in Istanbul where she met her husband, Pussy had never punched a clock. (Which, of course, was also the reason she could go by a name like Pussy.) Her husband, the managing partner of UBS Maximus Warburg, was a fish out of North Shore water. Brown skinned and severe, his country of origin earned him the nickname "the Domini-king." It also earned her permanent banishment from the Macy's half of her family. Students noted that the Domini-king's accent turned certain words into other words, beach into bitch for instance, as in "we vacationed in West Palm Bitch" or "let's go to the bitch."

The Señors were just splashing around in money. Their home was the size of a medieval castle. It was surrounded by unfriendly lions and marbled dogs. Twenty or thirty times a summer it was mistaken for a resort hotel (hence the dogs). Their other child, a son named Gunner, was shipped off to boarding school after he tattooed a giant barcode in the middle of his forehead to protest the school's use of bar-coded i.d. cards, which mistakenly didn't include names.

"It matches the one in my belly," she said as I strained to remember *anything* else about her.

"What matches what?" I was still thinking about the Domini-king.

"The diamond on my tongue matches the one on my belly button." She arched her back and took her eyes off the road to reveal her rippling, suntanned, Pilateed abs with a barely perceptible trail of flaming red fuzz disappearing into jeans slung low on her hips. (!!!)

"Right. Got it. Please be careful." My voice raised an octave as I reached for the steering wheel. Her half-clothed body swayed as I steered us off the sandy shoulder of Cove Road, the aroma of salt water and motor oil fresh in the air. (Thinking too late that this would be a glamorous way to die. If nothing else, I would get my name in the paper.)

> **"Every great love was in some way a terrible mistake."**
> **~ Michael Chabon**

I had positioned myself eye-level with her navel for most of the party; it sparkled every time she rolled her hips. Unbuttoned and bra-less in three-inch heels, Pussy's curves were as subtle as the roll of surf in the Sound. Her voice was a gravel path to that pebbly shore. All the other women at the party wore modest pastel shifts and chic, but sensible shoes. (In

Long Island we have this stuff New York City doesn't have. It's called grass. It's green, and it's everywhere. It makes stilettos impractical.)

    The headmaster's ocean-view veranda was lit only by the tiny yellow lanterns of fireflies. The trees added shade to shadow. The first fall leaves—tear-shaped, still green—spun languorous pirouettes in plush darkness. I wore a brown, popcorn tweed, three-piece suit with a tie depicting the Treaty of Versailles. New names and faces fluttered around me like moths trying to thwack their way into the bare light bulb of my mind. Long Island in September smelled sweet and old.

    This was not the orange cheese-cube and Triscuit mixer to which I was accustomed. There were no beer cans, no red plastic cups, no rhythmic chanting of any sort. Drinks flowed in brightly colored waves of singing crystal.

    Food was addressed impressionistically. An olive viewed through a haze of gin and vermouth. Crescent moons of green fruit. Schmears of grape, orange and apricot in the dying light of a clear twilight sky.

    Surrealism was reserved for conversation. The three chain-smoking, hard-bitten, spackled-with-makeup, South Shore, female members of the Foreign Language Department offered weary expert opinions on oral intercourse. Male faculty discussed their plans for the Powerball Lottery jackpot. They were all shaped like ampersands.

    Finn grabbed me by the shoulders and said in Finn fashion, "It's a C+ world out there, Goodspeed. It's a C+ world. What are you going to do about it?" I did not have an answer. He did not wait for an answer. The men, who were not on staff, talked in low tones, smiled but didn't laugh and mingled reluctantly, their hands gaudy with cocktails. The women flitted like birds of fine feather from branch to branch and flower to flower. They too spoke epigrammatically.

    "Computers. That's all the school should teach. Computers. The world is run by computers, and right now mine is a very expensive typewriter."

    "Mine is a fish tank."

    "Mine is a lifesaver. My husband doesn't leave his *Playboys* everywhere anymore."

    "Computers are old economy. In another year keyboards will be obsolete."

    "As will parents."

    "And clothing, if my daughters are any indication."

    "For $28,000 a year, my son should be given straight A's."

    "And a backrub."

"I had a dream last night that carbs were these furry, potato-shaped monsters that I couldn't get away from. The little buggers were everywhere."

"I fear television more than terrorists."

Pussy skidded to a stop directly below the Dalrymple's master suite. Her tires kicked up a cumulus cloud of dust. The car jerked forward when she let out the clutch, almost heaving us into Brickhouse's beloved hydrangeas. The drive suddenly felt like a date. Do we hug? Kiss on the cheek? Handshake? Think, Fonzie, think. Body language. What is she telling me?

She stretched her arms above her head. Two tiny lights twinkled inside her silhouette, one between her lips and one between her hips. My hand groped buff, Corinthian leather in a desperate search for the door handle. My mind was a rainy windshield with "intermittent" wipers.

Pussy swiped her hand through the silence by asking, "How are you with buttons?"

Buttons? Oh, Mrs. Robinson, you *are* trying to seduce me. Please keep your voice down. Brickhouse may hear you.

"I'm not opposed to them. I mean philosophically speaking. Although zippers are okay too." My voice quivered. Like, duh. Think: suave. Think: Gregory Peck.

A silence happened. The night filled with crickets. I swear I heard a clock ticking.

"I mean buttons, like, as in gadgets, doodads, e-lec-tronics." She checked her teeth in the mirror.

Ohhh . . . *buttons*.

"My husband simply can't get this to work." She held a fire engine red cellphone in the air. "Why don't you try it?" She tossed it to me. Pussy's would be my first (cellphone, that is).

"Sure, I'll give it a shot." What exactly does she want done with it?

"Super, 'preciate it. Toodles!!!"

Her tires left tracks as she peeled away, spewing pebbles all over my recently shined, thrift shop shoes.

Toodles??? For me, everything here was generously punctuated.

I was afraid to look up and see Brickhouse silhouetted in her window. Thunder grumbled in the distance. I remembered the Cheeseman saddled with his shotgun. The house was one big shadow. Then a curtain twitched. When I moved in, the Dalrymples and I didn't sign any contracts or discuss house rules really. Until now I felt we had a true and proper agreement, which made accompanied documents unnecessary.

I snuck back to my apartment. The moon is a silver balloon on a string. Leaves confettied all around me. Before I reached the front door the phone started playing Frank Sinatra's "Under My Skin." When I flipped it open, Pussy's face appeared. The image flickered like a flame.

"What's your stance about dogs?"

"Well, I like them better than cats." I generally don't have stances.

"Would you be willing to feed and water Mercury and Jupiter? The Domini-king is dragging me to this benefit thingy in the city."

I laughed one hard syllable, "Ha!" She knows what people call him.

"Where is Fern?"

"A hockey tournament in New Hampshire." She spat out these words. Now I remembered; Fern is the goalie on the boys' hockey team. She sat in the back row of my class, a large girl with large ears, dry lips, boyish, pink skin, clear eyes that don't blink, a nice girl, watchful, that's the impression she gives, a watchful girl, a good listener.

"Okay, I'll stop by after school."

"I'll leave instructions on the countertop in the kitchen." What sounds like an electric shaver turned on in the background. The phone silenced before I could respond.

*Word spread about my body.*

*Everyone is talking about it. It's not just my imagination.*

*"Wendy Love has boobs!!!" Jade Green announced to practically the whole Upper School gathered in the student lounge before homeroom. (I was sitting right there.) Her voice crumby with disbelief. She italicizes everything. She is as subtle as change in a dryer. She likes her entrances to be grand, her exits grander. Boobs must be the last straw for me—faculty brat, interloper—and for Jade. Or for me as far as Jade is concerned.*

*(The savviest teachers knew better than to send their kids to SHS. Faculty brats tiered socially below legacies, north shores, celebrity spawn, neuvos, south shores, and scholarshippers. Faculty kids could raise or lower their station slightly according to the present popularity of their teacher-parent and their own beauty and or athleticism. However, the most beautiful or athletic were deemed changelings and could not raise the station of their siblings or parents. Girls could temporarily boost their stock by putting out, but most, by the end of middle school,*

understood the ultimate futility of this approach. I know I did. My father, the Woodshop teacher with 8 fingers was many things, savvy not among them.)

Jade is the school ogress, militant heterosexual, fashion Nazi and not-so-subtle mastermind. Jade sanctions things: friendships, conversations . . . giving approval or disapproval, her blessings or curses. She can be found in the student lounge speaking too loudly on almost any topic as if everyone cares; I'm not sure if she takes any classes. In her own right, Jade is a fairly accomplished butt model for Calvin Klein, one sly chromosome away from true beauty. Her ass decorates busses all over Manhattan. (What does that say when your backside is your best quality?) Oddly the rest of her body is more like a partridge's, with legs like a grasshopper. Her other claim to fame is that she'd had a one night stand with Myles from "Real World London." Or so she says.

Jade has three mommies. There's lawyerly mother. Medicated mother. And Twenty-four-year-old-television-anchor-trophy-wife stepmother. The latter referred to by Jade as her stepmonster in another announcement she made today, "I will never call my stepmonster 'mom.' Never, ever." (I can't imagine a 24-year-old wants to be called "mom," by a teenager no less, but . . .) That is Jade; all of her ideas—jokes, nicknames, whatever—came from someone or somewhere else.

I'm writing you in my pillowy room with the Escher prints and the Princess Amidala poster. I scribble black ink on this white page which reflects the failing light of the second day of school. The girls in 12$^{th}$ grade are no different from those in 7$^{th}$. They wear Prada skirts and carry Pucci pencil cases. They think Raphael, Donatello and Michelangelo are mutant ninja turtles. They smell like cocoa butter. Their lips are glossy. School just started and already the air is thick with untruth. My friendships are false, born by accident, raised in confusion. High school, like kindergarten, is a land of make-believe. A Never, Ever Land.

I hear the Caucasian noise of the TV in the next room, and my brother's coyote-like voice trying to harmonize with a cartoon sponge. The soft clatter of pots and pans with the heavily accented, Vietnamese cursing of my mother. (You haven't lived until you've heard swearing in Vietnamese.) My father's docile sighs as he turns the pages of the newspaper. They know nothing of how my days unfold.

I cannot explain the recent fructification of my skin. My physique is unfamiliar even to me. I check the mirror to see if it is still there. (Most of the time when I'm looking in the mirror, I'm checking to see if I'm still here or I'm wishing I was somebody else.) It's still there. This body. The sine curve silhouette, the womanly lines, the breasts now impossible to hide beneath sweaters and behind books (God knows I have tried), breasts that ache with all of the talk. (Actually they would still ache if there was no talk about them. Is this what they mean by growing pains? I always thought they meant that figuratively.) Just last year my breasts were barely Hershey's kisses. A triangle of fur now hides what I remember to be down there, as if keeping a secret even from me. Is it supposed to look like that? Otherwise I look like myself, only more so.

I live in conflict. An uncivil war. At times I feel an urgent need for others—the desire to experience pleasure produced by someone other than me. Other times I wish to be alone, completely alone. A-l-o-n-e.

A dog howls as the moon approaches. The crickets begin their serenade. I imagine the laughter of my peers filling the air as they spend their evenings on the beach singing songs accompanied by guitar and harmonica. The white tennis-club girls wearing white and their plaid, sail-cloth boys. Most with last names as first names (insuring they remain on a last name basis with everyone). They arrange themselves hull to hull. Some will wander off to whisper sweet words into attentive ears. Others will swim in a sea warmed by the admiring shine of stars. They will pass bottles and smoke. They will drink; they will dance; they will drug. They will re-enact scenes from their summers. Underlining their lives with fluorescent yellow markers. Highlighting the highlights. They will know how to do this. How they know I do not know. They will live richly, more richly than me. I will stay in my shadow world, listening for the sounds of life I imagine can never, ever be mine.

Secretly I search for those songs. I sneak out of my house and bicycle to find those beaches. I only end up more lost, lonely and alone.

My world is enclosed by a transparent plastic sphere. Filled with snow and water. Pick it up. Shake it. You might as well, everybody else does. That's me inside there. A statue of puberty. Lady Puberty. A monument to my misery. Patinaed green with envy, not age. Bestride the harbor to what my mother pronounces "Wrong Island." We couldn't touch if we tried. Our fingers would stub against the sphere. The least you could do is wave.

While I slept, Pussy text-messaged me. I read it when I woke: "Gr8 2 finally meet u. U r just as Fern said. Y wait. Come 2 my house 2morrow, we'll go 4 a swim."

School was hellish today. I guess I made the mistake of wearing spring colors in fall. Or maybe I answered too many questions in Spanish class. I dunno.

My weeks are like a carousel ride. Rotating round and round and up and down at the same time. I leave off each week somewhere on the short circular continuum that I travel round and round each day of each week. Bus-school-bus-more school-bus-work-instant message-work-i.m.-bus-school-home-i.m.-eat-i.m.-school-work . . . repeated ad infinitum. Zippity doo da. My emotions bob down low and back up high. Down low, up high. (Well, high in a relative sense.) Yet I am not the dazed and giddy child proudly astride a candy-colored stallion. I am that stallion. Inert. Feigning exertion. Miscolored. Out of sort. (With a pole shoved up my ass.) The whole bit. The calliope churns out its fatuous ditty. Passers-by, all smiling and waving for some reason, appear as a blur.

# Asset Management

Pussy answered the door in a black string bikini as if that were a perfectly normal thing to do; her eyes sparkled with depravity. She held the door open with a sandaled foot and continued to talk on the phone while she stood practically naked in front of me feeding baby carrots into her mouth. A white oxford shirt trailed from one hand to the floor as she balanced the phone between her cleft chin and nude neck nape. I was, as usual, high and became fixated on the shadowy glimpse of her nipples the semi-sheer fabric provided. They held my gaze masterfully and without effort.

She led me from one platinum, marbled room to the next, her heals beating a castanet rhythm on the floor, the white shirt still sweeping behind her, the poetic lines of her legs stretching out before us until the back of the house disappeared into the glittering ocean.

When I paused to gawk, Pussy spread her arms out wide and announced, "Biggest swimming pool in North America."

Like a mirage, at the back of their home a transparent second home soared made entirely of glass with turrets, towers, peaks and gables and a two story glass door that sighed when it opened automatically as we approached. My rubber flip-flops squeaked and slapped my feet.

The Señor's dock was a single, long index finger pointing straight out to sea, a green light at its tip.

The sunshine was brilliant and the gardens fragrant. The air was thick with butterflies—lifting, fluttering—and sweet with hydrangeas. A breeze blew warm on our faces, no trace of September in it. The silvered surface of the swimming pool reflected the light of the sun like a sharded funhouse mirror. White ducks with orange feet stood and watched us from the many limbed shade.

To the left of the pool was a large black X painted onto perfectly coiffed turf, as if their property were just a map for another, greater treasure.

Beached on the hot, dumb sand was Fern with her bangs and one-piece, racing-striped, eggplant Speedo. She was 16, but she looked 12, a very large 12, retaining the prominent tummy of childhood. Without enthusiasm she stood up to greet me. Without enthusiasm I waved back. She went pink, bowed her head and removed her glasses. Faced again with the substance of her—and her teenage daughter—not just her voice on the phone, I felt my toes getting cold.

My flip-flops continued to squeak and slap.

> **"Denial is an undervalued asset."**
>
> ~ **Finn Fenstermacher**

Fern's antecedents were the school's old guard gold coasters. Their wealth had spanned and would continue to span generations regardless of whether or not any existing family member got out of bed. So Fern dudded her grubby, orange Philadelphia Flyers windbreaker and chummed around with similarly soft, sometimes simian, sometimes piratical boys who went to IHOP, McDonald's and Boston Market in rotating succession before and after every school day. They convoyed Jeeps of varying vintage, all sported buzz cuts or long tangled hair, all played hockey and lacrosse.

To our right, the perspectives of sand and water drew to a point with the tender blue line of the horizon. The sun was a gold bauble in the sky. Saltwater licked the thin figure of the shore.

With a cigarette bobbing on her lip, Fern paced in a circle around me, turning me end over end, shaking me, emptying my pockets without really moving much herself. She petitioned me to explain the rings of Saturn, cold fusion, and the Marshall Plan. (I had grown accustomed to this type of oral exam.) I concocted elaborate narratives filled with the names of minor celebrities, sophisticated plot twists, wildly inaccurate descriptions of flora and fauna and some bits of dialogue in ersatz Frenglish.

The V formed by Fern's crossed legs created a dial for the sun that painted a black line between me and Pussy.

Pussy swimming was an event. First there was the perilous untying and retying of each of her bikini strings, then the banding of hair, the toeing for water temperature, the bouncy toe-touching, the knifing of the water, and the dramatic, slow-motion stair climbing.

She stood for a moment with her hands on her wet hips. Glistening in the sunlight. Water shimmied in rivulets, runnels, nooks and streams from her chest to her thighs. Drops sparkled and fell, sparkled and fell. The light spilling out around her reduced her to a curvy eclipse. Actual diamonds twinkled inside her silhouette.

Untied, her red hair splashed over her shoulders. Her wet feet left dainty foot marks on the deck. Around her eyes, I thought I read disappointment, even sadness, and a willingness to set sail again. Surprisingly I had only vague plans of unbuttoning her blouse, removing her cowboy boots, and peeling off her blue jeans. Maybe because we were suddenly past that step in the bright light of day.

A servant served sashimi on blocks of blond wood at 4:00. The sight caused Pussy and Fern to snatch black enamel cases from their bags. The hand-painted cases cradled ivory chopsticks pincered in red velvet.

We basked beneath the clacking fronds of good-natured fan palms. Pussy swam and lay about in various stages of undress. Fern told stories, funny stories. She stirred in references to "heavy tongue sushi action," and tossed salads as if we were slutty sorority sisters. Pussy had a snort in her laugh that could stop a record.

Pussy drank saki. Fern and I smoked. Fern's glasses winked in the afternoon sun as she colored moustaches and black teeth onto the people photographed in copies of *Town and Country* and *InTouch*. She magic-markered her toenails black. Next to her lay the uncracked spine of *Tender is the Night*, the 12$^{th}$ Grade's summer reading selection. When her mother supplemented her speech with the word, "bastard," Fern wiggled her eyebrows up and down and smiled slyly at me.

When I wasn't smoking or talking, I utilized my dark sunglasses to watch the play of elastic across the arch of Pussy's behind. I chose to interpret every heave and sough of her bosom as an invitation to join her in bed at my earliest convenience.

A stereo played softly, allowing Ella Fitzgerald to drift and bob on the ripples and swells of the mirrory water. The sun's last golden columns of light, perpendicular when I arrived, lounged at lazy, bow-shaped thirty degree angles. Only occasionally did Fern fold her hands over her stomach and sigh in a bored, theatrical way.

We spent the rest of the afternoon in silence, Pussy's thoughtful, mine clenching and uncomfortable, Fern's adolescent.

At some point Fern disclosed the existence of a pied-a-terre the Señors owned at a swank Upper East Side address. This pricked up my ears. I had only lived on Long Island for a short time now, but already I discovered that no self-respecting Manhattan sophisticate would date someone out on the Island between September and June. Long Island seemed like a good idea when I was lost and ridiculous in Boston, the way Boston did when I was lost and ridiculous in Jersey. It was only now that I begin to recognize that Long Island is coming true. I had this brief, stupid fantasy where Pussy and I are doing the dishes together, she washing, me drying, the breeze through the window blowing her hair back like a long scarf. Her dangly ball and chain earrings swinging back and forth like the clappers of two bells. I imagined us sleeping like naked spoons. A New York hideaway made this easier to picture. We would figure out something to tell Fern, and we would all simply have to adjust.

Low flying aircraft broke me from this revelry. Worker bees were buzzing back to their hives. The distant fft-fft-fft-ing of helicopter blades sounded as if someone were trying repeatedly to interrupt our conversation. Train whistles blew. A foghorn groaned across the Sound.

The noises all seemed to be headed in our direction. We shielded our eyes and squinted into the sky.

A gigantic black mass blotted out the sun and started descending like a space-age spider, creating a tornado of sand and leaves and wind around us. We took cover beneath beach towels.

Out of the spider stalked a shadow with stern black hair, woolly eyebrows and a Kaiser Wilhelm mustache, all motionless beneath the churn of the chopper blades. He looked like a political cartoon—giant head, exaggerated features, tiny body.

Just like that. An air assault. Domini-king ex machina. Enter D.Señor, exeunt B.Goodspeed.

# That Thing

The instant messages bloomed the second I sign on. Kids instant message; adults email. None of my students check their emailboxes—many don't have one—unless instructed to do so, yet they begin instant-messaging the second they get home. At this moment every night, I regretted giving my screenname to students. I did not even have to look anymore, each message was exactly the same. "Wassup?" Or "was'^?" Usually I created one response that I copy and paste into every window. Something corny and earnest that would successfully scare off everyone, everyone except Love of course.

Her screenname is Amidala-grrrl, mine is Bnannafish.

**Amidala-grrrl:** Hi
**Amidala-grrrl:** Do u speak Spanish?
**Amidala-grrrl:** I'm doing ur homework.
**Bnannafish:** In Spanish?
**Amidala-grrrl:** HoLa!!
**Amidala-grrrl:** Si
**Amidala-grrrl:** No
**Amidala-grrrl:** Why would I do that? (Porque?)
**Amidala-grrrl:** I don't think u can read or spek it
**Amidala-grrrl:** Speak, I meant speak. That's what I get for trying to type in bed.
**Bnannafish:** I know a little
**Amidala-grrrl:** When is the next dance?
**Amidala-grrrl:** por supuesto
**Amidala-grrrl:** Tu aprendes en escuela?
**Amidala-grrrl:** Do u know what I just said?
**Bnannafish:** Si
**Amidala-grrrl:** Esta bien
**Amidala-grrrl:** How far does ur Spanish vocabulary stretch?

**Bnannafish:** Not far

**Amidala-grrrl:** Didn't think so

**Bnannafish:** Huh?

**Amidala-grrrl:** What I mean is

**Amidala-grrrl:** I can say just about anything in Spanish

**Amidala-grrrl:** That's bcuz of mi momasita. She started me on Spanish in utero.

**Bnannafish:** Kewl

**Amidala-grrrl:** I know

**Amidala-grrrl:** Next year I am supposed to read don quixote

**Bnannafish:** Next year?

**Amidala-grrrl:** So I asked for the book for Christmas

**Amidala-grrrl:** If I don't graduate

**Amidala-grrrl:** I don't wanna get behind, so I'm reading it this year just in case

**Amidala-grrrl:** Unfortunately, I don't understand it in English

**Bnannafish:** Behind? It's September?

**Amidala-grrrl:** But Spanish is kewl

**Amidala-grrrl:** Most of my mother's family graduated high school early

**Amidala-grrrl:** Do u go on the Hotchkiss trip?

**Amidala-grrrl:** Bcuz I'm plotting . . .

**Bnannafish:** Duh, yes

**Amidala-grrrl:** I was in sixth grade last year how would I know?

**Amidala-grrrl:** I really think u should dance at the next dance

**Amidala-grrrl:** Maybe then the boyz will dance with other people Pleeeeeaz???

**Bnannafish:** We'll see

**Amidala-grrrl:** It's usually just us girrrlz dancing, and we sometimes want to see some boyz dance

**Amidala-grrrl:** Even alone

**Bnannafish:** Hmmnnn . . .

**Amidala-grrrl:** U are the very slippery evasive fish, u know that <>< ?

**Amidala-grrrl:** I'm the slippery diabolical fish <><

**Amidala-grrrl:** I will call u "<><" from now on, okay fish-y?

**Bnannafish:** Lucky me.

**Amidala-grrrl:** Do u think that rebekah is a static person?

**Amidala-grrrl:** Oh and by the way, if u r gonna dance, please allow us to show u some moves b4 the dance

**Bnannafish:** Harding or from the bible?

**Amidala-grrrl:** U know like the step I was doing in class

**Amidala-grrrl:** The bible??? That's random

**Amidala-grrrl:** Duh, harding

**Amidala-grrrl:** Rebecca's name is not spelled like the one in the old testament anyway

**Bnannafish:** Oh

**Amidala-grrrl:** Didn't u ever notice the spelling?

**Bnannafish:** Uh . . .

**Amidala-grrrl:** Did u know I can play the piano?

**Amidala-grrrl:** Oh gosh, I forgot about the school song!!

**Amidala-grrrl:** I apologize

**Bnannafish:** What school song?

**Amidala-grrrl:** Exactly. Remember I was gonna rite a school song?

**Amidala-grrrl:** Cuz y'all don't have 1

**Bnannafish:** Y'all?

**Amidala-grrrl:** It was gonna be to the tune of Lauren hill's "that thing"

**Bnannafish:** I dunno

**Amidala-grrrl:** Maybe I should do something more pompous

**Bnannafish:** Oh, right. Drat thing?

**Amidala-grrrl:** Very funny

**Amidala-grrrl:** I'm laughing my stomach out

**Amidala-grrrl:** Can't breathe!!!

**Amidala-grrrl:** I'm rolling on the floor now . . . !!!

**Amidala-grrrl:** And no, not "drat thing"

**Amidala-grrrl:** Although that could be the unofficial name

**Amidala-grrrl:** But u know that song right?

**Amidala-grrrl:** u know the one that goes "girlz u know u better watch out . . ."

**Amidala-grrrl:** Cuz guys some guys r only about . . .

**Bnannafish:** Yes

**Amidala-grrrl:** That thing

**Amidala-grrrl:** That th – i – i – i – ing . . .

**Amidala-grrrl:** Oh good

**Amidala-grrrl:** Does it have to talk about our motto and stuff like that?

**Bnannafish:** I hope not

**Amidala-grrrl:** Hallelujah

**Amidala-grrrl:** I had the manuscript started, but I had 2 stop

**Amidala-grrrl:** I'll work on it Monday

**Amidala-grrrl:** Do u believe in god?

**Amidala-grrrl:** How tall are u?

**Amidala-grrrl:** Have u ever been crank called?

**Bnannafish:** Uh . . .

**Amidala-grrrl:** Is it prank or crank?

**Bnannafish:** depends on the call

**Bnannafish:** WL, 'tis almost morning. My brain is sand.

**Amidala-grrrl:** but . . . , but . . .

**Amidala-grrrl:** I . . . I have more questions.

**Bnannafish:** I don't doubt that.

**Amidala-grrrl:** =(

**Bnannafish:** =)

**Bnannafish:** G'night

**Amidala-grrrl:** Goodnight, indeed.

**Amidala-grrrl:** Adieu

**Amidala-grrrl:** Adios

**Amidala-grrrl:** Au revoir

**Bnannafish:** Cheerio

**Amidala-grrrl:** Vale

**Amidala-grrrl:** Aloha

**Amidala-grrrl:** Bon voyage

**Amidala-grrrl:** Godspeed, Godspeed.

**Bnannafish:** L8er g8or.

**Amidala-grrrl:** In awhile crocodile

**Amidala-grrrl:** G'night, g'night. A thousand times g'night.

I hadn't seen Pussy again for a week when she called my cellphone and said, "You'll never believe what I am doing. I'll call you back."

Uh, okay.

I was standing in line at Neiman Marcus trying to catch up on my errands for her. I still had "a thing or two" to pick up at the dry cleaners, the organic market, the pharmacy and the pet store.

# C'est la guerre

The first time I saw Sagittarius "Tinky" Love, he was floating face down in the fountain of the school's front circle. Over him loomed a smiling, marble, mustachioed Teddy Roosevelt stuck mid-gallop with gun drawn.

Tinky was a blue-blazered jellyfish listing in three feet of water. Someone was shouting, "Call 911, call 911!!!"

I waited, stifling a yawn. Love spent most of her free-time in my classroom. She and I were on our way to soccer practice. Tinky seemed to sense us watching him from the second floor window of my classroom. He reared back and sat up spraying a tusk of water over his head. He squinted at me as if he were taking aim down the barrel of a rifle. I squinted back.

"Oh for heaven's sake. Tinky, you play too much." Came the cry from the chalky crossing guard.

"You the jerk's teacher?" He called to me.

"Which jerk?"

"Wuv."

"Oh-h, Wuv. Yes, of course. Smart girl."

"Wha'?"

"Smart girl that Wuv."

"Yeah, sosmartthatshecan'ttelltimeyet."

"Wha'?"

"If anyone's interested," he called out gazing sleepily now, "Which I doubt." His voice somehow had already known the bottom of countless bottles of whisky. "It's 3:00. Sh' was s'posed to meet me at 2:30."

Love stuck her head out the window. "Tinky, it's 2:30 right now. Your watch is wrong again. Maybe if you stopped swimming in fountains . . ." Her voice trailed off.

All around Tinky, children recently emancipated from refrigerated air and florescent light were flailing and yawping as if they were at an amusement park or a revival meeting.

If you went to SHS, you knew Tinky. He earned his name in kindergarten. For Halloween that year, he dressed as the infamous pink Teletubby not long after it was outed. When the parade of costumes wound its way around the gymnasium, the mostly Republican crowd cheered wildly for Tinky. They thought his costume was a bold political statement from a member of the faculty. His father told everyone, none of whom were listening, that Sagittarius just liked the color pink. For the rest of the year, Tinky refused to remove his costume. The liberally-defined Lower School dress code did not stipulate about costumes specifically. They were allowed. And it was one of the joys of working at the school that occasionally you saw a fairy flying to the lavatory, an elf sneak around a corner or had a cowboy busting caps into your back as you climbed a stairwell. Of course no other parent allowed such frivolity to continue for more than a day.

Another unwritten school rule is that all names must be shortened; people here are very busy. Five syllables were way too many, and since Sagittarius refused to respond to Sage, people were eager for a suitable substitute.

A silence followed during which a faint shadow squirmed across Love's face. "El Diablo," she said in a stage whisper. It was the wind that cast that shadow, the way it does on the surface of the sea.

"Que?"

"Nada."

From this angle I can only see the round bespectacled sun of his face; his glasses reflect a movie reel parade of clouds.

"Ahoy, dirty dog." I cried.

"Wha'?" He shouted back. Squinting at me while using the knuckle of his thumb to scratch his rear end. Tinky was pigeon fat, all belly and chest, his nose flat and wet like a puppy's. "I've been waiting *all day* for *her*." He called out mingling exasperation and affection, his thumb still busy with his butt. A desperate, charging hope shined in his eyes.

"You her mentos, too?" This one took me a second. I squinted at Love through a plume of smoke.

"It's a gift really." She volunteered while biting a frayed cuticle.

"Oh, he's a treasure all right."

"Yes, a treasure, let's bury him."

"Aye." I shouted out the window. "Mentos, aye!"

"You know what?" Tinky again.

"What?"

"That's what."

Oh, that one never gets old. "Aren't you glad he's sharing? He's a real rocket surgeon." Love said absently. Tinky almost smiled, but his eyes were fixed on me, unblinking, his forehead wrinkled. He seemed to be holding his breath.

What distinguished Tinky was the art of dishevelment which he practiced. His palette of rumpled cloth and cowlicks harkened the work of Dada, Dada to Love's Da Vinci. Staring up at me now with his slack mouth ajar, he wore soiled khaki shorts that hung well past his knees and a white button down whose tail was not acquainted with the inside of his pants. His tie and blue blazer were not even afterthoughts. Two finger-painted hands held the arms of his back-pack which, similar to Love's, was a stuffed monkey. His appearance plucked dusty chords in me.

More scratching. There were blue moons of sleeplessness under lots of lashes. His eyebrows were knotted.

"Did she really beat you at Scrabble?"

I didn't know we had played Scrabble. I looked at Love. She blushed as if it hurt her, like a burn. She held out her writing journal, open to two pages where she had affixed wooden Scrabble tiles spelling out "Benjamin" and "Wendy May," the former equaling eleven points, the latter eighteen. (Am I, as her English teacher, obligated to say that proper nouns are forbidden in Scrabble?) She looked at me with a faintly questioning smile. Her lower lids were slightly pink and puffy as though she had been crying. Her lovely braceletted arms, upon closer inspection, were actually banded by hospital identification badges. Etched onto the knuckles of the backs of her hands, one letter per knuckle, was the word "jealousy." She feigned a dainty yawn when I looked back up at her.

"How old are you?" I said, not knowing what else to say.

"How old do you want me to be?" she responded.

I felt myself changing colors, trying to blend in, not standout so. I looked at the doorway to see if anyone might have overheard that. The only witness a lost pair of sunglasses hanging on the knob.

As we faced each other, she seemed to grow in stature. Her gaze fell on me as warmly and affectionately as a beam from the sun. Her lips trembled into a smile, but her iridescent eyes remained distant and serious, as if bent on the composition of a great puzzle. In this Technicolor world made mad by falseness, her candor, her candied limbs and her perfect lack of guile were fatal gifts.

Not knowing what else to say, I said finally, "Old enough to know better," as I opened the window and climbed out onto the fire escape, my favorite shortcut to soccer practice.

> **"I have a story inside me, but I can't get it out."**
> ~Tinky Love, Grade 1

Outside the crisp voices of little boys and girls fluttered like red leaves on a fresh breeze. From the landing of the fire escape, I watched a river of trees flow into a sea of trees. We could hear the singing of uncaged birds, the splash of cool water on hot flagstone, the first of the evening trains arriving dragging grey flannel clouds behind it. The world lay like a sunlit valley at our feet. We blinked away the sun's brightness, stretched and yawned. We exchanged lazy, unfinished sentences and leisurely pauses. We watched children mix and mingle like great flocks of white sheep.

Tinky followed us as we descended the black iron staircase, as if he were following the flight of a plane in the sky. There was a jauntiness about his movements as if he had learned to walk by balancing a baton in the palm of his hand. His demeanor changed as he walked as if his mood were flashing quickly between cartoon animation and feigned boredom. He's not sure which he should wear with me. He carried his surpluses—hair, belly, clothing—as gallantly as only a seven-year-old can. When he coughed, his whole body heaved, almost taking his feet off of the ground.

In the fields around us were virgins practicing archery, ripe fruit falling at exactly the right time, real toads bouncing high in blue Italian gardens. The wind swirled around us. We walked in the eye of a small funnel-cloud of leaves. Everything was warm and soft. The air smelled like ozone; there must be a storm coming.

When Love and I reached the ground at the edge of the woods, the yellow sun threw our black shadows ahead of us so that we tread on dusky, impossibly tall images of one another. Love filled me in on Tinky. Her sentences drifted from disinterested diagnoses to expressions of peculiar fondness. "Mother says he's always been unusually communicative." His sketches harken the work of De Kooning." "He looks like my father, I look like no one." "He loves music and fencing."

"Music and fencing? Well that's implicit. Who doesn't love those?"

"Tinky, sing 'The Pants Song.'" Love called out, her voice full of sibling authority.

"London britches falling down, falling down . . ." he began.

Love answered my smile by singing, "Oh beautiful for spaceship skies . . ."

I sang, "My country 'tis of thee, sweet land of misery . . ."

Tinky confided to me, "My mom says I can learn to play the piano as soon as my feet reach the brakes."

"Three cheers for mom."

"Tinky, who are your favorite composers?"

"Sherbet and Betoban."

"Ohh, "Symphony in B-minus?"

In an aside to me, Love said, "Would you like him to sing Acapulco?"

When Tinky finally reaches us, I cried out, "Fencing! The sport of kings! Why, that is me sport. Ye'll meet the rope's end for that, bucko." Tinky stepped passed my drawn sword to disappear for an infinitesimal moment into Love's lap as she held his head to her. There were persons, places and things at this school that taste would conceal and compassion spare; Love and Tinky were not among them. Intuitively, they both knew this.

Tinky about-faced toward me. Love pulled a recorder from Tinky's book bag. She began to play "Mary had a little lamb." His smile moved from his eyes to his lips.

"Epee or saber?" he said.

"Saber, naturally."

His breath whistled in his nostrils, and he opened his mouth to stop it. His left hand attached to his hip as he raised his right to me. His face became a spear. He looked at me as if he blamed me for something.

"Blimey," I trembled.

"Engarde." Tinky corrected me, legs now spread.

"Ditto." I responded raising my left hand.

"A leftie?" Tinky said standing up straight for a second to puzzle over this. When I smiled, Tinky attacked with two quick thrusts of his sword, collapsing the distance between us. I parried the first and dodged the second.

"Easy there, mate."

"You weren't calling me mate two minutes ago." His words came out fast as though he had been saving them up for a very long time. Retreating as an obvious set-up, he then launched three crippling thrusts.

"My dad says fencing is chess with knives." He continued.

"Who but ye dad would know? God bless him." Recovering, gathering myself. The habit of living together gave Love and Tinky some of the same vocabulary. Both utilized the phrases "mother thinks" or "my dad says" as a way of bolstering an opinion of their own. Tinky and I began a fairly civilized little swordfight that took us back up the fire escape, into deep poison ivy and all the way out to the soccer fields. He counted out two-four-two beats under his breath and gave his every move a name. We got to know one another amid the bout. Love began to recorder "Dance of the Sugar Plum Fairy."

"Do you like Chapstick? Lunge. Riposte. Lunge."

"Arggh, yes, me lips get chapped." Retreat. Flinch. Parry.

"I like to eat it. Cut and thrust. Feint."

"Shiver me timbers." Bite at feint, dodge and counter-attack.

The afternoon sun threw our shadows eastward.

"So who is your teacher, Tinky?" Pausing. Breathing heavily.

"Mrs. Shultz."

"Oh, Mrs. Shouts. She's my favorite."

While the tactical advantage was clearly Tinky's, I scored the first hit – a meager little slap to his right thigh.

"Off-target." Tinky called while raising both hands above his head as if in appeal to a judge.

"Bloody hell." I responded, pleased to see Tinky limping as though he had caught a bullet.

"Please don't take your anger out on me." Clearly parroting a line he had heard elsewhere which caused a long pause. "My dad plays the hannukah."

"As well he should."

Meanwhile, in the widening gaze of sunlight, Love stood poised with her heels touching one another and her legs turned outward so her toes were pointing in opposite directions. She tottered a step and then returned to first position. She rose up to support herself on the balls of her feet. Now coming back down to bend her knees leaving her heels on the ground.

"First position, the releve and the demi-plie. You should be proud!" She shouted to me.

"Wow, that was great. Now do another." I said.

She responded with an exaggerated smile, all lips and no teeth. "I Googled you. You're right; your college writing was very solemn. Are you aware of your recurrent use of the words: rigor, wistfully, obvious and recurrent in your work?" Paying me the subtle tribute of knowing more about me than I knew of myself.

"Heck, those are great words, no?"

"Touché." Tinky cried while spearing me, scoring the first valid hit of the match.

"Touché." Love murmured. She placed her right foot in front of her left so that her right heel was directly in front of and touching her left big toe. Lifting her right foot, bending at the knee and pointing her toe, she drew her baby toe up her left ankle and shin, stopping at her left knee.

"A back port de bras in high fifth position into retire releve.

"I saw you talking with Madame Soulier last week. She just acts that way because she is French. She's married, you know."

"Hence, the Madame, no?"

"Studying French is so bourgeois."

"What here isn't?"

We both sighed and stared at the black leaves on the sunny path at our feet. She bit at the cuticle of her index finger. Lifting her right knee and straightening her leg, Love lifted a pointed right toe to her side. Her big toe reached above her head. Tinky was swashbuckling the bushes.

"A grand battement developpe."

Pirouetting closer, Love executed multiple turns – I lost count at six–on her left leg while simultaneously whipping her right leg around and around. She circled us while remaining close enough for me to feel the rush of air each time that lethal right leg flashed by.

"The famous fouette à la the black swan pas de deux from *Swan Lake*."

"Indeed."

Tinky has backed me up against the fire escape. I climbed two steps. He held the railing and jumped to meet me with one clean thrust, delivering a fatal blow to my abdomen.

"A fleche! That's called a fleche! It's a jump lunge!"

I staggered around a bit, doubled over, holding my stomach, throwing in a pronounced limp for good measure. Tinky slashed at imaginary foes, slicing the air around him with his saber held with two hands now. He played back the phrase "C'est la guerre" over and over to himself.

Love narrowed her eyes and shivered at this sight. She was pawing tentatively at the ground with the big toe of her right foot. Her eyes were fastened with an awed expression, she stretched out her pinky finger and said to me plaintively, "Look! I'm bleeding." With her teeth she had drawn one tear of blood from her cuticle.

"C'est la guerre." I said.

"Indeed." She responded.

A phalanx of eleventh grade girls approached menacingly, arm in arm, smelling of cocoa butter. Our private idyll was soon to be over.

"It's as if they were cut out from the same piece of folded paper." Love murmured a little wistfully.

"What?" This was the Love I knew from class; she spoke in such low tones that her comments were often lost on all but her closest neighbors.

"They're stencils on a wall." Her lips stiffening to say that and nothing more.

"What?"

"Things are going from bad to worse."

"Ohh, the star-bellied sneetches. Do as I do, just smile and nod."

Through the pallor of her face, she stuck her tongue out at me. Tinky was now leaping up around us making challenging barks. She shielded the right side of her face from the glare of the sun and held us silent for a moment with her hand. The sunlight left leaf patterns on our faces.

"Move it! Move it! Move it, ladies!" Someone was shouting. I squinted through a haze of smoke and pinched out my cigarette. Over the crest of the hill at the end of the path, a black cloud rose in the form of good, old Mr. Mincing. (The kids call him Mincemeat.) Mincemeat was my shadow. He was roughly my age and size. When I got a spiked haircut, he got a spiked haircut. I got dope Puma King soccer cleats; he got Puma King soccer cleats. I wear sunglasses to practice; he wears sunglasses to practice. That was where the similarities ended. He did not go to that school in Cambridge. He does not take drugs (although they might do wonders for him). The kids do not like him. They do not laugh at his jokes. He does not make any jokes. They do not consider him witty. He is not witty. He yells a lot and gives demerits. He left his Masters' thesis in the copier in the teachers' lounge. It is about a mysterious Headmaster X who mismanages a school on Long Island. What a stroke of genius. I saved a copy of his thesis for future use. If I think about him too much, I begin to twitch. Mincemeat was simply enforcing the rule that all upper-schoolers run the half mile up the hill from the locker room to the playing fields before and after practice. No one actually followed this rule. Some even drove their cars.

Leaves drifted past us. Love's neck and face suddenly blotched red. She bit her lip in thought and rolled her eyes upward. The path around us filled up with purple shadows. Each chirped greetings to me. "Hey, hey, G-funk." "Beaver fever, catch it." "Thirteen will get you twenty." "Keep it rizzle, my dizzle." "G-g-g-G Unit." I listened to the treetops rustle.

"I'll 'exquisite day' *you*." Mincemeat shouted to the girls in the back of the pack who had slowed to a fast walk. Laughing nervously they returned to a trot. He was as grey and drawn as a figure in a pencil sketch.

"What did I tell you?" Mincemeat again. There was an edge to his voice; he seemed to be trying to get something clear to himself, like Travis Bickle talking to the mirror. I avoided him on principle.

"What did I tell you?"

"Don't drink and drive?" One girl responded quizzically.

"Say 'no' to drugs?"

Palmer paused a beat to say as she passed, "The stick up his butt has a stick up *its* butt."

"Of all of the times I am not interested in discipline, this is the time I am most not interested." I whispered to Love; she was forcing soccer cleats onto her bare feet. When she paused to begin her dash, a smile passed from my lips to hers. I watched her run. She ran without regret.

I forced myself to yawn in a relaxed, superior, lazy sort of way as Mincemeat approached. His gait was lopsided. He aged a year for every step he took. I will never forget the way he kept his face averted while he talked to me. His eyes were filmy. Years later in my dreams, his blank, averted face with all of its arbitrary and rectilinear conformity would appear, dark with all of the things he couldn't express.

Finally out of the woods, I step onto emerald fields under a Tiffany blue sky. Smoothly, ominously the next two hours slipped by. In them I did things I never thought I would do: blow a whistle, holler at children, traffic in platitudes. With a ball at their feet, some came alive as if a spotlight had hit them. Others melted under that glare. Some stared absently at the brilliant grass waiting for the time to pass.

Sports were religion at Sagamore Hill. In the fall the school offered soccer or field hockey. Nothing else. No football. No cheerleading. Football is working class. It lacks dignity. How was a coach supposed to dole out positions anyway? Here everyone's son was a quarterback. The other positions interested no one. Soccer was European, worldly. Soccer was spoken in Paris, Rome, London and Milan. Soccer met the foreign language requirement here. Soccer was romance, football was warfare. Just as none of the sons of SHS would serve in the armed forces, none would play football. Besides, the finest schools in Manhattan played only soccer as well. And there lies the underlying motive for everything. For the scions of the Sagamore Hill School, soccer, hockey, and lacrosse were indisputable ways to outperform the queers from Collegiate, the sluts from Sacred Heart, the speed-freaks from Trinity, the huffers from Dalton, and the dumb-white-idiots-getting-high-together from DWIGHT. Yes, those schools had access to better museums and more drugs, but we had soccer fields and ice rinks and more places to hide—and Gatsby. What trumps Gatsby?

The sun set slowly, allowing cool air to drift in like fog. The clouds mingled and reclined and stretched themselves across the sky like an ivory down quilt, billowing and riffling subtly as if children were scurrying about underneath. The fields filled with refracted light and conflicting lines, shadows and figures. This place decorously tucked itself away. The day's choreography concluded with a polite, ladylike, closed-mouth yawn.

Pussy got a Brazilian and a boob-job.

# Now-or-Never Land

The day I interviewed, I found Dr. Fenstermacher asleep at his desk. When I knocked, he jerked awake and waved me into his office.

The room smelled of leather and horses. A thin layer of dust rested over everything. The school crest emblazoned in burgundy and dishwater gray picturing an open book, an anchor and a hippopotamus hung soberly above the antiqued marble mantle. While my Latin was rusty, I was almost positive the school's motto was "ready and willing." I blinked at it. I sneezed once. The second word "deducam" definitely meant willing. (I would later learn that the school mascot was a beaver and not a hippopotamus. Yes, that's right, we would be the Sagamore Hill Beavers. I couldn't make that shit up. Eventually, even I would find myself shouting "C'mon Beavers" to the girls on my basketball team. They were just as embarrassed by it as I was.)

After five hours of interviews with six of the most unnaturally cheerful people I have ever met, I struggled to separate my facts from my fictions. (I laid awake all night concocting and rehearsing various fictitious versions of myself.) I said I was staying at the Four Seasons and was a great-grand-nephew of Grover Cleveland. I said my parents were both doctors, surgeons, heart and brain. My family members were all monogrammed giants in silk smoking jackets. I spoke of Zelda and F. Scott as if they were neighbors. I told a Lulu of a Henry Kissinger story. I dropped the names Andrew Lloyd Webber and Zbigniew Brzezinski. Acted like I had each holding on another line. I wore a navy blazer with someone else's coat of arms; my shirt was stitched with someone else's initials. I probably should have used a pseudonym. When they asked me for three adjectives to describe myself, I did not say, "unemployable." I failed to mention my membership in the Brotherhood of Unfulfilled Early Promise.

We sat looking away from one another toward the fireplace. He wore a kingfisher blue jacket and prawn-colored tie. Although Finn was a fine talker with a deep, rumbling voice, he talked very little. The unexpected quiet was a welcome change. My face ached from talking so much.

I listened to the sound of my shoes shuffling on the carpet, the faint crackle of my starched shirt, his labored breathing. I remembered thinking, this man is temperamentally incapable of warmth. He is a statue in a park.

I imagined myself with a giant gleaming scythe cutting my way through a field full of golden wheat. Fensterfucker was on the other side of the field.

I became fascinated with a rose in the carpet. I planted my heel delicately in the center of the rose and pressed down. I traced its outline with my toe. Finn engaged in a valiant effort to remain awake. His parched lips moved the tiniest bit as if he were counting something. When he completed his exhaustive examination of the fireplace, his thoughts strolled casually back to me.

"How old a man are you?" Was the first thing he said, snapping me to attention. He might as well have yelled "incoming!" After the initial surprise, I yielded easily to the authoritative, single-malt tone in his voice.

"Twenty-six, sir." I lied inexplicably, trying to deepen my voice to match his.

"A fine age for a man. The very acme of bachelorhood."

"Yes, sir. None finer." I lied.

"How did you like Bean-town?" He said.

"I loved it." I lied. I aimed for cheerful and confident, without a hint of unemployed.

"It's not Manhattan."

"What is?"

"Winter's are cold."

"I love the cold." I lied, smiling broadly. I sensed that rigor is valued here. (Or is it vigor?)

"Why Long Island?"

I couldn't tell him that he was the only one who called me for an interview, although he was. Six months of searching for a teaching job made me realize the Sagamore Hill School might be the only chance I get. I needed this job. I had $120,000 in student loans to repay, $15,000 in credit card debt and a very large man referred to as "The Wall" to whom I owed another sizeable amount. The Wall was my most pressing concern.

"I love Long Island." I lied.

He looked askance at me and tried a different tack.

"How tall are you?"

"Six foot two." I told the truth here.

"Six foot two eyes of blue?"

"Sir?"

"I knew a girl like that once." He lost me here.

I smiled. The level of the room kept changing. The surfaces swelled and receded with oceanic rhythm. This was the sea in calm water. I did not like the sea in calm water. I envisioned myself, like Prometheus, chained to a rock against which broke jeweled waves. I stared hard at him. I remember thinking, "I will steal fire from you." I was prepared to articulate just about any opinion that I thought he was eager to hear, but the opportunity did not arise. He spoke with the calm detachment I imagined he used when dictating a letter. I felt extremely noble for not telling any real lies, and I remember feeling noble for several more minutes.

"Do you like golf?"

"Not particularly." I should have lied. I was philosophically opposed to golf. Hackysack had no golf courses. Before I could regret being such a spoilsport, he proved again that he wasn't much of a listener. With the tiniest glint of enthusiasm, he responded, "Of course you do, who doesn't? Let's see what you've got, shall we?"

The drapes hung twenty feet from floor to ceiling like the curtains in game shows. They too were burgundy with a dishwater gray border. He paused the way the host of "Let's Make Deal" might. "Ben Goodspeed, you can give up your life of dead-end jobs and petty theft to take what's behind curtain number one." When he leisurely opened the drapes, I had the distinct feeling of being on a stage with the curtain opening to reveal the audience for the start of a play–a play for which I had not memorized my lines. The sun was a lone spotlight trained directly on me. The windows, also stretching from floor to ceiling, revealed the ocean. From where I was seated, the sea was a blue meadow, which was magnified across the distance by the horizontal light of the mid-afternoon sun. The meadow seemed to grow past the windows into the office. The bright surface of the water held us for a second, held us like a looking glass.

I followed him out to the deck of the flagstone patio. We watched a flight of swallows sweep low over the field and disappear behind the rooftop of the gymnasium. The skeleton of a new gym rose right next to it. On either side of the patio stood two bronze hound dogs with paws pointing toward the horizon that was now shimmering gold. Fresh, easy blowing wind made the green grass wave, revealing its cool, silver backsides. I would soon learn that afternoons in summertime here were long and peaceful. You could watch the sky change from orange to peach to pink to violet as the sun descended.

The world filled like a sail, all green and billowy under a dazzling sun. Sunflowers as big as trees; with dozens of tiny suns blooming from each, bordered the left and right sides of the field.

Pulling a club from the bag balanced in the middle of the deck, Finn handed me a $500 driver whose head was as big as a loaf of bread. We both laughed at the sight of it as he pulled the buck-toothed beaver head cover off.

"Is this for polo?" I tried to smile in a way that conveyed uncertainty. The blood in my legs was beginning to flow again.

Backlit by the sun, he brandished one gleaming white golf ball stamped with the school's crest. "Ready and willing," I thought to myself. I imagined him handing me a pill that large. I placed the ball on a small rubber tee as I would a pill on my tongue. There was no rubber mat, no square of artificial turf. I looked up at him for approval. He nodded consent as if it were perfectly ordinary to be teeing off of this surface.

I held the Alice-in-Wonderland club with two hands and braced the shaft on my shoulder the way a baseball slugger would. I warned him that I had not swung a golf club in years. He laughed. I tightened my grip on the club.

It was 3:00, my veins felt hollow. My nerves tingled. Sweat gathered at my hair line.

Jesus Christ, for this I went to college? I was driving golf balls to land my first coat-and-tie job.

> **"What if the great day never comes**
> **And your life doesn't shine with vivid blossoms?"**
>
> ~Carl Dennis

I needed this job. I was getting too old to have no career. It was now-or-never. This strange world I walked into, for me it was now-or-never-land.

I straddled the ball and glared out at the freshly landscaped chessboard the lawn had become. Had this scene been assembled on a sound stage? Was this his screen test for me? Would I guess that this was just a backdrop hung in front of miles of suburban blight? Or would I whack a golf ball into it? I measured his gaze. He raised his eyebrows and said nothing. It suddenly occurred to me that inside his ribs beat the heart of these people. The light shined over his shoulder with certainty. The emotions in my own, twenty-nine-year-old heart caricatured the ones in his.

"The trees are 300 yards away." The bravado in his tone reached me like a fragrance. A circle of balls surrounded a red flag standing at the far edge of the field. Five years ago I would have hit the ball softly down the middle of the field taking pains not to scratch his club. Five years ago I didn't have the sack. To say I had nothing left to lose was an understatement. I had less than nothing. ($135,000 less than nothing.) I'd sooner burn these woods to the ground than lay up short.

The breeze sank to stillness. My last thought was, "His club, his ball . . . You asked for it; you got it."

The club head hit the ball with a thwack as definitive and satisfying as slicing an axe through the rinds of a pumpkin. The ball was still rising when it passed the trees at the edge of the woods. It flew 300 yards in a precise straight line exactly 45 degrees to the right of where I was aiming. I prepared several excuses.

Finn merely held out another ball. His face sphinx-like.

"Thank you sir, would you like another?" His speech clipped.

I took it and teed it up. It became a routine. We fell into stride like old pals. When my arms finally grew tired, I had buried seven perfectly good golf balls 300 yards into thick evergreens exactly 45 degrees off course. On my last two swings, sparks flew from the club as it grazed the stone, and his face broke into a wicked grin. That's when I knew he had five more clubs just like this one at home.

He patted me hard on the back and said, word for word, "I like your style."

I couldn't be sure whether I detected a false tone in his voice. I offered to lose more of his golf balls.

He said that I was going to like it here.

I had no idea what he was talking about.

It all sounded rather iffish and offhand.

He said, "Welcome Aboard." I thought people only said things like that in movies. (Should I respond, "Aye, aye, Captain"?)

My lips moved, but my "yes, sir" was inaudible.

The train back to Manhattan was breathless and swift. The porters gallantly served beer and wine, tipped their caps and never asked for tickets. More movie talk. Old men hip-hip-hoorayed me. Women pursed silky lips and offered flirty *"cheers."* I leaned out the window and plucked wild flowers from their stems and tossed them like confetti. Honking automobile horns met us at every junction and made a medley with the whistling train. Striped umbrellas twirled. Weathered towns flashed by like old photographs. The tracks seem to have risen a little toward the sky like a winding ticker tape.

With flowers in our hair, we tumbled through the blue, soapy water of the sky. We guffawed. We here-here'd. We clinked glasses and bottles. We told tall tales. We exchanged names, which were forgotten on the spot.; banks of shining poplars gave way to the limpid, money green twilight of swaying pines. We were a blur of voices. We were a true part of the country through which we passed.

The contract arrived in the mail two days later.
Welcome aboard.

# Miss Fortune

Rensalear Wright had the hiccups. Ren hiccupped chastely, and Fe' Fendi giggled fancy-free. Every 30 seconds. I should have sent him to get a drink of water, but I couldn't bring myself to it. Fe' sucked a gleaming fountain pen and lolled sideways with both legs over the arm of her chair. She wore a white pleated skirt and black velvet hair band. She had pink-rimmed, sea-foam green eyes and an apricot complexion. It was last period. *Hiccup.*

"Ren is a banana republican," Love had previously informed me, "he is lofty and clean as soap." *Hiccup.*

The wind rustled and the sunlight fluttered. The shadows of gold and ruby leaves waved across the white board. Twelfth graders were free-writing, my all-purpose answer to having nothing planned. The class' glance skipped from window to wristwatch to clock and back again. *Hiccup.*

First I modeled the intended behavior. I wrote in my journal. *I am a snowflake in the ocean. I am on the wrong side of the hill. 30, a blink in the long, dumbfounded stare of adulthood.*

*Hiccup.*

Second I patrolled to help people focus. Fe' calligraphied, *life, like high school, is just a bowl of cherries,* dotting her i's with stars. Ren scrawled, *Mrs. Boom-Boom McDonald, the second grade teacher. The way her hips go boom-boom when she walks. She is shaped like a dollar sign. Twenty-four is a great year for asses, the best in fact, never better. Never again ass good.* He dotted his i's with cartoon bombs.

*Hiccup.*

Third I calculated the hours until the weekend, Thanksgiving and Christmas.

Today's soccer match dug the St. Ann's Steamers out of Brooklyn. That's right, the Park Slope Clams versus the East Egg Beavers. The clams turned up like mismatched socks. They exited their bus reluctantly and traveled in ones, twos and threes. They might not all know one another. Some outfitted in uniforms, others clad in jeans, a couple dressed as they meandered toward the field. Several leaf through books during warm-ups. At least one was headphoned.

My team circled the field in two even lines. Each player fitted in burgundy warm-ups top and bottom. The captains at the front of the lines called out, "Who is your daddy?" The others shout back, "Sag Hill is your daddy." We stretched to precise, rhythmic counting and clapping. I uttered nothing. When the prescribed regimen concluded, my players hustled to meet me. This is how the beavers roll.

The clam's coach blew in last; he had been chasing several loose leafs of paper. His name is JV. His paint-splattered t-shirt said, "pain is temporary, quitting lasts forever." Our favorite local octogenarian refereed. The game did not clarify whether he remembered a whistle.

Our parents gathered in quilted barn jackets in autumnal colors. They provided orange peels at halftime. When they offered me a drink from a thermos, Mrs. Wright stage-whispered, "Vodka. Don't leave home without it." They winked at me when we scored. Their mittened clapping suited the occasion. They cheered for both sides. Rensalear conquered the hiccups and scored two goals. Halfway through the game I spied Love on an adjacent field. (She has been after me to let her play for my team.) Each time we free kick, she lined her ball up in a similar spot. She synchronized her kicks with our kicks; each time launching her ball farther. The exquisite clarity of her movements had its auditory component in the pure thumping sound of foot and ball percussion.

The next day at practice, I let her play defense during our scrimmage. The boys feared getting caught trying around her. With her little-boy shorts and their ribbed cuff folded down once, slim waist, sly midriff and sleeves rolled atop satiny shoulders, she schooled us. We spectated. The ball loved her. That loping kick of hers possessed beauty, strength, and a classical purity of trajectory. Her form absolutely perfectly imitated absolute perfection. When we gathered at the end of practice, Love stood facing us. The afternoon sun, a dazzling white diamond, shot iridescent spikes of light through the leaves of trees that shivered and shook around her. Her cheekbones flushed, and her full lip glistened. It was as if she were a celluloid image rippling on a silver screen.

We laughed at our good fortune. She fluttered her eyelids. We ran together in triumph through the burning autumn foliage.

By the time we got back to the locker room, word had spread. Miss Fortune, the girl's athletic director, all two-hundred and sixty pounds of her, was waiting for me. The metallic click of her cleats combined with a bouncing key-ring sounded like the jingle, jangle of spurs.

"Hey, new guy, who died and made you bossy?" She smelled of crushed dreams and sweat.

"Pardon?"

"You think your shit doesn't stink?"

Charming. I hadn't considered the issue. Really. This is my least favorite cliché.

"You're math guy, right?"

I was English guy.

"Poaching players equals bad." She spread her hands above her head as she spoke as if we were brainstorming slogans for a marquee.

Aargh, I really hadn't thought about it. Clearly a coach had to *let* Love shadow my team for two days. But everyone knew Coach Fortune rolled the balls out at practice and then napped in her golf cart while parked in the woods "running an errand." I should have known. Still, if it was a challenge Love was up to, why hold her back?

"I wasn't poaching. She volunteered. I assumed her coach knew."

"The problem when you assume, sir, is that you make an 'ass' out of 'us.'" She made exaggerated marks in the air with her index fingers.

"I've heard something like that before." She gave me a look that said, "Stick with me, kid."

"You don't know Love's *history*. The problem with Love is: she thinks the rules don't apply to her."

No, the problem with Love is that the rules don't apply to her. I too struggle with their application. "Well, I am sorry. You are the boss."

"I don't need you to tell me I am the boss for me to be the boss."

Uh, okay. Clearly this is about something else entirely. The dialogue lulled shallowly. Dusk deepened in the weakly-lighted hallway. Lockers slammed, and showers dripped. This was her dismissing me.

Through a doorway I watched a black tree scarecrow menacingly against a copper horizon. Pumpkin-colored short busses rolled down the hill. Last Saturday we fell back. Daylight slaving time.

When I entered the faculty lounge, the lights were off. I stubbed my knees on a polyester sofa and two plastic lawn chairs before a voice said to me from faux velvet darkness. "I want to thank you for what you are doing with my daughter."

This statement was troubling for a variety of reasons. I took a step back. I interacted with too many daughters to guess at the owner of the voice. I turned to locate an illuminated exit sign.

The voice's green eyes glowed like a cat's. Shadows took shapes as my eyes adjusted to the darkness. The voice came from the customary perch of our woodshop teacher, "oh, right," Chuck Love, Wendy's dad.

"It's like pulling punches around here." He is a flabby man with thickly-rimmed glasses and hangdog jowls.

"What is?"

"Getting doors to open for my kids."

Hmmn, would these mixed metaphors were true. Your oldest just skipped five grades. Your youngest wore his Halloween costume to school for a full year.

"You don't know our history."

"I seem to be the only one."

"I've been here thirty years. Miss Fortune's been here thirty-five."

"Let's call her 'Ilse?'"

"Ilse has never liked Love."

"What's not to like?"

"Naturally, I concur."

Try saying that ten times fast. I never get to use "concur." "So, what the problem?"

"My wife thinks that Ilse treats all of the pretty girls poorly so her lifestyle isn't seen as a liability."

"Her lifestyle?"

"She's a lesbian."

"Does everybody know that?"

"Everyone but Ilse."

"Ilse doesn't know she is a lesbian?"

"No, she doesn't know everyone else knows."

"Crikey. Why else would the school keep a physical education teacher who is morbidly obese?"

"Our own little Egyptian river?"

"Hmm. So she berates schoolchildren to prove she doesn't have sex with women?"

"So the theory goes."

"What do you think it is?"

"She requires obeisance of all the girls. Love refuses to play that game."

Obeisance? Concur? Damn.

"I refuse to let her play that game."

"Which one?"

"The treat-Miss-Fortune-like-she-is-king–because-she-has-been-here-forever game."

"Whatever happened to 'tag' and 'four-square?'"

"Banned probably."

"I guess I haven't been playing the Miss Fortune game either."

"I wish I could say it won't hurt you."

"It probably already has."

"You're probably right. I saw her go into Finn's office after practice."

"Are you kidding?"

"I wish I were. Don't worry, you'll slide. You're the new-guy."

"How long will that last?"

"Until there's a new new-guy."

"Which I hear can happen any day around here."

"That is true."

The window framed a serpentine path leading through the forest to the faculty parking lot.

"Well, thanks for the warning. I'll go spiff up my resume."

"Good luck with that."

# Fetish Ball

**Amidala-grrrl:** hi <><

**Bnannafish:** hi, what's up?

**Amidala-grrrl:** not much, <><—y

**Amidala-grrrl:** I just read a stack of stories by Nin.

**Amidala-grrrl:** I forget her first name.

**Bnannafish:** Anais

**Amidala-grrrl:** I'm also getting dressed. I'm going to a Halloween ball, which promises to be delightful.

**Bnannafish:** dressed as?

**Amidala-grrrl:** Chun Li. I went through so much trouble to create the costume last year that I thought I should wear it again.

**Bnannafish:** ?

**Amidala-grrrl:** anime vixen, measurements 88, 58, 90. patent leather, knee-high combat boots, blue-black hair . . .

**Amidala-grrrl:** *http://www.chunli.com/gallery/html*

**Bnannafish:** uhhhh . . .

**Amidala-grrrl:** It's pretty ironic given my hatred for video games.

**Amidala-grrrl:** but it's nice to be objectified once in a while.

**Bnannafish:** uh . . . brownie points for irony. how did it go over the last time you did it?

**Amidala-grrrl:** last time I wore the costume was at a different event, called "fetish ball" at the college.

**Bnannafish:** fetish ball??? What happened to square dances and sock hops?

**Amidala-grrrl:** I wore it to make fun of my male friends in the physics department who spent too much time playing video games.

**Bnannafish:** ohhh, the physics department? that's different. Carry on.

**Amidala-grrrl:** So it went over well because there was this added implication that people fetishized Chun Li.

**Bnannafish:** fetishized? Try saying that ten times fast.

**Amidala-grrrl:** And everyone was very impressed that I'd put it together all by myself. And I looked plausibly like the character.

**Bnannafish:** uh . . . Kewl . . . I guess.

**Amidala-grrrl:** alright, stop distracting me. I must get dressed.

I place all of the garments on the floor in the shape of a person and imagine myself inside them. They are undergarments. They look like a woman viewed with x-ray vision. But this is all I plan to wear for my costume. I add the skirt. I sit on the edge of the bed in front of the full-length mirror. Again, I am surprised by my reflection. I wish there were less of me. My thin skin lets the blue lines of my veins shine through, as if my body were more a blueprint for a woman's body.

Each breast is a handful and emits its own heat. I've chosen underwear I might not mind having someone see. (The word "panties" is difficult to say without laughing. Who really uses that word?)

I slide the thin veil of my stockings over my toes and up my leg. I wrap the garter around my waist and attach the stockings. The corset is silk with lace, scrimshaw and ribbons. It starts out tight and gets tighter. It squeezes and accentuates my hips and bust and makes my waist look much thinner. The overall effect is that all of these ribbons and straps, whalebone and veil call attention, draw every eye, to my strapless shoulders, each naked inch, their glowing nudity. I picture the shapes and curves of a pristine desert seen from the window of a plane.

I tie a white wool sweater around my neck. The skirt is even shorter than the ones I wear for school. It fits more like a sash. The shoes are black patent leather combat boots. They make me feel several inches taller and *powerful*. I should wear them every day.

The wig is blue-black and shiny. I comb the hair into pigtails the way Chun Li wears it. The lipstick is called "licked cherry" from a company named Kiss & Tell; it makes my lips look like silk, lip-shaped pillows. Mascara makes my eyelashes more. I spray my perfume in the air and step into the mist the way Audrey Hepburn did in some movie I saw. I am not sure if this works, so I do it several more times.

I look like a different person. I should do this every day.

# Water World

Imagine a phone call, an invitation, a promise. Consider me marooned in Manhattan. Showered. Monkey-suited. Cleanly shorn. Shivering. In the mulberry blush of twilight. On the steps of the American Museum of Natural History. Next to gargling pigeons. Beneath dinosaur-shaped topiary. Sober as a tick. Watching streaky yellow cabs play leapfrog along the grease-grey avenue.

Wind reversed umbrellas, and rain lagooned sidewalks. People swim like salmon against the stream.

At just the right angle, the museum's steps glittered, the color of coins—shiny pennies dropped in wishing well water.

Smack in the middle of honking traffic, crossing against the light, moving with the ease and grace of a cloud of smoke was Augustus Isachenko Protopopov, known to me as Gus. He holds his head up and his mouth open drinking in the evening rain.

Gus is fair haired with a face like the dial of a clock. He was tailored in navy with gold epaulets on his shoulders, stripes on his cuffs, aviator pin on his lapel and wire-rimmed Ray-bans over his eyes. Women trenchcoated in navy, beneath light blue pillbox hats, decorated each arm. When he saw me, he called out, "Bridge and Tunnel!" And the laughter of the flight attendants blew toward me across the mauve lawn.

The Ivy League Masquerade Ball. (Was I the only one who considered that name redundant?) I presumed tonight's disguises would be the usual ones. I dislike costume parties. I never know what to wear. When I was six, the first Halloween I can remember, my sisters and I dressed as the characters from "The Wizard of Oz." They coerced me into the Cowardly Lion costume, much to the amusement of everyone. My brothers—all dressed as bums and thieves—took enough pictures to ensure I would never forget this scene. Sometimes I feel like I have spent my whole life trying to shake the image of me as that lion. Secretly I identified with the lion's brand of cowardice. His existence affirmed mine. But the costume ruined it, made the connection too obvious. It occurred to me now–more than twenty years later–that I was still searching for a heart.

"This is your captain speaking. On behalf of the flight crew we'd like to welcome you aboard . . ." Gus announced, a golden lock of hair falling over one eye. He handed me a yellow pill stamped like a New York City subway token and walked past me into the museum. His hand was cold with jewelry.

"I've got a nice suit, haven't I?" he demanded not pausing for a response. "What are you supposed to be?"

"Confused."

"Again this year?"

Gus' antecedents were mysterious. He wore a ring with a plum-size ruby set in gold claws surrounded by Cyrillic characters. His family's home in Southampton was as big as a public high school, filled with chairs not to be sat upon and china not to be used. He dabbled at real estate and excelled at self-abuse. His friends were all graduates of Hahvahd and Hazelden. Otherwise he was a man of little compass. If I was at all prone to self pity, which I am, I would have resented him his money, which I did. There was no end to the list of things that separated us; I forget what originally brought us together.

We don't talk so much as exchange headlines, subtitles, captions, punch lines, fibs, boasts and non sequitors. We both listened with one ear.

"True or false. What time is it?" He said over his shoulder.

Inside the museum is all marble floors, whispery silence and mother-of-pearl stairways—all polished and shiny—like the inner curls of a conch shell. The party, two floors below, sounded like the muted crash of waves on the shore at nighttime.

We boarded a glass elevator and descended like a bathysphere sinking into the tank of the Ocean Life Discovery Room. The room was a sea of blue and black, silks and fine wools perhaps, whose contrasts caused the floor to roll in dizzying waves. I was surprised to see so many costumed people. I recognized a shark, a pirate, little red riding hood, an ape with a grass skirt and coconut bra, two crash-test dummies sprawled out on a car seat and Snuffaluffagus. There were also the requisite men in drag and women as sexy kittens. The kittens just barely nudged out the women in wedding dresses for most popular costume. More common still were men in black tuxedoes with short hair parted on the side, and women in black slip dresses with short hair parted on the side. The girls would all have boys' names and year-round sunburns.

Not so long ago I hoped I would never see any of these people again. But after having been away from school for awhile and having lived in the middle of the woods for the past two months, I needed to be around people. People who read more than the sports section. People who might recognize my face.

King Tut was talking to Samuel Clemens. Stan and Laurel Hardy were arguing. Either Bjork at the Oscars or a swan floated past us. Buddy Holly and Marie Antoinette were grinding on the dance floor.

From my pocket I removed a white bib stamped with a red lobster and hung it around my neck, flattening out the creases. I'd found it in the jacket of my borrowed tuxedo.

"Now what are you supposed to be?" Gus laughed.

"Hungry?" I replied, unsure of myself.

Gus was more an ally than a friend. The kind of person you keep on your side because you don't want him against you. A giant white plate with two strips of bacon and a fried egg sauntered by holding the hand of the Empire State Building. Snuffaluffagus knocked people over on its way to the bar.

A woman approached holding a large picture frame in front of herself. Her hair and face were painted cobalt blue. She had little midnight blue cubes and geometric designs stenciled on her cheeks. Her dress was royal and had turquoise swatches sewn all over. Tampons dipped in blue dye hung from each ear. She stopped directly in front of me, waiting for me to acknowledge her. I smiled. "I give up." "Picasso's Blue period." "Nice, subtle." She smiled and continued on.

Gus floated away on waves of black silk to a crowd of people I didn't recognize. Some very Abercrombie. Some Smith and Vassar. The band was set up in front of the "Pearl Divers in a Coral Sea" diorama. The lyrics to a Dido cover reached me. "I will go down with this ship. I won't put my hands up and surrender."

A man in a pink three-piece suit approached holding out his hand. "How are you, old sport?" he said. "Just fine, how are you?" I replied. I didn't remember his name either. His hair was thoroughly waxed and pomaded. He confessed that he had spent years searching for the perfect pair of khakis, and today he had finally found them. I congratulated him and assured him I had been occupied by the same pursuit. He was eating handfuls of chips and crackers and cheese and caviar and mixed nuts. He nodded and smiled at people with his full mouth.

The colors in the room swirled and rendered his face like a Warhol silkscreen, changing from frame to frame right before my eyes.

I remembered then that he'd written an article for the school newspaper during his senior year titled "Have Tux Will Travel." We reminisced clumsily and covered subjects I had hoped to forget: college, beer and Kitsy Campbell.

"She's right over there, you know?" He said, pointing me in the direction of the coral reef. I did not need to see her to be reminded of the days of our great ambivalent affair. Heir to the Campbell Soup fortune, Kitsy had rose-colored corneas and Jermack bounce-back-beautiful hair. Jay Gatsby and I had covered all the ground we had in common. I figured it couldn't hurt to say hello to Kitsy. I knew I'd made a mistake as soon as I heard her voice.

"BenGoodspeed, BenGoodspeed!" She sang out extending her arms stiffly for a hug, careful not to spill her drink or burn herself with her cigarette. She always used your name twice, pronounced as one word, blurring the line between given name and surname. She was amiable on the surface with a champagne bubble of dismissal in everything she said. She carried herself like a prettier woman; for her rivals filled every room. Either Tarzan and Jane or Pebbles and Bam Bam peered over her shoulder. Richard Nixon and Rocky were ingesting helium and offering their signature lines "sock it to me, baby" And "Yo, Adrian" sounding like Alvin and the Chipmunks.

She stepped back to ponder my attire. She blew a smoke ring at me and squinted through it as if it were an aperture to another place and time. "I give up, what are you?" She said, her voice sandpapery. I recognized the glassy-eyed grimace caused by her too-tight dress.

"Despair. What are you?"

Holding her arms out—martini in one hand, cigarette in the other—turning her hips from side to side. Gold bracelets chattered on her wrists. "I'm my mother," she said, and her friends encouraged her with laughter. Like that she turned to them as if I no longer existed, marooning me to my island of distemper, this autumn of my discontent. People to Kitsy were destinations on a map. She could visit for a time, soak up all of the sights and just move on. Right now she was leading her friends through the streets she sees as making up the town of me. Recounting sights she encountered on her one evening there. The fuming end of her cigarette painted the air with broad strokes.

I heard someone say, "I went to Miss Porter's; I am mostly pink and green." That I would like to see.

Gus blundered by, "Don't sweat the K-train; she's a Cabbage Patch Christie Brinkley. *Chicken Soup for the Gonads.* There are better fish in this sea."

"But, it's Opposite Day; I like her." Gus was a little harsh, but she did have doll eyes, doll hair and a doll heart. Kitsy looked more like a Cindy Sherman still-photo of Christie Brinkley.

"Once is a mistake, twice is a character flaw."

The band was playing the Dave Matthew's Band's "Crash."

The lyrics "you've got your ball, you've got your chain, tied to me tight, tie me up again" filled the space.

Gus steered me over to the car seat that now held only one of the crash-test dummies. I slid in next to him. Gus left to get drinks. My blood was already 80 proof. When the room started to look like an Impressionist painting, I closed my eyes.

> **"You can't help what happens to you at night.**
> **That is what made things how they are now."**
>
> ~Carson McCullers

Sometime after that, bubbles filled the air as if I were seated in a glass of Alka-Seltzer. Hundreds of little spheres. Each an airy planet reflecting the bigger world in rainbowed swirls. Some contained a cloudy vapor which made them look like something was alive inside preparing to hatch.

Their presence enlivened this corner of the blue room. Groups of people gathered beneath each cluster. Judges, lawyers, scholars, scientists—all red-nosed and beaming—struck out in pursuit. The ones that appeared alive burst with puffs of smoke. Their disappearances provoked glee as if each person, by reaching out and touching one, had participated in something fantastic.

Still, others stopped only long enough to shoot angry glances up the stairs. It suddenly occurred to me, as I watched these individuals lead the more elderly away from the marble floor that was now glossy and slick, that these suds might have a terrestrial source.

A pilgrim in a black double-breasted blouse and flowing skirt primly crossed her square-buckled boots halfway up the staircase. A pipe poised at her lips, her lips a sherry-colored pout. In fine red cloth embroidered with gold and silver thread on the breast of her dress the letter A roosted four inches high.

"Atomic bombshell," I whispered. Gus was beside me now.

"Tempest in a c-cup," he demurred.

"I've been looking everywhere for one of those. The only thing missing is a trail of smoke." I am now at the end of a long line of people waiting to talk to her. She smiled a smile someone else might save for the christening of a ship. She actually reached up and tousled people's hair. The women around her blushed. While she was doing this—I kid you not—her eyes never left my face.

"Girls gone mild. Just say 'no.'" Gus disapproved, which only spurred me forward—as if I needed any help in this case. Enough with his half-witticisms, I cut to the front of a line.

"What are you supposed to be?" She said in a voice that is whiskey straight from the bottle with a whiskey chaser. That is a good question, one to which I was running out of answers.

"I'm a conscientious objector."

"Oh, I don't know. Do conscientious objectors wear tuxedoes? To say nothing of lobster bibs." I tore the bib off and forced it into my pocket. "That's what I like in a man—courage of conviction. You should keep it on. You looked 'lost' in an endearing way."

We stood for a moment in imperfect silence. I said nothing. No speaking was left in me. She said nothing back. My face was palsied in thought. She looked me in the eye; I looked down at the floor. When I raised my gaze again one of the sexy kittens was licking Hester's neck; her tail lashed me away. Hester closed her eyes and grinned.

"Male fantasy sequence." Gus again. Gus and Hester acted as the indices of my sorry life: what was in abundant supply and what was least available. I can't think of anything to say other than my name. I mouthed "Benjamin" to Hester sounding out each syllable like a first grade teacher. She laughed and replied, "Ben-ja-min." Even her condescension was affectionate. I loved my name on her pillowy lips.

"Bi-sex-u-al?" Gus interjected, "Gre-a-at, that doubles the number of people she can cheat on you with." I was still focused on the bright side of things.

"The beast with three backs."

"Know when to say when."

"It's Opposite Day; she likes me."

"'A' is for abort."

"Or act of god."

"E unum pluribus."

"E clitoris unum."

"Your life has become a Kevin Costner movie, Dances with She-Wolves, Field of Wet dreams."

I looked past Gus at the eerie galleries of frozen, hand-painted polyurethane. In one a whale was chased by a giant squid. In another penguins lined up to pierce a circle cut through ice. A sea lion waited in the water below.

"Waterworld," I said while walking away.

"Exactly!" Gus called out after me.

That was when I saw Hester again, stepping into the glass elevator holding hands with a kitten. They leaned against the railing with their backs to me and their fingers linked. That would be what one calls watching the first shoe drop. I wouldn't be around for the second.

Through a bulletproof partition in a state prison, my uncle once said to me, "Ben, the funicular goes up, the funicular comes down. Teach yourself to wait for it." I looked up funicular when I got home. I still had no idea what he was talking about; that is until now.

I could wait. Hemingway would say that he is able to wait for as long as there is such a thing to wait for. Hemingway killed himself though eventually, right? I spent twenty minutes talking to the Statue of Liberty, Mick Jagger and the Riddler.

I left the party and walked through dark, marble corridors, listening to my shoes clack and echo. I envisioned myself walking through time. I hiked through the South American rainforests and hallucinated vegetation. I stood before the "False Society of the Iroquois" and heard drumbeats. I stamped with a herd of elephants. I swam with dolphins and skulked with walruses.

When I reached a sign that said, "This Way to the Egress," I thought I was sure to be in for something good. I followed the arrow down a dark hallway to a brightly gilded door which I realized only after the lock clicked shut behind me was a door leading to the street. The only way back in was two dinosaur-size blocks and probably another $50 away for my unstamped hand. Now this, this is the story of my life.

To my surprise the world had been remade while I was inside. It was frosted with sterling silver icing. The trees lustered like the silver trees in fairy tales. The starlight sparkled on the nuded branches like pearls. Lines of glittery light carved the world into triangles and rectangles and cubes like Picasso. I remember thinking, all of these stars, where did they come from? Are they out here every night?

The Avenue was now a frozen river. And standing on the bank of that river was . . . Hester Prynne, now covered by a white fur coat. Her hair and eyelashes flecked with snowflakes. In the movie version of this scene, I would run to her and we would embrace. That's the one I would rewind and play over and over.

Hester's feline friend purred her way out from behind her just as I was about to speak—not that I had thought of anything to say, but I was determined to speak this time. Kitty's face glowed like a lighted pumpkin.

Hester's breath smoked the air when she saw me. She smiled that ship christening smile. Kitty noticed and pulled on her arm. Hester tossed snow into the air over my head and said, "Look, magic pixy dust. Make a wish."

She stumbled backwards for a couple of steps. Her jacket shed a petal. "Make a wish." She repeated. The scarlet letter A lay on the sidewalk at her feet.

She kept walking. I picked up the letter and stood watching her white coat shimmer smaller and smaller down the middle of the river, away from me. When she was almost out of sight, the streetlights, hung on thick bows of tinsel, winked up the avenue in her direction, each turning from red to green, all the way down to where she was standing waving her hand back at me. From red, from red, from red to green, to green to green. Her white jacket twinkled like a star atop a Christmas tree.

# Manhattan is Burning

We met downstairs at the boathouse; it felt illicit. Indian summers synchronized with guilt for me, as if I were the only one getting away with something. Long Island Sound looked like a blue Wedgwood platter under a crescent slice of lemon sunshine. The day's curtain rises on the finest ropes. She always reacted as if we hadn't seen each other in a very, very long time, although we lived 100 yards apart.

To my disappointment Jamie Brickhouse Dalrymple wore a t-shirt, deck shoes, Levi cutoffs and sunglasses. Despite her burlesque gardening, Jamie was a modest girl with a square bottom, a bouncy, tip-toe walk and a Special K air of health and clean living about her. She was relentlessly positive and unreasonably generous. She found daily, justifiable opportunities to use words like "terrific" and "glorious." She used both with a straight face. Her fleet of sailboats and recreational watercraft? Mine for the asking. Pool? Anytime. The leather-bound books from her personal library? Have at 'em. Her springer spaniels Crick and Watson? My dogs too. There were so many things about me that she just shrugged away and accepted, things I haven't been able to slip past anyone. In the bright blue, open ocean world of her eyes, I was her peer. I was not the petty, small-time criminal raised in subsidized housing somewhere in the swamps of Jersey; I was, like her, a Manhattan sophisticate lured out to Long Island by the sunsets and Daisy Buchanan. Were we both then "boats against the currents, borne back ceaselessly into the past"? I know I was.

Not wanting to appear overdressed I wore bathing trunks and flip-flops. Jamie was officious about sailing. I didn't need to say that I had never been in any kind of sailboat. Or that I had never used a compass. We started with a lingo lesson using the parts of a 420, a two-person sailboat not much bigger than a bathtub. "Bow," "stern," "port," starboard," "windward," "leeward," "luff," "Ready about," and "hard a-lee." I retained none of it. I was tempted to ask if we could use "right," "left," "front," "back," but I didn't want to yokelize myself more than I probably already had. I actually thought we would be sailing in the family ketch "The Pinta" that forever bobbed 100 yards offshore, equipped with our own crew. She laughed when I suggested it. I decided against sharing the detailed daydreams

I'd been having of standing at the helm with Jamie as we sipped mai-ti's and had the wind provide us with perfect sailing posture. In the dream Jamie wore a scarf in her hair and dark glasses like Holly Golightly.

In truth we rigged and raised, sheeted and trimmed sails—both jib and main—on dry land first. We attached rudder and tiller. We practiced reading telltales and recognizing puffs and lulls. We listened to the racing pulse of passing motorboats.

Right before setting sail, a jet whistled a single note across the flawless flesh of the morning sky, followed by a white streak shimmying in a great lazy arc. The sound grew distant and faded in the wind, soon no more than a sigh.

A second later a blast of sound. Then silence.

The first hour of the lesson amounted to me watching Jamie wave at every passing sailboat and scowl at all the motorboats and jetskis calling them "stinkpots." This was not difficult. The Sound furrowed with activity. Both air and sky seemed to offer endless, magnificent possibilities. She illustrated how to steer with tiller, sail and body weight. She spoke of captains and crews. We feathered and hiked out, at one point our feet were on the windward edge of the hull and our whole bodies leaned outside the boat. We were tethered to the sail by a single string. The boat threatened to keel. She smiled like a circus performer.

The second hour my hand held the tiller. We headed for open water. No life existed anywhere except under the filtered sunlight of our robin-breasted sail. The sun swung up the sky. Jamie said we would know it is noontime when the color of the sea changed from French blue to money green and sure enough we were soon surrounded by a billion dollar ocean.

We sailed. For long stretches sailing equaled sitting, marveling at the spectacular, rainbowed wetness of the water, feeling the wind finger through our hair. Our conversation was the kind travelers have—the weather, the scenery, former and future trips. Tacking, however, required maneuvering my 6 foot 2 inch frame under the boom of the main sail and to the other side of the boat, while pushing the tiller "hard to leeward." It was easier to crawl under a chain link fence than it was to change seats in this dinghy. You'd be surprised how disorienting it can be getting hit in the head with a sail. You'd also be surprised by how easy tipping over a sailboat is.

We capsized once by accident; I lost my sunglasses and flip-flops in the ocean.

Then we capsized over and over on purpose, laughing harder each time. Capsizing excused us from sailing for bathing. We utilized what Jamie eagerly titled the "scoop recovery method," which amounted to having one person scooped into the boat as the other used the centerboard, a jib line and his or her bodyweight to right the boat. Then the person inside the boat helped the other climb aboard using "the windward side of the transom." Where that is I still don't know. Logic suggested that I, the heavier of the two of us, should scoop Jamie into the boat, however, then the problem became getting me into the boat especially after having just maneuvered the lifting of person, boat and sail out of now wavy water. Pulling someone out of the water by the elbows or underarms is no easy task. Initially Jamie insisted we use proper technique. We fought like children over who would be the scooper and the scoopee. Eventually we took turns. Performing either task gracefully was impossible. We improvised and apologized for improvisations. Removing our life vests, t-shirts, and Jamie her shorts seemed like a good idea, until we lost them in the water.

Exhausted and panting our bodies sprawled in the well of the boat. The wet sail falls over us like the sheet of a bed.

We'd lost our compass and had trouble finding any sign of land or life. Port and starboard replaced east and west. Shipwreck was a new experience for me.

Ingeniously Jamie stowed a picnic in the boat's hull. Skewers of chicken satay and peanut sauce with phat cari noodles and Thai iced tea in a red and white thermos. Jesus. A bottle of wine led to more of the easy green laughter of childhood.

After picnicking we carefreely chose a course, and watched the weather turn. The billion dollar sea became filthy money, a mess of dirty counterfeit coins. Waves asserted themselves; wind billowed; light waned. White water lipped the waves and tumbled down like snow. We had to wait for a wave to crest to look for land.

"Christopher Columbus!" Jamie cried using her favorite curse word stand-in. How *Little Women* of her.

Jamie insisted she heard the clink of cowbells. We tillered toward them. Gymnastically the dinghy bobbed and bucked, vaulted and swooped, defying gravity and logic. Perspective contracted and enlarged with the constant motion of the immoveable sea. Marble peaks sparred with the grey sky.

Viewed from a bigger boat, this play of sea was probably splendid.

We attempted to laugh off the first hour of high seas. We conferenced informally.

'The wind says one way; the waves say another." Jamie mused.

"Who knows we are here?" I wondered.

"Keep the boat facing the sea." She instructed, although she manned the helm.

"I didn't tell anyone." I responded.

"Let the bow cut the wave." She continued.

"Did you?"

"Don't let her swamp."

"Does this boat have any kind of radio?"

"Don't let her keel."

"Homing device?"

"These waves are kinda important."

"A pigeon?"

"Trim the mainsail. We're top-heavy."

"Somebody will see us."

"Where are all those stinkpots now?"

"We'll be okay."

I obeyed docilely.

Bone-white sea gulls circled like buzzards, cawing messages we could not understand. Brown mats of sea weed floated past us; Jamie professed that these were signs we were getting closer to land.

Sea and sky were equally dark, our eyes strained to read shadows. We were looking at a sonogram of the world.

The waves were quiet and difficult to see in the darkness. Despite our best efforts, icy flames of water slashed into the boat. Sailing lost its charm. You didn't need to be a sailor to know that our situation forbid catastrophizing. So we were silent. For long stretches: silence, silence, silence. Cold water sloshed from me to her. We used the thermos to bail. An hour on the sea in the dark is a long hour. We kept our feet warm by pressing them under one another. We sat back to back to row and steer. We lined up the grooves of our spines. We pressed warm skin together. We took turns shivering and chattering our teeth. The brevity of our clothing was absurd. We were as naked as November elms.

The night, the future, the world, was all ocean—indifferent, unknowable.

Delirium set in. Surely others had drowned in painted sailboats. Had I been alone, this thought would have sustained me. Drowning would provide relief. If we both drown that would be a shame; Jamie had so much to lose. I remember also feeling gratitude.

My eye chanced on a small thing stuck up on the horizon, a point so tiny only a desperate eye would notice.

The light grew larger slowly.

"See it?" I pointed as if she had been traveling the same train of thought.

"See what?"

"A light. Over the stern."

"I don't see anything."

"Look again, 10:00."

"That's a star."

"But, it's red."

"I'm telling you, that's a star."

"Are stars red?"

"One star *could* lead to others." She reckoned to herself, "C'mon north star."

"Do stars move?"

"The shore doesn't move."

"Well, it is moving."

You're right; it is red."

"And it's moving."

"It's a plane."

"That's good, right?"

"A plane is the one thing that can't help us. It could be flying from or to at least six different airports from north, south, east or west."

The waves merely paced back and forth now. The sea was black satin. The world was flat.

Where the sea and sky came to a point, a shadow lifted. A flat black line. A mound. Hills and plateaus. A mountain range. Beautiful flecks of lights climbed out of the sea and shook themselves off. There was sound. How far had we drifted?

"Port Washington?"

"Newport?"

The sound was surf, which implied a shore. Light arrayed vertically, twinkling, drawing lazy, velvet-rope arcs in the sky. We were nearly under it before we recognized a bridge. First the Whitestone, then the Throgs Neck.

In the distance a city of square forms smoldered against the night sky. The squares rectangulated and continued to fume. Was this a trick of the eye? The wind bore the smell of fire and smoke, of green logs aflame.

We drifted farther without rowing.

A city climbed the night sky, a glowing dome of light around it. Beams from two searchlights clashed back and forth like giant swords.

The isle of Manhattan. The greatest show on earth.

"Manhattan is burning," was all Jamie said as if she were describing a broken fingernail or a paper cut.

The phrase hovered above us like a kite, like a macabre marquee.

That couldn't be. How long had we been out here? How much wine had we drunk? We agreed that we knew where we were now, even if we did not know what exactly was happening.

We hoisted sails and sped east without speaking.

Land appeared again. Light flamed on the water. We followed the line of the shore looking for landmarks. We scanned the shoreline. We identified Great Neck and Glen Cove. The long finger of a dock pointed straight out at us a green light at its tip. The current carried us in. We made our way to shore slowly ascertaining that this was . . . Pussy's dock.

When we reached the dock, Pussy and Fern were waiting there in a golf cart. Neither looked very happy to see us. Again the absurdity of our attire. Jamie did her best to shoot the breeze. I tried to laugh off the fact that we were all together here. The shore was foreign to our muscles.

They took us inside and gave us warm clothing, blankets, coffee. On television we watched Manhattan burn. We had no language for what we saw. My mind became a Jackson Pollack, all greys and blacks and browns.

They provided a driver to take us back home. When we got to the front of the house our boat had already been hitched to the back of an SUV whose motor was running.

When we arrived at home, Jamie's daughter Juliet was sitting on the front porch with her arms crossed. When she saw us, she turned and marched inside, arms still crossed.

"I've got some explaining to do." There was a tone in her voice beyond speaking or tears.

"Can I help?"

"Not anymore than you already have."

Somewhere a foghorn wailed.

**"Whatever you say, say nothing."**

~Seamus Heaney

It will be months before I can talk about what happened last week. (It's taken me two months to even write this about it.) Revealing that my father is dead means revealing who he was, a vision that conflicts with the Errol Flynn character I've created for them.

School resumed as if nothing had happened. Classes met. Lunch was served. Bells rang. No one talked about why we had been off school.

Love would visit during break, coming in sheepishly at first and then more boldly as if this were where she was assigned to be. We talked about nothing mostly. Funny words. Svelte. Bumptious. Bogart. Whether or not boys can be sluts. Why Mrs. Shouts shouts so much.

I was just surviving, trying to make it through the day, trying to fill class time with something that felt like teaching. I had eight messages on my school voicemail that I hadn't listened to. I had forty-five essays left to grade. I needed to create a reading quiz for *Lord of the Flies* and a vocabulary quiz made up of words pulled from *Huckleberry Finn*. By Friday I will have to calculate the interim grades for all seventy-five of my students. I have only three grades recorded for 11th graders so far. I will have to squeeze some more in by the end of the week while every teacher is doing the same thing.

When we were reading *Great Expectations,* everyone stared off like deer mounted on a wall until I mentioned that a movie was made of the book starring Ethan Hawke and Gwyneth Paltrow. Everyone wanted to know which parts they played. (This will tell you how many people have actually been reading.) Most had stories about someone they know who knows someone who knows "Ethan" or "Gwyneth." Everyone had an opinion about each. Then the conversation veered off to talk about celebrities in general, somehow it winded its way to Mira Sorvino whom I made the mistake of telling everyone I dated for like five seconds in college. (Who cares that you never even met her?) Immediately everyone's opinion of me changed. I do not have to tell the boys that Gwyneth appears naked in the film to know that they will be renting and watching it that night anyway, in lieu of reading the book. This will require me to watch the movie so I will know how to discern who actually read. It will be difficult even to separate the two after more discussions about how Ethan \_\_\_\_-ed and Gwyneth was\_\_\_\_\_-ing.

Love didn't know who Ethan Hawke and Gwyneth Paltrow are because she is not allowed to watch television. She will ask you privately to explain. How do you explain this? They're movie stars. Americans love movies. Americans confuse what is beautiful with what is good. Therefore Ethan and Gwyneth are two of the best people her classmates know. She will say things like, "but they are playing characters?" and I will say, "I know." And we'll both end up confused.

*Halloween in Manhattan dressed as Chun-Li. B.Good didn't notice me. Well, he noticed me, but didn't recognize me. He gave me that head-to-toe look-see and smiled and kept walking. What did I expect, my hair was black; I was wearing a corset and four-inch platform patent leather combat boots. I should have said, "Hi."*

**Amidala-grrrl:** I saw you.
**Bnnannafish:** When?
**Amidala-grrrl:** Last night.
**Bnnannafish:** Where?
**Amidala-grrrl:** The museum.
**Bnnannafish:** Inside?
**Amidala-grrrl:** yep
**Bnnannafish:** Why didn't you say anything?
**Amidala-grrrl:** I wanted you to recognize me.
**Bnnannafish:** That was silly.
**Amidala-grrrl:** Sorry. I also wasn't sure.
**Bnnannafish:** About?
**Amidala-grrrl:** Wasn't sure if I would get in trouble?
**Bnnannafish:** For what?
**Amidala-grrrl:** For being at the party. My parents thought I was babysitting in Greenlawn.
**Bnnannafish:** I am a teacher not a cop.
**Bnnannafish:** But you should be careful in the city
**Amidala-grrrl:** Okay, dad.
**Bnnannafish:** who were you with?
**Amidala-grrrl:** friends
**Bnnannafish:** What were you dressed as?
**Amidala-grrrl:** Chun-Li?
**Amidala-grrrl:** Remember?
**Amidala-grrrl:** *http://www.chunli.com/gallery/html*
**Bnnannafish:** ohhh, the anime chik?
**Amidala-grrrl:** I prefer "vixen."

**Bnnannafish:** Pause. <<cough>>
**Bnnannafish:** That was you?
**Amidala-grrrl:** Yah
**Bnnannafish:** I looked right at you.
**Amidala-grrrl:** I know
**Bnnannafish:** You dummy, say hello next time.
**Amidala-grrrl:** K
**Amidala-grrrl:** I didn't want to disturb you.
**Bnnannafish:** Disturb?
**Amidala-grrrl:** You seemed so focused.
**Bnnannafish:** On what?
**Amidala-grrrl:** That girrrl.
**Bnnannafish:** What girl?
**Amidala-grrrl:** Hester Prynne, the one with the bubbles.
**Bnnannafish:** Oh.
**Bnnannafish:** Her
**Bnnannafish:** I don't really know her. [The truth was my head had been filled with bubbles since the night I first saw her. Already she is a kind of grail.]
**Amidala-grrrl:** Maybe she is bi-sexual.
**Bnnannafish:** Here's hoping
**Amidala-grrrl:** That would be ironic
**Bnnannafish:** Why?
**Amidala-grrrl:** Nevermind
**Bnnannafish:** Nevernevermind
**Amidala-grrrl:** Sorry
**Bnnannafish:** And stop apologizing
**Amidala-grrrl:** Surry
**Amidala-grrrl:** She was pretty.
**Bnnannafish:** if you like pretty
**Amidala-grrrl:** but a little prim
**Amidala-grrrl:** if you ask me
**Bnnannafish:** no I didn't
**Amidala-grrrl:** just saying
**Amidala-grrrl:** I don't think the pilgrim outfit was an act

**Bnnannafish:** I doubt it
**Amidala-grrrl:** Why?
**Bnnannafish:** Just do
**Amidala-grrrl:** Are you going to ask her out?
**Bnnannafish:** No
**Amidala-grrrl:** Y?
**Bnnannafish:** Don't know her number or her name
**Amidala-grrrl:** Bummer
**Bnnannafish:** Yep
**Amidala-grrrl:** Well, she wasn't that cute.
**Bnnannafish:** Uh . . .
**Amidala-grrrl:** There were other fish in that sea.
**Bnnannafish:** Kinda made me seasick.
**Amidala-grrrl:** Coulda been all those vodka tonics you were drinking
**Bnnannafish:** Doh!
**Amidala-grrrl:** Did you count them?
**Amidala-grrrl:** At one point you had a glass in each hand
**Bnnannafish:** Holding both for friends
**Amidala-grrrl:** r-i-i-i-i-i-ght
**Bnnannafish:** doctor's orders
**Amidala-grrrl:** heard that one before
**Bnnannafish:** uh . . .
**Bnnannafish:** It's for the pain
**Amidala-grrrl:** What pain?
**Bnnannafish:** You'll see.
**Bnnannafish:** I was trying to forget something very sad that had happened to me long ago.
**Amidala-grrrl:** you should be careful in the city
**Bnnannafish:** Okay, mom.
**Amidala-grrrl:** I loved your costume
**Bnnannafish:** you see . . . I . . . uh . . .
**Amidala-grrrl:** It was so Meta
**Bnnannafish:** Well . . .
**Amidala-grrrl:** pure genius. I am jealous

**Bnnannafish:** Took me weeks to come up with it.
**Amidala-grrrl:** You should google her.
**Bnnannafish:** Google who?
**Amidala-grrrl:** Hester Prynne.
**Bnnannafish:** I don't know her name
**Amidala-grrrl:** The E-vite had a list of names
**Bnnannafish:** Gold star for you.
**Bnnannafish:** Two gold stars
**Amidala-grrrl:** And a happy face.
**Amidala-grrrl:** Only if you want to find her . . .
**Amidala-grrrl:** You may not want to find . . .
**Amidala-grrrl:** Miss Sensible Shoes . . .
**Amidala-grrrl:** The scarlet letter-er . . .
**Amidala-grrrl:** Miss I-Have-A-Girlfriend-and-dress-like-a pilgrim
**Bnnannafish:** I get it.
**Bnnannafish:** Arggh ye matey. The e-vite has 500 names.
**Amidala-grrrl:** heedle in a naystack
**Amidala-grrrl:** Beauty is over-rated
**Bnnannafish:** Oh?
**Amidala-grrrl:** I prefer brains don't you?
**Bnnannafish:** Uh . . .
**Amidala-grrrl:** You don't fuck her face/
**Bnnannafish:** Woah, not okay.
**Bnnannafish:** You shouldn't even know that saying.
**Amidala-grrrl:** Please
**Bnnannafish:** Stop
**Amidala-grrrl:** Stop what?
**Bnnannafish:** noodge
**Bnnannafish:** noodges
**Amidala-grrrl:** ?
**Bnnannafish:** noodging.
**Amidala-grrrl:** Me?
**Bnnannafish:** the poking.
**Amidala-grrrl:** Wha'?

**Bnnannafish:** the prying.

**Amidala-grrrl:** Me?

**Bnnannafish:** You. Always. Prying.

**Amidala-grrrl:** Always?

**Bnnannafish:** Often

**Bnnannafish:** Curious?

**Amidala-grrrl:** Never.

**Bnnannafish:** Always

**Amidala-grrrl:** Me?

**Bnnannafish:** You! Always you.

**Bnnannafish:** It has to be you. Who else is there?

---

I think I'm going to shoot my computer. It won't I'M. I can't write Ben back!!!!!!!!!!!!!!!!!!! My computer is evil. Oh and now several eys on the ey board are stff. sn't ths perfect. Oh my God. serously thn ths computer s gong to drve me nsane.

Wow. This is sadder than sad. I am now copying and pasting i's and k's from other words since I'm waaaaay too lazy to actually try to fix the stupid computer.

Lovely. The eight key doesn't work so this means I can't use the asterisks. It's currently 11:41 pm and I should be sleeping, however, I am not because of this poor excuse for a computer I am typing on.

# We Wear the Masque

"The Masque," the school's literary magazine, has won national awards every year for the last 45 years. However, none of the faculty advisors from the last five years are still employed by the school. Last year's advisor printed a short prose-poem titled "O" that used the ocean surf as a metaphor for a certain autoerotic event. It was *Penthouse* Forum, if *Penthouse* Forum were written by Milan Kundera. The author was Anon E. Muss. It was the only decent piece of writing in last year's edition. It was surely the only piece everyone in the school read. I would have published it too. I have zero years of experience with literary magazines; I wouldn't have hired me. Really, I mean, where do I start? I can't even type very well.

The all-student staff was a hodgepodge of the eagerest beavers. Palmer Jones was editor-in-chief, but her twin sister Mace was the self-appointed spokesperson for the group.

Mace Jones was dangerous. She came with her own bass beat. There is beautiful and then there is what Mace was. Her beauty made both men and women swallow hard and think, no matter what I saw in the mirror this morning it wasn't *that*. She could cut her hair using dull hedge clippers and a rusty rake, and she would still start a trend. If she showed up to a black tie function in grubby cut-offs and a wife-beater, everyone would immediately feel overdressed. Somehow whatever she was wearing, seems like *the* thing to wear.[4]

With Mace, you were always looking for those little signs that she was fucking with you. Last Thursday she did her own version of the strawberry song-and-dance, but she was wearing a thong and the abrasion was a rosy spot farther north. I thought I detected a glimmer in her gun metal blue eyes when she explained how she got it—the bruise that is.

---

[4] If you prefer another perspective, allow me to quote Reed Godlewski, age 15, "Mace is so hot, I would lick her armpit."

That knowing look seemed to say, "C'mon, Mr. G, say that I am in violation of the dress code. I want to see you explain to Mr. Wilson how you know I am wearing a thong.'[5]

Yawn. There was nothing lower on my list of priorities than the dress code.

Mace was a sexual predator, and she would tell you as much if you asked. Oddly enough her father was something of a public figure at the school due to the fact that he had recently been arrested for indecent exposure at the train station for the third time. The school buzzed with hearsay about them. Mace, however, was as indifferent to her family's reputation as she was to their possessions. Getting a hand job from Mace somewhere in the school building was as much a rite of passage here as earning a varsity letter. (Please don't ask how I know this.) Jerking people off was what Mace did in lieu of running for student body president or vying for editor-in-chief of the yearbook. Catching her in the act would give me no pleasure, so I turned corners slowly, noisily, climbed staircases swiftly, walked everywhere with my head down. (When we were discussing *Tender is the Night*, the boys started calling Mace "Dick Diver.")

In English class, during a discussion of *The Scarlet Letter*, Mace not so coyly announced to the class, "People are defined by the secrets they keep. Isn't that right, Mr. Goodspeed?" There were volumes of innuendo in the way that sentence was spaced, each syllable given additional stress. However, most of the kids in that class were sixteen going on nine, not sixteen soon to turn thirty like Mace. With five minutes left in class, they were gathering themselves together like geese or cattle preparing for some great migration. They gave this comment nothing more than a barely perceptible sniff. Still Mace arched the thin eyebrow above her right eye. Her pupils were black pin pricks. Her irises blazing with things she couldn't say.

It was the last period of the day, when I was usually not far from a diabetic coma. I responded by saying, "What secret, Mace? She's got a bloody capital letter A sewn on her chest. Should she have spelled out the entire word for you?"

---

[5] At the risk of sounding like Grandpa Walton, thongs were not common when I was in school, so Mace's was actually the first one I had seen someone wearing. In theory thongs made me sad; they smacked of desperation. I imagined them on thirty-five-year-old asses. In Mace's case a thong was an act of defiance, for surely her mother hated them, and an act of liberation comparable to what burning a bra was to a pervious generation of women. At my grammar school, girls wore shorts under their skirts. Here the opposite impulse was at work. This act fell just short of wearing mirrors on your Mary Janes.

I immediately regretted saying anything. The boys in the back of the room stage-whispered applause and pantomimed cheering.

I was bumbling my way through a retraction when the bell rang. Everyone stuffed their books in their bulging knapsacks and shambled toward the door, chirping cheerful good-byes over their shoulders.

"Of course, some people are defined by the secrets they keep, but Hester Prynne is not one of them. She is a heroine we have not seen before. She was created 50 years before Virginia Woolf was even born . . ."

My classroom was empty. These last words I shouted to the backs of the heads of the last students to leave.

Ninety percent of the submissions we received for "The Masque" were written by girls. Submissions were received via a slot in the door of the magazine's basement office referred to as the Kasbah, essentially a boiler room. Naturally our advertisements for submissions all said, "Rock the Kasbah." In our first meeting, we voted to continue to accept anonymous submissions. That was all we accomplished. Then we spent forty-five minutes speculating about the identity of Anon E. Muss. The next day we received a flurry of nameless creative writing, almost all derivative of "O," some with only a few words changed.

# Precarious

We walk out of the movie theater and into the night, our breath making wispy clouds in the cold, liquid light of the street lamps. We face each other, a few feet apart. By unspoken agreement, we never touch in public. One of your coworkers could walk by and jump to incorrect conclusions (although I don't think it would be a problem; I look a lot older than I am). "What an attractive couple," the cashier said when we got our tickets; so it's not just my conceit when I say our age difference doesn't really show. Not that we are a couple, of course. You deserve someone older and taller and beautiful. Still I wore a short skirt for the occasion. Our friendship is that of kindred spirits, two people with shared dreams and passions, who read and laugh and experience life together. But we're still members of different generations. We never hold hands in public.

You're talking about the moral motivations of the main character, but I can't concentrate enough to contribute more than the occasional nod. All I can think about is how much I want to kiss you, how stupid it is that I want to.

There are couples walking by us on the way to their cars, and they would not think it strange if they saw me kiss you. They probably think I'm twenty, at least. If you didn't kiss back, you would risk making a scene. Firmly, I inform my wayward emotions that this relationship is platonic and I shouldn't complicate it, but my body is already leaning forward. Standing on tip-toe seems so natural after a year of your six-foot-three company. My face upturned to you, I stand at arms length, head cocked, a posture worn comfortable with use, no longer seeming odd or unnatural. Although already on the balls of my feet, I reach farther up, stretching, balanced perfectly on the toes of my combat boots, back arched to keep from falling into you. At last, I reach your face. I can't imagine you letting me do this, but I can't imagine you stopping me either. I keep my eyes open, afraid that if I close them, you will disappear and I'll fall forward, and keep falling, with no one to catch me.

I'm leaning close, close, close, so close, but not quite touching you. Your eyes are open and I can't read them. They are the color the sky would be if it could burn. My left hand curves around the back of your neck, fingers running through your short, soft hair. You're frozen, an ice sculpture, and my lips brush snowflakes before you turn away, your left hand gently pushing me from you.

"What are you doing?" You speak to me in the same placating tone you use for puppies who press their muddy paws against your legs.

You remain motionless and unreadable. We've been standing here so long. We've been standing here for years, and no one else is leaving the theater. I want to talk to you, I'm desperate to say something, to end this terrible, undefined silence. But I don't. We are graceless statues beneath the flickering streetlight. I look up to stare blindly into your charred blue eyes, hoping for a sign of forgiveness, or even reproach. I see nothing. I have never felt so awkward and frightened and stupid in my life.

"I'm sorry," I whisper, only I sort of cough out the word, and it hangs in the air, an empty, phlegmy phrase, but all I can trust myself to say.

# Precarious 2, the sequel

**SUBMITTED TO *THE MASQUE***

Her lips are eating me every time I look at her my eyes rest on those lips and my skin imagines them. She opens her mouth and closes it on my flesh, but no, we are two feet apart and walking towards the door. Outside her footsteps are loud. She wears black combat boots laced with purple ribbon frayed at the ends and I think they are too large for her. It seems everyone is looking, trying to find the source of those footfalls. Most women I know are high-heeled with small clipped canters like carriage horses, but she strides and her legs are two slim curves of muscle, parentheses around the center of all my anxious thoughts.

We have stopped under a streetlight. My heart stutters. Someone from work may walk by and see us a man and a girl and what would I say? A coincidence? She smells so good, like cinnamon. We are not talking. I should talk. We should be talking. I want her to speak because I do not like the sound of my voice. I always sound as though I am recovering from a cold, but her voice is shivery and wonderful. And she has sharp eyes; she notices what happens in the backgrounds of scenes. She sees layers of meaning. She is smarter than I am. She is growing, moving so fast. This year an intern and then college and then she will have a better job than I do. She is growing, moving so fast I am jealous. Waiting in line, she asked about my day I had nothing to tell her because my day was four walls in an office building, my day was a cubicle, my day was waiting for her lips. I walked to the men's room four times because it is two doors past the mail room where she sometimes works. I feel like she is flying past me; she will be gone so soon and she will forget. I try to hold her to me with stories, with secrets, things no one else knows. But now she is my secret and I have no stories left to share.

I do not want her to look at me. She must see that I am not beautiful. If only we could speak blindfolded, sit beside one another in darkness where I would not have crow's feet and strange, orange-flecked eyes, where she would be invisible to me and I could speak without aching.

In the lamplight her hair is the color of the last November leaves. Her lips are moving, saying something, and they are very pink and I can see where she has bitten them and I want to bite them, but softly, not leaving marks. She balanced on her toes as she spoke to me, aspiring to my height. She is talking about the movie and I respond without thinking because, oh God, every night I think of those lips; I concentrate on that tiny part of her because if I considered the entirety I would . . . it would be too much.

I don't want to stand here with so many people, where someone from work could walk by and see us and then what would I say? We ran into one another? A coincidence? I will say that.

She is on her toes as she talks to me and I wish I could be her size. I wish I were not so tall and stiff-limbed. She is slight and could fit anywhere, slip through narrow places, hide easily. Oh, her lips, she will make them bleed if she keeps biting them and I want to taste the blood on her lips and that's a horrible thing to think. She puts her arm around my neck because she is falling, I think. She has been balancing on her toes too long and I try to look through her, to freeze because I can't think about her hand on my neck and the thick bands of her pewter rings cold in the night and raising gooseflesh on my skin. I distinctly remember begging God for a thirteen-year-old girl but that was years ago and why, why did she finally come now? I want to crush her to me close, so close. Her lips touch me. I will melt, I will forget everything but her and we will drown.

If someone is watching they will have seen her kiss me, they may know us, they may know her age and who would believe I had never done more than kiss her?

I gently push her away and her collarbone through her shirt makes me ache and the feeling of running my tongue along its length is so clear as if it were a memory not a wish. Her eyes are breaking, everything is falling apart. She looks down ashamed and I fall down with her gaze but I am still standing.

"I . . . am . . . sorry," she stammers as if it were a sentence that had taken her weeks to compose.

~ Anon E. Muss 2001

Palmer Jones' screen name is **Hotti4u.**

**Hotti4u:** 'allo

**Hotti4u:** what's ^?

**Bnannafish:** Hey, how are early apps going?

**Bnannafish:** joyfully?

**Hotti4u:** ecstatically

**Hotti4u:** i finished my apps, then promptly got a sty, an ear ache, and a sinus infection.

**Bnannafish:** thank you, Santa.

**Hotti4u:** i am now a percossetted zombie.

**Hotti4u:** yep

**Bnannafish:** thumbs up to percosset

**Hotti4u:** yeah, except it's nauseating.

**Hotti4u:** anyway it's nice to be done

**Hotti4u:** what have you been up to?

**Bnannafish:** grading papers, writing reports

**Hotti4u:** aw, poor you

**Bnannafish:** i know, I slaved for 4 hours.

**Bnannafish:** er . . . Or maybe it was 3

**Bnannafish:** or 1

**Hotti4u:** speaking of work, do you think I would incur sychological trauma if I worked as an exotic dancer to pay for college? I don't see how a norml job could possibly leav me enough time for my studies.

**Bnannafish:** ok, so I didn't actually grade any papers today, but I was going to . . .

**Hotti4u:** ugh . . . sorry . . . about the spelling . . . it's the percosset

**Bnannafish:** uh . . . how exotic?

**Hotti4u:** my butt must be covered. No g-strings . . .

**Hotti4u:** some sort of bra or shirt

**Hotti4u:** and absolutely no touching

**Hotti4u:** i would never work in a place that permits body tipping

**Bnannafish:** . . . uh . . . all good rules. you've clearly thought this through

**Bnannafish:** why not be a model for art classes or photographers?

**Hotti4u:** BTDT

**Bnannafish:** ?

**Hotti4u:** been there, done that. I'm too fidgety to model. I need jobs that require mental and/or physical exertion.

**Bnannafish:** learn to meditate, if it pays well and frees up time for other stuff . . .

**Hotti4u:** dancers have somewhat regular hours at least

**Bnannafish:** true . . . uh . . . not that I would know . . .

**Hotti4u:** ha! i absolutely can't stand still for modeling, not even a possibility. It would make me despondent.

**Hotti4u:** dolorous

**Hotti4u:** woebegone

**Hotti4u:** :' (

**Hotti4u:** tenebrific

**Bnannafish:** thank you, Stanley Kaplan.

**Hotti4u:** i have a friend who is a dominatrix.

**Hotti4u:** i'm considering that as well

**Bnannafish:** a "friend," eh? Who doesn't?

**Hotti4u:** i've actually been learning flogging this month

**Bnannafish:** who hasn't?

**Hotti4u:** BBFBBM

**Bnannafish:** ?

**Hotti4u:** the friend = bbfbbm

**Bnannafish:** ?

**Hotti4u:** body by Fisher-Price, brains by Mattel.

**Bnannafish:** Still does not compute.

**Hotti4u:** She has the body of a Tonka truck and the intellect of Barbie

**Hotti4u:** it's harder than it looks

**Hotti4u:** nothing like trying to be a bad-ass dom and getting ur whip wrapped around ur arm . . .

**Bnannafish:** yeah, that's no fun.

**Hotti4u:** dominatrices have to buy their own wardrobe (usually). That would be a nasty expense.

**Hotti4u:** if only I could choose my clients, I would be a dominatrix in an instant.

**Bnannafish:** what about portraiture?

**Hotti4u:** as in painting?

**Bnannafish:** yeah, your artwork is amazing.

**Hotti4u:** i don't think I am good enough, but it's a possibility, and painting is one of my favorite activities.

**Hotti4u:** actually I'd be hard-pressed to think of 5 things I like more than painting portraits

**Bnannafish:** see. put up a sign and see how it goes.

**Hotti4u:** hmmmn

**Hotti4u:** very tempting

**Bnannafish:** an internet search might give u some ideas. What about copy editing or . . . ?

**Hotti4u:** but how much would it pay?

**Bnannafish:** not sure anymore

**Hotti4u:** i'm concerned about time. All the college students I know exhaust themselves with academics and only have very part-time jobs

**Bnannafish:** really? where r u finding these people? Flexible hours would help.

**Hotti4u:** i am perversely attracted to exotic dancing, probably because I'm such a workaholic nerd most of the time.

**Bnannafish:** but there may be better, less scandalous jobs out there.

**Hotti4u:** but that may just be the percosset talking

**Hotti4u:** I know. I know. like painting?

**Hotti4u:** Thanks for the buzz kill

**Bnannafish:** Glad to be of service.

**Hotti4u:** I'm going to bed.

**Bnannafish:** Feel better

**Hotti4u:** Ditto

**Hotti4u:** hasta la vista baby

**Bnannafish:** c u

Look at the spaces between your fingers and know that my fingers fit perfectly there.

The word "love" should have a dictionary of its own. And lovers should have a special thesaurus.

**Amidala-grrrl:** Do you hate me?

**Bnannafish:** Only when you begin conversations that way

**Bnannafish:** Are we in 7th grade again?

**Amidala-grrrl:** Ugh, you're right.

**Amidala-grrrl:** But . . .

**Amidala-grrrl:** Uh . . .

**Amidala-grrrl:** Do you?

**Bnannafish:** Not any more than yesterday.

**Amidala-grrrl:** Okay good.

**Bnannafish:** Why?

**Bnannafish:** What did you do?

**Amidala-grrrl:** Didn't write you back last night . . .

**Bnannafish:** The horror!

**Amidala-grrrl:** Went to that party . . .

**Bnannafish:** Well, no time like the present for finding out how boring it is to be an adult.

**Amidala-grrrl:** Yah, so it was basically drinking and standing around. Just like middle school.

**Bnannafish:** Uh . . .

**Amidala-grrrl:** Or so I have heard.

**Bnannafish:** Quite

**Amidala-grrrl:** Was there anything I missed?

**Bnannafish:** Other than the d & s?

**Amidala-grrrl:** Yeah

**Bnannafish:** Subtle machinations mostly. Tumbling. Air guitar. Some complicated rhyme schemes

**Amidala-grrrl:** Gee, they couldn't spring for a raffle?

**Bnannafish:** I know! Or bingo.

**Amidala-grrrl:** B – I – N – G – O, B – I – N – G – O, And Bingo was his name-o.

**Amidala-grrrl:** Or a broomstick for limbo?

**Bnannafish:** Maybe next year.

**Amidala-grrrl:** Dare to dream.

**Amidala-grrrl:** ? for you

**Bnannafish:** yes

**Amidala-grrrl:** would you

**Bnannafish:** yes

**Amidala-grrrl:** I haven't asked my question yet.

**Bnannafish:** Whatever it is, yes. A letter of recommendation? An A for effort? Blood for the blood drive. Whatever you need.

**Amidala-grrrl:** Uh

**Amidala-grrrl:** Well

**Bnannafish:** Just give me the forms

**Amidala-grrrl:** Um

**Amidala-grrrl:** but

**Bnannafish:** I have 67 five-page essays to read by 8:00 a.m.

**Amidala-grrrl:** Oh

**Bnannafish:** Yeah,

**Amidala-grrrl:** We can talk later

**Bnannafish:** Anon

**Amidala-grrrl:** Okay. Anon.

**Bnannafish:** goodnight, goodnight,

**Amidala-grrrl:** a thousand times goodnight.

# Seersuckers

Today was a professional day when teachers met *in chambers* and discussed confidential school matters. Chambers convened in the wood-paneled loft of the library that commanded a view of the ocean, which today was as still as a mountain lake colored shadowy green and purple. The conference table, perfect for a feast, abided 100 years of Sag Hills' headmasters gazing down haughtily from gilded frames, as well as 100 years of graduates squinting from group photographs, all of the girls gowned in white brandishing blood red roses, all of the boys seersuckered in blue with white straw hats. The boys looked like graduates of a school for carnival barkers.

Assistant Headmaster Howard Ney, or "Ass't Head" as it said on the plaque above his door, chaired chambers. Someone blackened the 't not long after I arrived. No one knew exactly what Asshead did at the school. I saw him occasionally at assemblies and lunch, and he would look up at you every time you passed his door. He was as sunburned and lanky as a Norman Rockwell farmer, and he moved with the grace of a camel with sore knees. He dubbed all new teachers "rookie" and the headmaster "chief." Today his misbuttoned Oxford shirt was Labrador yellow. His eyes were driftwood grey. A monocle would have perfectly completed his look. His voice was the perfect timbre and cadence for slumber. On the first days of school he wore a tin sheriff's star pinned to his lapel. Because the headmaster never appeared at chambers, every indecision Asshead made was final.

Chambers wasted extraordinary amounts of time. Teachers bitched about kids. No one—except Asshead—cracked a grade book or Filofax, took notes, or referenced hard evidence. Discussion rarely produced plans of action. Agreement was seldom sought. My goal became to try to get people to say certain words. The most successful word-of-the-day was "rigor" which six different people used after I said it. Today's word "proactive" had only been repeated twice, which disappointed me. Normally the group is more suggestible. Otherwise, Jesus DeJesus, the school's guidance counselor and token teacher of color, and I spent the rest of the day playing "find the negro" in the graduation photos.

Today demerits for dress code violations dominated our time. The male faculty's unwillingness to reprimand girls for short skirts angered the female faculty. The men balked at using rulers to measure skirt height above the knee. The women bemoaned playing the heavies in this category. There was not a girl in the school whose skirt stretched to within two inches of her knee, including the kindergarteners. We spent two hours and forty-five minutes on this subject. I contributed nothing more than a couple of heavy sighs.

Next we voted concerning Jake Keene's student status. Jake, the son of a SHS faculty member, a 30-year veteran no less, allegedly tagged the school with graffiti. Because the tags all included the letters JK and a crude spray-painting of a one-eyed snake, they were assumed to be Jake's. Dr. DeJesus contended that tagging was a cultural art form and means of self-expression essential to the self esteem of a disenfranchised few. The other faculty laughed cheerfully at this and then immediately drew straws to see who had to tell Jake's mom about his expulsion after ten years at Sag Hill.

The crooked face of the clock glowed like a jack-o'-lantern. A door on rusty hinges creaked open inside me. My 30th birthday loomed like a good beating. Another decade of lonely. A sleep-walk through a dreamscape. Black nights and grey days, waking with my shoes still on. A pantomime of hard work for my parents' sake. A Tai-Chi of who I am supposed to be. This way to dusty death. I sought solvency, a hair cut, a dog, a good therapist, a fair woman or an exorcism. I was too old to be picky. I would settle for decent Chinese takeout.

After having endured two waves of marriages among my peers, life looked like a giant game of musical chairs. The music has stopped and there were only a couple of open seats left.

The clock called attention to itself as each minute passed. Time moved on creaky hinges.

The rest of the day was spent dreaming of once and future sailing lessons with Brickhouse and beginning to sketch a profile for myself for Mainsqueeze.com. While teenage girls crushing on me is flattering, I held out hope for someone . . . uh . . . taller. *Squeeze* also connected me with the Manhattan girls that I wanted to date. I gladly checked out of chambers.

> "Either our lives become stories or there is no way to get through them."
>
> ~Douglas Coupland

Internet dating is catalogue shopping for people. People shopping. People shopping for people. Everyone I know in New York does it. The photographs are a type of promissory note. Windows into souls. Similar to sixth grade, I had new crushes hourly, all people I would probably never talk to. Also like sixth grade, there was homework. Writing the headline for your profile is the hardest part. The headline runs right next to your primary photo—the one everyone sees. Not even an Annie Leibowitz photo could get past a gimpy headline. I skipped beautiful girls with the headlines, "eat me like a donut," "vacuum sealed for your protection," "do you think I am as cute as I think I am," "snuggle," and "Top choice, grade A." I lingered over "athletic enough to have swum (swam, swimmed?) in college," "jappy, nagging, lazy, grumpy," and "this is how Charlie Brown's little redheaded girl would look if she grew up gracefully (and without the big cartoon head)." Most voiced surprise about using such a method (as if anyone grows up dreaming of finding a mate through a dating service). References to soul mates, knights, princes and frogs were deal-breakers for me, as were photographs featuring: straw cowboy hats, endangered animal prints, purple velour, anything bedazzled and dogs in handbags. Bikini shots were nice, but they greatly reduced incentive.

Your alias was the next challenge. Headlines I liked such as "I like using ( )," "more chutzpah than your average debutante" and "I'll be honest, I'm so sexy it scares me sometimes," I skipped because they were connected to the aliases "(shopilicious),""Juicy" and "Fendigirl." Bootilicius might have worked. The aliases "Sassy," "Saucee" and "Lois Lane" made me pause. I made obsessive lists of headlines for myself:

- Tall
- Employed
- Tall, employed and literate
- Outstandingly tall
- Former t-ball all-star
- Role models: Arthur Fonzarelli, Ted Koppell, Winston Churchill, and Elvis
- the love-child of Kyle McLaughlin and Isabella Rossellinni
- Two parts John Cusack, one part Clint Eastwood and one part Charlie Brown
- Talents: the worm, air guitar, raising one eyebrow.
- I change my own oil
- Postcard from the edgy
- Guided by voices
- Crikey, photos, downloading, typing, filling out forms, more typing. What a production.

- An atypical all-American . . . uh . . . *type*
- I am Spartacus!
- A legend in my living room
- Ring size? Roommates? Existential angst?
- Lloyd Dabler is my idol
- Dislikes: Cher, clowns, redundancy
- The keymaster
- Bulletproof, bespectacled . . . ring any bells for you?
- Yes, your mom did put me up to this.
- 6-12 uncut

- I finally settled on:
- **Likes:** snow days, Tolstoy, Pythagoras, anything bobble-headed

It took me about three weeks to decide. I chose "good egg" as my alias. During those weeks I looked at millions of pictures and read a couple of profiles. I fell in love quickly, planned elaborate scintillating conversations that never occurred and received little positive feedback from the people I did finally contact. Over time experience taught me certain things. Clearly any reference to photographs or appearances was verboten. Enthusiasm was almost always met with silence. Excitement was best kept to oneself. Your contact email had to be general, but not generic. The right mix of interest and nonchalance.

I fiddled with my profile. Early on it read:

> *Me*: impossibly handsome, dashing, witty—followed by cheering throngs—the whole bit. Tall, know loads of big words, notable sense of rhythm, yet soft-spoken, humble, sometimes even shy. *You:* Ditto. **Me again:** Looks most often compared to Christopher Reeves in Superman 1 or a young Gregory Peck. People, lots of people, not just my mom and the Seniors I visit in nursing homes, see me this way. Degrees from fancy schools, blah, blah, blah. Looking for serious relationship, filled with laughter. Appreciation of irony crucial, sarcasm optional. Charming accents a plus.

I changed it to:

I enjoy life's simple pleasures. It's a good day if it includes any or all of the following: swimming, Earl grey tea, *The New York Times*, a slow walk, a quick run, Me winning the National Book Award, badminton, beverages, a movie, whitewater rafting, You winning an Oscar for Best Adaptation of a Play or Novel (for my novel, of course), food of some sort, nakedness, showering, flannel, bocci, sleep, Scrabble, scuba gear, play, a good book, a bicycle ride, massage, socks, laughter, applause, no safety net.

Still nothing.

My maiden voyage with health insurance (and with dating) motivated me to schedule a visit with a psychotherapist. Similar to dating, I left messages with forty or fifty therapists and heard back from none of them.

Finally I received my first response from a woman who called herself "Martha Stewart" with a headline that said "do I look fat in this?" next to a photograph that revealed that she looked a lot like Martha, which was very hot. Martha Stewart is on everyman's "to-do" list. Her bio said she liked "cooking, crafts and insider trading."

The email she wrote read: "You had me at Pythagoras."

Friday. D-day. Dateday. Desperately trying to find the right shoes to wear. Traipsing all over the city. (The baited breath phone call to 1-800-Kenneth Cole. Thwarted. Foiled again.) Therapy session with Princess Leia look-alike. She was testy. Arguing to try to get me to be more honest, to disclose fully. Be careful what you ask for Sissy. I'll rock you. This session is on my dime. I should get to decide what we talk about. I don't really even have the money to pay for this so the time is fairly precious. Forty-five minutes once a week. I could fill 45 minutes a day. Or an hour.

Eight o'clock with Martha Stewart. Obituary writer. *The New York Times*. A brassy midtown bar filled buttocks to buttocks with grey flannel. Her photographs suggest Martha is Ivory-Girl pretty with librarian sex appeal. Must remember to show enthusiasm. Don't shrink. Show interest. Don't let things drag on. Two hours tops. Two drink maximum. Leave on a high note. What will we talk about? Write notes. Christ, blind-dating is like job-interviewing. All the players are stiff and humorless. I must break that mold. No Barbara Walters-type questions. Don't make her cry.

D-Day came and went with a whimper (and only a moderate amount of drooling). Martha was . . . neighborly; Martha was nice. Bespectacled but nice. Cowel-necked but nice. Big spaces between her teeth but nice. She gave me all of the textbook signs of interest as portrayed through body language—removing clothing, sexy underthings, hair flipping. I was embarrassed in response. I shrank, not wanting to give off mixed messages. I do want to stay in touch, but how do I do that without miscommunicating? If I call and she's afraid I want more will I be shot down unnecessarily? (Hey, you can't reject me because I wasn't interested in the first place.) But do we want to go further? Do I desire more or simply desire to have had some effect on her. She had spent the day writing Stephen Sondheim's obituary, then she saw him on the street.

Date total = $54 ($16 dollar LIRR roundtrip, $8 cab from Penn Station so I wouldn't get sweaty and lost, $32 two rounds of drinks, $2 bus and train back to Penn Station.)

I sent out another hurricane of emails.

No responses.

A week later I receive a letter from girrrl_next_door. She is an architect from Vienna, educated at the Sorbonne. Not exactly next door to me, but okay.

My life becomes a montage of expensive first dates and unproductive therapy sessions.

D-day with GND. Sunday, a no man's land for dating, a day not even under consideration in *The Rules*. Lillith's glasses were very Frank Lloyd Wright, her hair Frank Gehry, her personality just plain frank. She looked at me over the tops of her lenses as if I had interrupted her from reading something important. She did everything but hiss at me. Me calmer, smoother, but still dull. Our conversation labored until we had had enough to drink then we laughed and smiled and flirted. The Austrian accent helped. I remember candy white teeth and a heart-shaped face. And just when things were warming up and rolling, I sent us packing. I thought the moment would linger on a walk toward the park and a cab. No such luck. She was surprised when I suggested that we go out again. I mumbled a response still thinking that all the signs were already there.

Oh well, I'll call her tomorrow. Which I promptly fail to do. Called Wednesday, left a short, non-committal message. Assuming things were still fine. Thursday comes and goes, call unanswered. As did Friday's email. When I saw the empty answering machine on Saturday I knew what it meant. I inadvertently listened to an old message from her. She was perky, chatty, poised and clear. Oops, such a girl would not put up with my stammering, my indecision, my unintended rudeness. I felt like an actor in a b-movie taking a bullet in the shoulder that sends him spinning to the ground. "You shot me," they would always call out incredulously, as if the gunman hadn't gathered as much. No, that's not it. I would prefer being shot. I could see the blood, finger the hole. Where I was was a murkier place, a no land's man.

Shit, just fill out this questionnaire for me so I can know what I did wrong. I am not so worried about losing this girl—already I am saying 'what was her name?'—I am worried about losing. What had it been? Was I not good-looking enough? Was I dull? What did my clothes say that I did not want said? How does this speak of me? I could have played richer, puffed out my chest, talked a better talk. Probably I should have been a better gentleman. Bolder. More decisive. Clearly expressing interest. Clearly explaining my concerns. Gus says that I should move forward with the mission to have sex and anything else is a bonus. It's not like I go out expecting anything, but . . .

Leslie was a five-foot-eleven kickboxer from Michigan wearing a black velvet choker and patent leather Mary Janes. A very Melrose Place black velvet choker with a small silver heart charm. I was equally confused. The restaurant was shadowy and overstuffed; it smelled like the inside of a new Buick. Two of Leslie's three pictures looked like Elizabeth Taylor in "Butterfield 8." She looked like the third picture. She was magnetic, half would be attracted to her, half repulsed. Asia, our waitress, was closer to what I expected from Leslie. Leslie said "how are you" about five times when we met. We chatted. Bjork. Wilco. Maybe too much talk about me and teaching. She played on the golf team in college. Ho-hum and she got up to leave after about an hour and 25 minutes. "It's been great, we should do this again sometime . . ." I spent $100 on drinks and dinner. I never saw her face again.

I tried again with Lois Lane.

Dear Lois,

I feel like I already know you. To be perfectly honest, jumping over buildings in a single bound is way overrated. And while flying is wonderful, it is less so without a partner. Sure, my job = endless hours, high stress and not enough applause, but it is profoundly fulfilling. I'd like to share that with someone. When I take my glasses off and relax, it is like I am another person. 'More laid back and loose-er than you might guess.

How's that for starters? Tell me more about you. Siblings? Shoe size? Superpowers?

Truly,
Clark

No response. One day. One week. Two. I tried keyword searches that might net a winner. "Salinger," "Saunders" and "Soderbergh." Nothing.

Finally I typed "scarlet letter" and "Hester Prynne." Up popped the bubble girl's photograph next to the alias "H. Prynne" and the headline "a new kind of heroine." I clicked through the photographs, which catalogued her wiles. The heel in the air, the hand on the arm, the unbound laughter, the Homeric smiling. A golden retriever and a nephew—I hope—completed the picture. I was already picking out wedding invitations.

Her profile was one line, "if I were a bell, I'd be ringing."

I couldn't have said it better myself.

I spend five days drafting a letter to her. I wrote my life story in 600 words. I informally hired one sister and two friends as editors. We whittled my story down to five words. Then we delete those too. I experimented with opening lines. "Fancy meeting you here." No. "Needle in a haystack?" No. "Magic fairy dust land, part deux?" Nah. A Cinderella story? No. I scheduled another therapy session with Princess Leia. She wondered why I have spent so much time writing a letter to a stranger and so little time writing her checks. Finally I write:

> Dear Hester,
> I feel like we have already met.
> Best,
> Arthur

One day passes. I check my email every fifteen minutes. I program my computer to signal new mail with trumpets. I receive fifteen pieces of spam in the first hour. This disrupts my teaching. I switch it to a simple bell, like for a bellhop or a concierge. On the fourth day as I am heading to lunch I finally heard a "ding!"

> Dear Ben—ja—min,
> What took you so long?
> ☺ Loxi

God bless the Internets.

I often think of him before going to sleep; I want every cell of our bodies to touch.

A thousand sprites skate across my skin. In graceful figure-eights. Lutzes. Axels. Triple Salchows. Giant lazy O's. Leaving pearls of shaved ice all over my body. Spelling out a message in a forgotten tongue. A message in a body.

I bob and drift in light surf and wait for him to find me. I hope pirates don't get here first.

My breath fogs the glass.

Everything aches. Everything is agony. Agony is everything. The line between pleasure and pain is waf-fer thin.

No one ever calls, no one comes looking. Every part of me desires to be touched. I am mosing my lind.

I touch myself. I orgasm easily, in no time at all, seconds, a spontaneous combustion. Sometimes I wonder if it is one long orgasm with peaks and plateaus or thousands of little ones. Thousands of petite morts. Little deaths. I die a thousand deaths each day. Yes, that is the best way to describe my life. A little death. A thousand little deaths.

Even during school hours, I straddle the arm of a chair, lean myself against the cold steel of a desk, a telephone receiver, a lunch tray, a keyboard, a volleyball.

"Cowards die many times before their deaths, the valiant taste death but once."

Shakespeare always leaves me feeling crappy.

# East Egg, NY

Brickhouse never said *not* to drive the Mercedes, and I was only going to the train station, and since it is Loxi's first trip out—our very first date—what better way to begin than with the top down and the sun up.

Alabaster gulls whirled, and ghost-green treetops waved over the station.

Loxi was standing in the small arc of a rainbow. I wheeled alongside her in a honey-colored, 1963, two-door sports coupe with a mirrory finish. She was bronzed and strapless in a daisied sundress. She had a nutmeg spray of freckles across her nose and cheeks. She was black sunglasses and pearls. She was 23 and that is what 23 is. Twenty-three is bare shoulders. Twenty-three is daisies. Twenty-three has freckles. Twenty-three is starting out. Beginnings. No biological clock, no clocks of any kind.

"I feel like I am going to summer camp," she said, her voice had a soft Irish whisky running though it. Two flaming suns burned in the lenses of her dark sunglasses.

"Summer camp?

"I don't know; my clothes are in a duffle bag; I'm getting off a train." "I hope you're not looking forward to arts and crafts."

"Well, maybe just one or two potholders . . . And some archery."

"I can't make any promises." I tried not to notice the rise of her naked collarbones.

"I will settle for mosquitoes and ghost stories."

"Those can be arranged."

Loxi's Manhattan eyes caused me to appreciate my surroundings once more. Lush foliage canopied the cobbled roads meandering through the woodlands between the station and home. Our tires left puffs of gold dust behind us.

"Your car is very Gatsby. Are we in East or West Egg?"

"East. I think."

"I spent Labor Day at the little village of Sag Harbor in a big house with a housekeeper," she declared. And I thought, "Well, you'll spend this weekend with a view of a really big house with several housekeepers." Then I remembered that the Dalrymple's were vacationing—they'd asked me to feed Crick and Watson. The house could be mine, all mine. And Brickhouse had been so generous up to this point, I was sure she wouldn't care.

An archway of purple azaleas, complicated Linden trees and copper-colored, comma-shaped boxwood hedges framed the Dalrymple's driveway. (Twice a year, it took three men two weeks to trim this arbor.) It felt like we were headed to the Batcave. I had a feeling I hadn't had in a long time—that something was going to happen next.

"Oh, your castle *is* a castle. Why didn't you tell me?"

Because it just occurred to me.

The guest bedroom had a terrace which looked out on the water. The water sparkled in the early evening light. The moon was a silver parenthesis in the sky.

"Is this heaven?"

"No, it's Long Island." We laughed. Good fortune does that to you. Causes you to laugh at almost anything.

"My camp wasn't like this."

"Who would believe you if it was?"

"Do we need to dress for dinner?"

"Dress?"

"An evening dress, heels?"

"Not unless you'd like to."

"I have a denim skirt and espadrilles."

"Works for me."

The house was empty, but a television was on. The Twin Towers burning in high definition. Smoke pulsing from every window. We stood and watched for a moment. She looked at it as if it were a puzzle.

"What will we be doing first?"

"First on the agenda is gin, followed by tonic, limes and then ice. The rest of the schedule is flexible."

"Oh goody, I brought the right clothes for those things," she laughed.

So we lounged on the piazza, sipped tart cocktails, petted friendly dogs, wagged our tails and talked about New York. Loxi was an actress who spent her days auditioning. She'd been rejected four times that day. She'd appeared in Summer Stock Theater and daytime television along with one national commercial campaign for Velveeta cheese. She spent most of her college career flying to and from New York for auditions.

"My mother wants me to enter the Miss America pageant to get more exposure."

"Couldn't you just go streaking at the U.S. Open and save yourself some time?"

"I know. Cringe. I am an actor, not a trollop. But she's probably right about the exposure thing."

I built a fire, and we conversed nonstop for two hours. No anxiety, no preggo pauses, no seams. She laughed at everything I said. I didn't really say anything funny; she laughed anyway. Above us palm fronds clacked and whispered. Sunshine changed to starlight. We ate. We played Scrabble. We laughed. We talked about a moonlight swim. We made SMORES. We told ghost stories, swatted mosquitoes, listened to a cricket symphony.

Stars reflected on the black surface of the water. The red taillights of planes moved across the sky as if it were flat.

I could smell the ion charge of rainfall. We were definitely going to get wet.

At one point she took lip gloss from her purse and lacquered her lips in exaggerated strokes. I was embarrassed by this as if I were watching too private an act. I pretended not to notice. (Several days later I realized that was my cue.) Instead I cleared the table.

As I was doing the dishes, she rose and slowly unbuttoned her cardigan and placed it on the back of her chair as casually as she would if she were alone getting ready for a shower.

She descended the steps and disappeared into the darkness of the backyard. I stood in the doorway drying a dish and watched her white blouse appear on the branch of a tree.

She reappeared in the delicate, powdery light at the foot of the dock and slowly untied the navy blue ribbons wrapped at the ankles of her espadrilles. She shimmied out of her skirt and draped it across the railing.

She sauntered down the length of the dock clad only in mint-green bikini bottoms revealing two vanilla crescents that italicized the scoop of her rear end. There was nothing between that blue yonder and the top of her head except her. The clean nude plane of her shoulders flashed like a mirror tilted toward the light. What got me was the imperious roll of her heel-to-toe walk. God wanted her to be this way. The dock was like a pinball machine. Her languid hips setting off all of the bells.

I followed the trail of clothing.

She moved to the edge of the deck and paused for a dive. Her back still turned to me. A triangle of silver scales floated across the water from another place and time to frame her in its wavering light. She stood casually as if to meet it. So casually it hurt. It still hurts me when I think of it.

When she finally yawned and stretched and voiced concern about turning into a pumpkin, I walked her to the stairs leading up to the guest room.

Her hair still dripped and her white blouse—all she was wearing now—was patterned with transparent polka dots.

"I guess if I lose my slipper here, it won't be so hard to find me in the morning."

"I'd still go looking."

"What if the slipper doesn't fit?"

"Who wears slippers anymore?"

"What if it turns out that I have the personality of a ball of yarn?"

"I'm sure it would be a brightly colored ball. And who doesn't like yarn?"

A pause.

"Sheep, maybe."

The sprinklers in the yard turned on and sprayed silver into the black night.

We stood for several minutes in a pane of moonlight listening to the sprinklers sprinkle.

When our lips finally touched a volt of static electricity sparked between us causing us both to hop a step and reach to touch our upper lips where they still tingled.

That was a first.

Without turning Loxi began climbing the stairs slowly, holding her fingers to her mouth. I was nostalgic for that moment even as it was happening. It was both too much and not enough at the same time.

After our night and day together, everything was . . . more. Music. Sunshine. More. Color. Life. More. I was left singing. Music is made for moments like this. I drove back from the train station blasting Katrina and the Waves and singing along. I am walking on sunshine, oh . . . oh.

> **I wondered why everyone wasn't always singing, it seemed like the most obvious way to communicate.**
>
> ~Nick Fowler

I waited all of these years, these 30-odd—sometimes very odd—years, and I finally win. I win.

I win.

I win.

I get Loxi to take home. To keep.

I spend the next several hours planning our future. I wondered how many years it had been since the phrase "I love you" had wafted through the air in my presence.

I saw certainty. I saw an end to lonely Sunday afternoons. I saw someone sitting on the couch reading the newspaper; a simple vision that suddenly made my face flush. This is the person I will spend my life with. The thought did not send a chill through me. There were no goose pimples. I didn't fall to one knee or hear choruses singing. Not even any tears (certainly tears were in order after 30 years very much alone). Still, I was certain that I was right. That my life would change from this day forward and that I would share it all with Loxi. What have I learned from the examples of my siblings other than that love is hard work? I have spent the years girding myself, knowing that eventually I would have to take a leap of faith, to guess that I could get by or survive with the most recent person I was dating. To accept flaws . . . to compromise . . . to say goodbye to certain things forever. Yet here I was feeling otherwise. This new thing, this love, would follow me wherever I went.

Should I pick up the phone and call her. I just dropped her off at the train. I'll call later. That night: should I call? Will I call? It is late. She was up late last night. Should I wait for her to show her hand? Be confident. Oh shit, no answer. Should I leave a message? Is she screening? A short, sweet message? A long, confident one? I suck. I left no message. I fell asleep with the thought: Loxi will be my Waterloo, or she will be my wife.

## O M G!!!

He is better than sliced bread. He is a bread slicer. He is penny candy. He is Pez. He is man-ish among boys, boy-ish among men. When I talk; he listens. What a concept! He will make my day everyday.

> **Flesh is heretic.**
> **My body is a witch.**
> **I am burning it.**
>
> ~Eavan Boland

If you really think about it, eating is a peculiar habit. Sticking random bits and things into your mouth? That can't be good for you. I renounce food. I vomit hunger and engorge the flames of a fever. When I stand, the world swirls. I use desks and doorjambs to steady myself. I want to be as light as helium, thin as a rib, nothing but breath and shadow. If I wander far enough, I will come to it. I'd like to shave a slice or two off. Just a little less hip and breast, milk and honey; a few more days and nights should do it.

I cannot be not beautiful. It simply will not do.

My finger-and toe-nails were weighing me down, my hair was a burden. I cut them. My womanly wiles are overkill. Less will attract more. I can live on caffeine and Crystal Light. Reading is fundamental? So is purging. (It is also remedial.) You should always carry a toothbrush anyways. Like, duh.

# Phobaphobia

My school day equaled five 50-minute improvisational theater pieces, usually put on solo—using a variety of voices and the occasional disguise. I am a troupe of one. Every day I am expected to be on. While there are intermissions, there are no understudies, no supporting cast. As lead actor I must also be prepared to respond to every whim of the audience who can and will talk directly to me in the middle of every performance. Most will ask to go to the bathroom. Some will point out typos on my handouts or on the board. One will always ask, "Will this be on the test?" Few will ask questions relevant to the topic. I felt like the guy in old clips of the Ed Sullivan Show who keeps plates spinning on wooden poles and is always rushing around to make sure each plate keeps spinning and doesn't break. This generally made the class more about me than anything else. Can I do it again today? Keep the plates spinning? Break none? Entertain them? Enrapture some? Make some swoon? Make others laugh?

Fear drove this performance model of teaching. Fear of being shown for what I am: a fraud, a dolt, a sap, a weakling, someone who can't cut the mustard, walk the line, hold his smoke.

Fear bred fear. Insofar as I was afraid to be exposed, my students too would be afraid. Everyone dragged a knapsack filled with fears, insecurities, desires, expectations, needs, resentments—the list could go on forever—into the classroom. But the main component was fear.

Fear kept you going when you were dying to watch an hour of TV. Fear kept you grading essays at 2:00 a.m. The fear of my potential underlying fraudulence actually forced me to be a better performer and a bigger fraud. Humor masked the message in a form the kids were more willing to accept. The medium was not the message. It was all part of my funky (and partially demented) internal mechanism, but I made it work. I've always made it work.

Fear also kept you up at night.

Blink twice if any of this makes sense. In New York we live with a giant archer's target on our backs. Manhattan is the center of the target. If Manhattan becomes Fireball Island, Long Island will burn too. Thirty years ago Jim Carroll was pissing with fear "every time a fire truck or ambulance passed." Well, I am pissing with fear every time a fire truck or ambulance or police car or plane or helicopter or bright light or loud noise or curiously quiet neighbor passes. My dreams are sleeper cells filled with goblins flying flaming model airplanes and crashing them into gingerbread houses. Tongues of fire lick the sky. Ash falls like snowflakes.

I think more about the fire truck passing late at night than I do about Osama Bin Laden.

The city is wallpapered with skyscrapers. It's completely skyscrapered. Will it burn like paper? I wish we could re-model. It's hard to hide 100 stories. Even harder to hide millions of people in thousands of stories. Naked stories, naked city.

I dot my I's with mushroom clouds. I keep my journal in a fire-safe box.

We live twenty miles from "ground zero." Do you think it is fun living near a place called ground zero? There's no real grey area when it comes to that phrase. You can't help walking around feeling like planes are pointed at you from somewhere above you. I guess I would feel left out if the planes dropped and didn't get me.

I am waiting for the next shoe to drop. The National Guard and the cops with AK-47's make me feel less not more safe. Is it possible that the terrorists planned far enough in advance to learn how to fly jetliners and they only planned to take four planes on one day? And they had no other schemes? If these people are willing to die as part of their plot, there is no end to the possibilities. What about all the bridges and tunnels? You only have to throw a homemade bomb out of a car on the George Washington Bridge to bring it down. Going down underground to take the train is a risky move all of a sudden.

# The Keymaster

When do I call again? Do I wait a day? Can I wait a whole day? What if I leave a message and she doesn't call back? How long do I wait? I wasn't as easy and relaxed with my body as I should have been. Next time I need to be. Should I have been more physical? Or less? Did I let her down, not measure up, disqualify myself? She must have people lined up at her door. Is this it? Was there no magic for her? Oh fuck.

I decided to write an email.

> Loxi,
>
> I had a great time with you. I can't decide if I should pick up the phone and call you or just stand outside your house with a boombox held above my head playing Peter Gabriel like John Cusack in "Say Anything."
>
> ☺ Ben

I waited all day for a response. Day one passed without an answer. Has the balance of power shifted? What balance of power? Maybe I should call to say I was kidding about the whole Lloyd Dabler thing. I don't even own a boombox.

On Tuesday under the subject: "she gave me a pen" she wrote back:

> Lloyd,
>
> Uh . . . please don't stand outside my apartment with a boombox over your head. I think that's a SoHo commandment. It was one of 33 handed down to Issey Miyake and Kate Spade, the Moses-es of our generation, many seasons ago. I've heard that the original tablets are housed in the Armani Exchange store on Broadway, in case you'd like to confirm their existence.
>
> Talk to you soon!
>
> L

Oooooooooooooooooooooooooooooouch! Why does that hurt so much? My face was burning. I gave her my heart; she gave me a pen. Why did I send that email? Email bad. Send no more email. Ever.

Maybe I was wrong about her. We never did use the d-word. She was kissing a girl the first night I met her. She did go to Yale.

The next night: when do I call again? Do I wait a day? Can I wait a day? What if I leave a message and she doesn't call back? How long do I wait? I've had this conversation with myself before. Be strong. Don't quit. I called again but can't get through. A busy signal. Haven't heard one of those in awhile.

The wedding plans are put on hold.

After repeated attempts I realized that my phone had been disconnected. That's what those red envelopes from the phone company were about. I can't use the phone line to check my email either. The next day I snuck out of school to pay my bill and have service restored.

The next night: I called again but left no message. Called again later. Called and left message. A little crack in my voice. Would she notice? Why did I leave my number? Like she doesn't have it by now. Was that the sign of desperation that would make her not call back? Sinking in the pit of the pit of my stomach. The tenth circle of hell. I failed again. I fumbled. I fumbled the ball and then I kicked it. I imagined 22 helmeted monsters chasing after it.

On Friday I found her email from Wednesday night. She suggested doing something together on Sunday. The Golden Globes at her house. Her mom and dad were visiting from Connecticut (naturally). I broke my new email rule and wrote back immediately. I waited all day Saturday, Saturday night and Sunday morning for a return email or call. In that same stretch of time Pussy called me five times. I called Sunday at noon. No ring and cellphone voicemail. I got her machine at home. Oh god! She's blowing me off and can't bring herself to say so. I can't breathe. How will I get through the day? If I go workout, won't I miss her phone call and then would she think I was blowing her off? Workout would take two hours. I'll be out until 3:00. Is that too late? If I work out now and get more, clear bad news later, won't I need my workout to cope? Am I ruining our plans by not talking openly about them, not expressing clear interest, not leaving jokey messages for her. I swear I felt things were going perfectly well. All of the signs were there. She was smart, funny and beautiful. The trifecta. Everyone else I have ever known was a step down. Will she write a blow off email? Just not answer her phone or return my calls? Will I ever know what it was?

I must forge ahead. Proceed like all is well. Go get flowers. A new shirt at The Gap. What is the answer? How can I avoid feeling this way? Why must I always be all the way up or all the way down? What will I do if she cancels? Took garbage out. Checked messages. Shined shoes. Distracted myself. Wait until 2:00 for call. Then work out. Be back and in the shower by 4:30, out at 6:30.

I called my sister for advice, and she said that I no longer have my name and number blocked on my phone. What? Yes, I did. The phone company must have changed that when they turned my phone back on. OOOOOOHHHHHHHHHHHHHHHHHHHH, SHIT. I DON'T HAVE MYNUMBER BLOCKED!!!!!!!!!!!!!!!!!!!!!!!!!!!!!!!!!!!! DOES SHE HAVE CALLER I.D. AT HOME??????????????????????????????????????????????????? ???????????????????????????????????????????????????????????????????????????? ????//!!!!!!!!!!!!!!!!!!!!!!!!!!!!!!!!!!!! HOW MANY TIMES HAVE I CALLED AND NOT LEFT A MESSAGE? 5 HOME PHONE? 6 CELLPHONE? ???????? HOW MANY TIMES DID I CALL THE OTHER NIGHT?????????/ NOW SHE THINKS I'M A STALKER. WAS THIS ALL A SHAM? WEEKS OF DAYDREAMING. THINKING THINGS WENT FANTASTICALLY. DREAMING OF THE FUTURE. MY DUCKS IN A ROW . . . ALL FOR NAUGHT

Great.

At 5:00 Loxi called, fairly positive and blasé. She'll meet me at the subway station at 7:00. Yes, ma'am.

The sign on the wall in the Long Island Railroad said, "Welcome to Middle Class Poverty." On a Sunday evening, the only other white people left on the train were pock-marked and gaunt. The ones who weren't pock-marked were snaggle-toothed. Those who weren't snaggle-toothed had few teeth. All were sad. They read mostly. The ones who weren't reading were pretending to read, The Post. Nelson DeMille. Stephen King, looking no one in the eye. There could be a full-scale riot, and they wouldn't even look up. The black men did one of two things: glowered or snoozed. The ones who slept looked dead, legs splayed, chins buried in chests. How did they ever know when their stop was coming? Were they all getting off at the train's last stop? The black women focused on the floor; their thoughts turned inward, their vigil a silent one. Hispanics stared at the walls warily. Most had a ready smile. When a man getting off the train got his foot caught in the closing doors and his shoe fell off inside the train as he pulled his foot free and the train pulled away, the Hispanic men smiled broadly at me. The lone wildcard was a Middle-Eastern man in army fatigues talking into his sleeve. The great unwashed. Are these my people? Is this my destiny? Mix in unrequited love and I am fucked. She is the zenmaster; I am a spaz. Who is the walrus? Koo koo ka choo. I knew the answer involved being cool, calm, avoiding panic, but I don't know if I can deal with the heartache. I needed to use the force. The Jedi mind trick. "Do or do not, there is no try."

Sneakered and sweatshirted Loxi was seated halfway up the stairs, above a tile mosaic of a castle. She is positioned atop one of the turrets. A flock of birds parted as I strode through them into my new life. We kissed easily and naturally. I gave her flowers. She said, "My cat will enjoy eating these." I said, "Put them where she can't reach them." "She's a cat, she'll find a way." "Bon appetite, kitty."

Her apartment was one 10 x 12 room with a couch and no bed. She gave me a tour. "This is the living room." She said pointing to the sofa. "Here's the dining room." Pointing again to the sofa. The den. Again to the sofa. "The kitchen's over there." Gesturing to the stove, which was right next to the sofa. The mood was set by Christmas lights shaped like hot chili peppers. Again I think I am looking at the girl I will spend my life with.

We sat close enough to touch. Naturally so. We clasped hands. Lounged. Intertwined limbs. Canoodled. We ate Chinese and made fun of celebrities. Mira Sorvino has a wedgie. Calista Flockhart had a half stick of Dentyne for dinner. Loxi was very open with her feelings about who is hot and who is not. She cried over some of the acceptance speeches. She shared her own brushes with greatness. Fighting over a parking spot with J.Lo. Accidentally tripping Richard Gere in an airport. I shared mine. Bowling next to Scorsese. Rudi Guliani at an adjacent urinal. A faux fistfight with Muhammad Ali in an elevator. I made mine up. She was impressed. She updated hers to be: a one-night stand with Ethan Hawke, and a short romance with Evan Dando, lead singer of the Lemonheads. I don't know what to think of that. I don't try to top her.

Before I go I muted the television so we could talk.

I told her "I like you."

She responded, "Am I supposed to say 'I like you too?'"

I continued, saying I didn't know what she was thinking. I said, "When can I see you again?" She made a short guttural noise. I pointed this out. She called me a drama queen.

She said, "I wouldn't *over-think* things at this point."

No more than a minute later I was out the door. She didn't try to stop me.

## SUBMITTED TO THE MASQUE

you say you want a love poem
lick poetry from my lips
while i whisper about love
into the dark curl of your neck,
into the small of your back.

i won't love in rhyming couplets,
or Hallmark cards.
no purchased compliments
prepackaged,
promiscuously
printed for all to share.

your love poem
is written
in goose flesh on my skin,
in the rhythm of breath
coming faster,
in the curls of my toes.

~Anon E. Muss

# Links

After another sleepless night, the first fairway of the Knickerbocker Club appeared as if it were reflected in a convex mirror. Cattails wagged their brown and fleshy fingers at me and weeping willows waved. Early dismissal saved me once again. School let out every Friday at noon to give families a head start on vacation-home traffic.

"I know I am in trouble on days when my morning shower is a religious experience."

"Have a child, then every shower will be that way."

Her words came to me as colors. I have entered a fugue state.

"Two hours of sleep tops. I was sort of hoping that this would end as I got older. Or just wouldn't happen when I'm tired and desperately need the rest."

I dug my heels into egg white sand. Pussy towered above me on the crest of the trap which itself was on the crest of the hilly course.

"Don't you think that *that* is the reason it did happen."

"Well, yes, I suppose, Dr. Freud." I replied giving my ball a swift hack, which sent it briefly into the air. The wind blew gritty sand back into my face.

"Sorry, back to your story. So another day on two hours sleep?"

"Third in a row actually."

I was not yet out of the bunker. Pussy looked admirable in her heather blue sweater with the glow of a recent holiday in Egypt still warming her skin. She stood directly in line with where my ball should go if I were to hit it squarely. She smelled like sand and honeysuckle.

"You need to settle down and marry some nice girl."

I blasted the ball to her right and out of the bunker. Sand sprayed her spiked saddle shoes.

"And that will help me sleep?"

"It couldn't hurt. You'd have someone to talk to,"

"I've grown accustomed to having no one to talk to. Although five minutes ago I was quite enjoying talking to you."

'Yeah, you see, but I'm married."

"I'm well aware of that. Although that's the first time you have brought it up. So?"

"I can't be there all of the time."

"Nor would I want you to be."

It was Pussy's turn to hit, and she stopped talking until she measured her distance and swiped her ball cleanly. It hung in the sky like a balloon.

"We're not really talking about this, are we? Us?"

"That would be a first. Is there an Us?"

"You will never get anywhere hunching over your putter like that, hold your shoulders back and bend from the waist."

"Aye, aye, captain." I did as she said and promptly sunk a forty foot putt. I refused to look at her.

We picked up our balls and headed for the next tee. She said, "Have you ever played with Mrs. Dalrymple?"

"*Mrs.* Dalrymple?"

"*Jamie.*"

"Does she play golf?"

"I hear she's quite good.'

"Why don't you ask her to play?"

"Why don't you?"

'Because I don't play golf, remember?"

"Right. I forgot."

In the Fall the school laurelled its lapels with sterling silver Centennial medallions with burgundy and grey ribbon. The medals provided to the faculty were stamped with the school's crest. I lost mine, which ruffled eyebrows because the committee purchased exactly the necessary number. I was medallion-less for almost a week. On Monday while I was waiting for busses with some of my soccer players, Nan Doughty teetered up in mashed-potato-colored pumps to proclaim that she found my medallion. She brandished it along with a Snickers bar and offered them both to me. Before I could say, where did you find it or did I leave it behind at rehearsal, she said, "and I brought you a little something," handing me the candy bar. Then she turned and tottered off.

**Amidala-grrrl:** HI <><
**Amidala-grrrl:** !!!!!!!!!!!!!!!!!
**Bnannafish:** hi
**Amidala-grrrl:** ". . . put your arms around me
what you feel is what you are
and what you are is beautiful
do you wanna get married or run away?
I wanna wake up where you are . . ."
**Bnannafish:** uh . . .

**Auto response from Amidala-grrrl:** @ dance, u should b there 2, if ur not then ur not worth my time.

# As Little a Web as This

By November, Autumn had touched up the J. Crew catalogue world of the North Shore with chestnuts, acorns, aubergines, merlots, tangelos, coals, and carobs. The woods rang with the laughter of the loon, who came as usual to molt and bathe. The loons' arrival alerted every male on the island with anything even remotely resembling a firearm, in camouflaged golf carts and heated hunting blinds, with laser-sighted automatic rifles and compound crossbows, steered by infra-red, digital motion-sensor cameras and GPS navigation, with night-vision goggles, radio-controlled decoys and satellite weather gauges, with birdcalls and catcalls, with L.L. Bean and Orvis, vodka and gin. The apparati for firing greatly outnumbered those for aiming.

Hunters rustled through the woods like rowdy autumn leaves, seventy-five men for every one loon, the snouts of their guns pointed in every direction. Rain or shine. Day or night. The legend of the loon grew. They were heard but not seen.

Some hunters stationed themselves in tree-stands, some in underground enclosures. They swept the sky with broad-head arrows and buckshot.

The distant pop and snap of gunfire made me think of the pop and snap of blazing fireplaces, of the holidays fast approaching.

The school's website portrayed the school as exceptionally diverse and unmistakably happy. You could access the school calendar, athletic schedules and a short slide show of seasonal photographs. One African-American sixth grader appeared in every other picture. The technology department's lone contribution involved transposing cartoon leaves falling down the main interface in Fall, snowflakes in Winter, rain in the Spring and confetti in June. The site was notoriously easy to hack. Hackers most often played with the slide show, inserting pictures of teachers photoshopped into compromising positions, seniors into celebrity candids and the school mascot holding a bong in various settings around the globe. Common practice also entailed picturing two people together in a way that implied they were a couple. Many secret relationships were outed this way. If I had to guess, Ren was the hacker. He was not shy about his hacking. He often sent me emails from inside many of the country's biggest blue-chip corporations.

A week in the life of the website best illustrates the role it played. Over the weekend someone posted photographs of Tate Kirkland, the business manager, acting suspiciously friendly with Bridgitte, the undersexed French teacher, with whom he was rumored to be affairing.

By Monday morning most of the school had viewed the photographs. His wife Pep, the $3^{rd}$ grade teacher, took offense. Then she took an informal poll of her peers concerning the authenticity of the photographs. She spoke to everyone in the building but her husband and Bridgitte. It was noon before she interrupted one of my classes.

"What do you know about these photographs?" She said.

"Hi, I'm Ben. [We had never met.] Nothing." I replied.

"You didn't post them."

"God no."

"Some people think you did."

"Why?"

"Things like this didn't happen last year."

"Oh."

'Yeah."

"I hate photographs. Don't own a camera. Wouldn't have known to look at the website if kids didn't tell me to. It's my first year; I don't have a lot of free time. I assumed a student was doing it."

"What would you do?"

"What would I do when?"

"If you were in my shoes, what would you do?"

"Talk to my husband."

"Methinks he will protest too much."

"Then there is your answer."

She will never speak to you again.

Ten minutes later, brow still furrowed, she confronted Bridgitte in the faculty lounge in the middle of lower school lunch period while ten teachers looked on.

"Stay away from my husband," she declared.

Did I mention that Bridgitte was French? She replied, "Make me."

"I don't make trash, I burn it." Bridgitte's English wasn't great, but she understood the word "trash."

Bridgitte slapped Pep so hard she fell to the floor, effectively ending the conversation.

While there were no known photos of this event, a comic strip of the fight titled "the slap heard round the world" appeared in the slideshow by Tuesday morning.

> "And still I love the place for what I wanted it to be, as much for what it unashamedly is."
>
> ~Dannie Abse

On Wednesday someone outed a list of the salaries for every school employee including name, rank, years of service and responsibilities. The headmaster was famously secretive about salaries and tried to foster a code of silence surrounding staff and faculty pay. The list was a tremendous embarrassment for him, not just because he topped the list raking in $163,000 a year some $90,000 more than the second person on the list. That figure was especially shocking because everyone knew the school also provided the headmaster with a home a short walk from school, which was also fully stocked with food and drink—though mostly drink—supposedly because of all of the school-related entertaining he was expected to do. The school also provided him with a horizon blue Volvo station wagon. Because salaries did not match education and experience, every member of the community was eager to crack the code behind them. Some felt salaries must be connected to a teacher's ability to negotiate, although several famously hard-nosed faculty were surprisingly low on the list. Topping the list of faculty salaries and consequent faculty scorn was Chuck Love; the list also referenced him as the coordinator of both the technology department and student government although no one could remember him contributing to either group. The people highest on the list had to feel either their jobs were now in jeopardy or their next contract would be an unpleasant surprise. Without a doubt their daily performance would be scrutinized by all. The list failed to interest students thereby suggesting that there might be an adult hacker in our midst. Everyone had a theory about the identity of the newest culprit. All were agreed that more bitch slaps were in the offing.

The most popular, unofficial feature of the website involved the police report from the *Oyster Bay Chronicle* more commonly known as the *Oyster Bay Comical* or just the Comical. There every indiscretion was accounted for, from DW and DU-I's to criminal mischief, drug offenses and suspended licenses. The report also chronicled rulings related to incarceration, probation and community service and subsequently its successful or unsuccessful completion. Everyone in town already read *The Comical* for the police blotter. It was a great way to keep up with one another, much better than Christmas cards. It provided some comfort to those struggling with ebbing self-esteem. It also made for some interesting interactions, say for instance when someone who everyone knew had a suspended license drove her children to school. Luckily most of the teachers lived in other towns. The school did not notice or care that three teachers arrived via taxicab everyday. Reading the blotter on the school's website was also a good way to conserve paper; the school is very much committed to recycling. Although it clearly was not an official contribution of the school's famously overworked technology department, no one in the school questioned its appearance or authority. Whenever a photograph connected to a SHuSh-er was featured in the blotter, it also made the weekly slide show. One photo everyone in the community had surely viewed was Palmer's father holding a Burberry raincoat over his head as he was led into the courthouse after his most recent indecent exposure.

According to the Thursday morning *Comical*, Fern Señor was fingered for trafficking ecstasy. She had been absent all week. When *The Comical* came out, I started receiving phone calls from Pussy every five minutes. I had classes nonstop from 8:30 to 12:00. A text message she left said, "Help, the king is on the warpath. Get the police report off the website."

I dispatched Ren, and the report disappeared by lunch.

Lunch was too late. DK, toting a shotgun, tore the screen door off the police station at 10:00 a.m. The Oyster Bay Cove Police Station is not much bigger than a highway tollbooth and rarely fit more than one person. At the time the one cruiser was parked at IHOP. The charges disappeared. DK and his shotgun then visited the home of Jesus—generally understood to be the biggest local supplier and consumer of recreational pharmaceuticals. These actions failed to make the following week's police report, which was again posted on the school's website.

By Thanksgiving I came to appreciate both the actual and the virtual Sagamore Hill worlds. Both were forests filled with amateurs hunting loons.

In December the wind swelled and the waves surged and dashed angrily. Our sportsmen beat a retreat leaving the trees filled with lead and arrow.

I am naked at the computer. Shoulders bare, shorts down. I move my hips and spin my chair back and forth. The curtains are unloosed at the waist. The curtains breeze. Light windowpanes the floor. Outside silverware clinks on china. The doorknob turns and catches the latch.

I type and wait. Type and wait.

I am naked at the computer.

Wait.

Shoulders bare, shorts down.

Wait.

I move my hips and spin my chair back and forth.

Wait.

The curtains are unloosed at the waist. The curtains breeze. Light windowpanes the floor.

Wait.

The doorknob turns and catches the latch.

Do you have it set yet?

The camera?

Mine is ready.

I could die of disappointment. Embarrassment. Goose pimples. This is crazy, this is crazy. I will not click the "send image" button until I see . . . I want to trust . . . I do. But there is always the possibility . . .

Everything okay?

"Can you see me?"

No.

"Can you hear me?"

No.

"Drat."

"I can't get this thing to work."

Now I see shadows, the shape of a person. Black silhouette against a black background. Not a fair trade.

Lights might help.

"They're already on."

# Sky

The days passed, and the wind blew, and I always felt a trifle out of place.

In exchange for a couple of errands, Pussy proffered the keys to her Manhattan apartment. The address is at 73rd and Fifth Avenue. She warned me not to be frightened. "It is Hemingway-esque, filled with testosterone and taxidermy." I planned to go there every Friday afternoon and return Monday morning. My goal was to find friends, although I am not sure how to do that. All of my high school friends are manual laborers in Jersey, unwilling to pay the $6 that would gain them access to bridges and tunnels. Going back to Hackysack and drinking flat beer from plastic cups in sawdusty bars would equal defeat for me. My college friends had all paired off. Their weekends were spent at Pottery Barn and FAO.

I had become Brickhouse's pet and Pussy's errand boy. Neither role was terribly taxing, but they were not titles I wished to hold. Brickhouse really just liked knowing I was there. In the evenings she would inevitably wave at me from the back porch with a cocktail in her hand. Pussy would call when she had an idea. Her latest brainchild was to stage "Guys and Dolls" as the musical for the parent-faculty performing troupe. "Gangsters, strippers, unrequited love. What could go wrong?" She wanted to know if I would prefer playing Nathan Detroit or Sky Masterson. I didn't know the play or the characters; I'd never been in a play much less a musical, so I figured there was no way I would win more than a bit part that wouldn't accentuate my shortcomings. I immediately forgot about the conversation until I heard that the cast list was posted in the theater, and I had been chosen to play Sky Masterson the male lead opposite Pussy.

For *Antigone* eleventh graders are asked to contemporize the script and perform their adaptation as a puppet show.

**Amidala-grrrl:** HI <><
**Amidala-grrrl:** !!!!!!!!!!!!!!!!!
**Amidala-grrrl:** i did ur homework since fri.
**Bnannafish:** 'ello
**Amidala-grrrl:** how big are the puppets?
**Bnannafish:** nonstop?
**Bnannafish:** have you eaten?
**Amidala-grrrl:** a very long time ago
**Bnannafish:** they're hand puppets
**Amidala-grrrl:** are they about six inches long?
**Bnannafish:** uh, they fit over ur hand
**Amidala-grrrl:** okay
**Amidala-grrrl:** is it okay to make puppet clothes?
**Bnannafish:** I wouldn't worry about clothes.
**Amidala-grrrl:** U do know u r going to dance on Friday, right?
**Bnannafish:** Uh . . .
**Amidala-grrrl:** My friends and I talked that over
**Bnannafish:** You have friends?
**Amidala-grrrl:** Har har
**Amidala-grrrl:** Hasn't anybody ever thought of making u dance?
**Bnannafish:** Uh . . .
**Amidala-grrrl:** No?
**Amidala-grrrl:** That is the obvious thing to do
**Amidala-grrrl:** And that is going to be a hallmark moment
**Bnannafish:** Er . . .
**Amidala-grrrl:** oh, BTW, (happy birthday to me!)
**Bnannafish:** when is ur b-day?
**Amidala-grrrl:** Tomorrow, I will be 14
**Bnannafish:** Ooooooh, you don't look a day over 12. My condolences.

**Amidala-grrrl:** =P

**Amidala-grrrl:** ok

**Amidala-grrrl:** can Kreon be a druglord?

**Bnannafish:** I guess so

**Amidala-grrrl:** ur joking right?

**Bnannafish:** as long as it doesn't take the play in a completely different direction.

**Amidala-grrrl:** ok

**Amidala-grrrl:** if kreon is a druglord, does the execution have to be the same?

**Bnannafish:** it takes place offstage doesn't it?

**Amidala-grrrl:** like, she has to be entombed or whatever?

**Amidala-grrrl:** when he says take her away, does it have to be to the same place as in the original play?

**Bnannafish:** they can take her wherever

**Amidala-grrrl:** ok

**Bnannafish:** no gangland executions onstage

**Amidala-grrrl:** i know, we have to save the puppets for the next group.

**Bnannafish:** summer's antigone is a black panther

**Amidala-grrrl:** If I make antigone a valley girl, does ismene have to be one too?

**Amidala-grrrl:** HELLO???

**Bnannafish:** it's up to u

**Amidala-grrrl:** i know?

**Amidala-grrrl:** i mean i know

**Amidala-grrrl:** then our ismene is going to be Guyanese

**Bnannafish:** hmmmmn, ok

**Amidala-grrrl:** it is really strange, because ismene is the only person from the "valley'

**Amidala-grrrl:** everyone else is Caribbean or livin' in da hood

**Amidala-grrrl:** she shouldn't be shallow and silly, ismene would be better as a valley girl

**Amidala-grrrl:** that's the problem! antigone needs to be insightful, stubborn and loyal, but if crystal plays her as a valley girl, i think we will lose the essence of the play and antigone.

**Amidala-grrrl:** DUCWIM

**Bnannafish:** DUCWIM?

**Amidala-grrrl:** Do you see what I mean?

**Bnannafish:** yah

**Amidala-grrrl:** GMTA

**Bnannafish:** ?

**Amidala-grrrl:** great minds think alike.

**Bnannafish:** O i c.

**Amidala-grrrl:** then we will pull a switcheroo. i will be antigone. i do a great Guyanese accent

**Bnannafish:** Kewl, bonus points for switcheroos

**Amidala-grrrl:** Really?

**Bnannafish:** No

**Amidala-grrrl:** What will you give bonus points for?

**Bnannafish:** Punctuality . . . good hygiene . . . the usual

**Amidala-grrrl:** Cuz I wanna a+

**Amidala-grrrl:** I luv that we can get A+'s now on our report cards

**Bnannafish:** As well u should

**Amidala-grrrl:** I want one

**Bnannafish:** Who doesn't?

**Amidala-grrrl:** Touché

**Bnannafish:** On that note, I bid u adieu

**Amidala-grrrl:** And I u

**Bnannafish:** TTFN

**Amidala-grrrl:** G'night, g'night. A thousand times g'night.

# Hammer Time

When my dead father's name appeared on my caller i.d., I was perplexed. Six hours of parsing poetry has a way of making everything seem fraught and ominously metaphorical. Marijuana didn't help. I paused for a long interval, vowed to stop smoking pot . . . again . . . starting tomorrow. Was it possible? A phone call from the dead? Was I crossing over? Again, the same vow.

M.C. Hammer's "U Can't Touch This"—this week's choice for a ringer—pushed everything else aside. There was no other sound. It was both mysterious and familiar. Its rhythm was not constant. It hurried, hesitated, paused, rushed on, stopped, then repeated itself as if it were some kind of a signal or code being tapped out. (To be safe, I checked my eyes in a mirror. Touched stuff in the room: groped the cool brass of a doorknob, fingered the uneven grain of the wood paneling.) As much as Mr. Hammer can sound prophetic, he did.

I approached the phone with the trepidation of a snake wrangler. My dad was not the phone-calling type. He had never owned a phone. In 30 years I never received a call from him. Never had a phone conversation. Hell, I'm fairly sure he only ever picked up the phone to get it to stop ringing. Also, I screen all of my calls. I never answer the phone.

Do I break this rule for him? End our life-and-death-long Mexican standoff? My dad was definitely not the answering-machine-message-leaving type either.

Outside the sea and sky had melted into a single palette whose surface was as slick and hard as enamel. Its darkness was absolute, unfathomable. While I looked on, a single silver star, unattended, no bigger than a little boat, drifted out into the ebony surface of the universe.

This was it. My lodestar. My legacy. My father and I, both so clumsy with affection, would finally have our moment, our game of catch. Finally some grown up person was going to lay it all out for me. (Yes, to be or not to be was the question. But what was the answer?) I leapt over a stack of newspapers and sidestepped several garbage bags to get to the phone. The act was dizzying, irreversible. It felt like falling.

Then M.C. Hammer faltered, and the song slipped away completely. The silence vanished too. The night filled back up with sound. I stood still. I repeated the words to myself, my lips moving slowly, "Can't touch this." My heart beat less strongly. My breathing shortened. I felt as though I had been asked to gather the flotsam of a distant dream and to put the scattered pieces back in their proper place. It was too late for that. The dream was gone.

Outside the darkness loosened. Black clouds raced across a grey sky. Winter thunder rumbled. A flood light from the boathouse cast a latticework of shadow and light on the water, which rolled out to sea and into nothingness. The world was starless. I was done waiting for answers to fall from the sky. With this thought came the simplest of solutions: *69. I could call back whoever called me by pressing star 69 on my touchtone phone. (It was working already. I was taking charge. "Watson! Come quickly." This is how a safe cracker must feel as the final digit tumbles into place.)

Like a champ, I punched * 6 9.

The phone responded with three shrill notes and a patronizing message, "The number you are trying to call cannot be reached by this method."

Something I said must have provoked another outburst from M.C. Hammer because the phone was singing again before I put it down. I was ready this time. I slapped the receiver to my ear and shouted, "Hello."

On the other end, I heard a tiny, bewildered, far-off voice, as if it were coming from deep in a well, say one word, "Bub?"

Yes! This person was family. No one else would know my childhood nickname. Way back when, I couldn't pronounce my L's, R's and V's very well, so when I would say, I love you, it would come out as, I bub you. My siblings, all avid fans of ridicule, made the most of that foible. (Yes, my family even found a way to twist love around to use it against you.) I was no longer Ben, I was forever, "Bub," which would often get changed to "Bubba" when I was not very fleet of foot or mind. Today, all of my nieces and nephews call me Bub, not ever Uncle Bub or even Uncle Ben, just Bub. To be fair, despite consistent prodding by my sisters to decide otherwise, I did not require the kids to call me Uncle Bub, although I could have. No, I would let it be a small act of solidarity with those little critters I would grow to bub so much.

"G-19," the tiny voice called out again.

This voice was the voice of my nephew Frick; he and I played Battleship via telephone. He was giving me the coordinates of his next missile strike on my fleet. Then he mimicked the sound of a missile in flight using a whistle we had spent hours perfecting together. He whistled into the phone for as long as he could hold it before taking another gigantic breath and starting over. I paused to test his lungs while I checked the game-board's radar screen assembled on my coffee table.

"Hit!" I cried.

Frick launched into his best explosion sound effect. I could hear that he was convulsing on the floor to illustrate further the impact of his missile. I couldn't help but share in his joy as he bombarded my Navy. As the year had progressed, so had our game. We polished and perfected it, adding dialogue and plot until we had manufactured a small, constantly changing play. Right now he was Napoleon Bonaparte (or as he often said "Polean Boparte") (occasionally he forgot his name altogether and referred to himself as Marco Polo). His feelings would often outrun his language. He was a born hero. Could play any part. Assume any necessary characteristic. I was known simply as Waterloo, which Frick promptly shortened to Lulu. When I introduced trash talking, Frick didn't quite get it. After several days of referring to Frick and his ships as Frogs-this or Frog-that (yes, I was teaching him ethnic slurs), he took great pride in the fact that his ships were filled with leaping, green, semi-aquatic amphibians. Our tacit treaty was that the game halted whenever anyone else appeared. Others could have no knowledge of any kind of it.

As it turns out, Frick was calling me using a cell-phone my mother bought my father about fifteen years ago. The receiver is as big as a brick and the carrying case and battery pack are similarly brick-like. And my Dad used it as one would use a brick, to hold open a door, to weigh down paper. I'm sure he never made a call with this phone, but the fact that my mother kept his service running says something, what I don't know. (To be fair it was impossible not to admire her faith. She would fight her own battle of torment over this man, and she would fight it gallantly.) Frick had a relationship like no other with my father, whom he called "Pop-pop." Frick unwittingly barged into my father's life and refused to accept him on any other terms but his own. Pop-pop was the first one he would go to when he got to their home, and the last one he would speak to before leaving. My Dad was as flabbergasted by it as we were. Frick would drop an armload of toys in his lap and just start barking out orders. "Okay, Pop-pop, you are Luke Skywalker and Dora the Explora and I am Batman and Mojo Jojo." At first we were afraid for Frick. (Trust me on this, my dad did not enjoy being "Dora the Explora.") (Biologists posit that some animals know only hunger and fear; Frick had yet to learn about fear.) Each of my father's children made a rescue attempt, suggesting that maybe Frick play elsewhere with others, but Frick wouldn't have it. And when my Dad's interest waned, Frick wouldn't accept that either. He would say flat out. "No, we're not done playing yet." The first ten times he said that the whole house tensed up. My mother even stopped ironing. (We were all eager to ensure that the last ass-kicking in this home had already occurred.)

Frick is my sister Elizabeth's youngest of three. I would give you his full name, but I must confess I don't remember all of it. It's terribly long and hopelessly bourgeois, combining the names of several imaginary relatives. I think there was a "Francis Scott Key" in there somewhere. The only one I remember is the one I seized on: Frederick, which I shortened to Frick and, much to my sister's dismay, it stuck.

Regardless of the season, Frick's round face was always as white and pristine as unwrit paper, except for the tip of his nose, which was rosy. His hair was prematurely gray. His eyes were two big crumbs of chocolate cake. He was more complex than other children. He poured maple syrup on all of his food, from broccoli to hot dogs. While routine contentment for him consisted of turning anything into a gun, he had infinite patience for all living things. His brain teemed with bizarre plans and peculiar longings. Like any child he went through fascinating phases. Age two for him was generally referred to by his aunts and uncles as the Year of the Penis. Soon after his second birthday, on an evening when his mother had invited some colleagues over for drinks, Frick appeared with his penis sticking out of his pants. When his mother asked him politely to put his penis away, he responded by saying, "I can't, it's too big." His penal fascination lasted a solid twelve months during which time he only referred to it as "my big penis." Although I did receive an angry phone call from my sister soon after his first reference to the size of his unit, I told her in no uncertain terms that I wished I could take credit for both the prodigious size of his package and his reference to its size. (In all honesty we had not yet discussed our penises; I was saving that conversation for later.) That was Frick's own stroke of genius. You can't teach that.

Oddly enough age two for Frick coincided with my own Year of the Penis, or Year of No Penis. To keep up with the Longfellows, I experimented with pharmaceutical-grade Prozac. The drug's only effect was that I completely forgot I had a penis. No really, for twelve months. I don't remember one false move precipitated by the presence of my penis. I pretty much forgot girls existed, at least as girls. I don't remember expending any energy in pursuit of anyone or waking up in the bed of any strangers. Seriously, Prozac could change the face of society. There would be no wars. Of course, when I finally realized that my penis had turned up missing, I was eager to have it back.

For his fourth birthday I gave Frick a Levi's jean jacket that matched the one I wore. Every time I visited, he was wearing this jacket. Originally I had also given him a handful of buttons from punk bands that I was fully prepared to pretend that I listened to, he decided to choose his own pin. So, on the left breast pocket, he fixed a fist-sized, black, plastic cockroach. That gesture cemented our bond. He would always do me one better.

I was two hours late for my trip to Hackysack. I decided to drive straight through this time, crossing my fingers that my 1986 white VW rabbit would make it.

There were only two clearly defined seasons in New Jersey: summer and winter. Winter was grim. Somewhere in late October, winter would fall like the curtain in a middle school play. The cold was emphatic. The cold stung. Prophets and rock stars had long ago burdened me with the guilt of these aberrations of nature. Winter was spent longing for summer. Gloating winters, with little snow as solace, hung on through May until every town was grizzled and sullen. This was truth. Reckless, occasionally heartless, truth. Between the blackness of the earth and the sky I felt blotted out, erased.

Suspended in mid-air on the turnpike, looking down on my hometown, I imagined myself to be a World War II pilot with a cherished cargo, looking down on a city that I alone knew was doomed for destruction. This was one of those quiet moments that take more courage than their made-for-TV cousins. This was a town that dwelled on past defeats. Leafless streets stretched long and blue. There were no streetlights, so the rectangular lights from windows guided me. At 10:45 I could smell suppers cooking. Grey curls of smoke leaked out of chimneys. I looked with sadness at the little houses so used to being taken for granted.

Thomas Wolffe was wrong. Sadly, I can go home again. Sadly. Nothing changes. No one changes. Their middles thicken and their hair thins, but nobody *changes*.

Memory had softened the edges, made the players better, more beautiful, kinder. Distance and delusion allowed me to imagine the great conversations we would have. Life-altering conversations that I plotted out word for word during sleepless nights, all of the things I had always wanted to say and hear said. Hope sprang eternal right up to the point where I saw our front door and remembered exactly who lived there and how they were and how I was when I was with them. My grand plans immediately became less grand. I would flee to the quiet comfort of a television. I made none of the phone calls I planned to make. None of those preplanned conversations occurred.

What was I thinking? We didn't talk. Really. People in Hackysack didn't prize conversation. We drank. Drank long enough to see things not change. Long enough to crash a couple of cars, get in a few fistfights, spend a night or two in jail and finger the random, unwitting, friend-of-a-friend. Long enough that at 18 I knew I wanted to see ol' Hackysack only through the fuzzy lens that decades of distance would provide. Long enough, well, long enough. Every holiday since high school I was reminded that I still had no other place to go when everyone else went home.

In my neighborhood there was Hasser, Howie, Jax, Cards and Squirrel with whom I had stolen ten-speed bicycles, drunk Southern Comfort and smoked homegrown weed behind the bowling alley before burning out on video games where a gorilla hurdled flaming barrels and climbed ladders in pursuit of a blonde girl or where missiles fell from the sky in the direction of cities we were supposed to protect. My friends were all Dead-heads. The deadhead dance, the braless girls in paisley smocks and greasy hair, the coverbands, the six-ounce clear plastic cups of Genesee beer, this is what I remember. Immaterial girls just beyond my grasping. Their currency was cool, and I was broke. I wore Levi corduroys and button-downs buttoned too far up, my hair too carefully prepared, my eyes too clear.

Squalls, Johnny D, Johnny L, Dano, Riles and Quinner were the friends I acquired after Hasser et al. got booted from our bourgy boys' school. (I can hear them know, "et what?"). The boys' school boys were preps mostly, from families who went on vacations, wore matching socks and dropped their kids off at school. In their eyes I knew girls who put out and guys who sold dope. Big whoop. I got them high and introduced them to the Grateful Dead, which I previously hated, the girls in paisley smocks, who barely knew my name, and Genesee beer, which we all learned to love. Girls became "bitties," guys were "buddies," parties were "ragers" (or not) and "smoke" was smoke.

Alas, Hackysack is who I am. I've tried to hide it, dress it up, move far away, pretend it wasn't there. The farther I got from home the further I moved from the truth.

> **"He will carry the city within himself.**
> **On the roads of exile, he will be the city."**
>
> ~Zbignew Herbert

It drew me as the moon draws water. Would there ever be any other place I could call home? I much preferred letting my selective memory define reality. The house was uninviting. Two gray windows were hung to the right of the brown front door. A battered hat-rack with a mirror in its center stood outside next to the stoop. As I turned into the driveway, the mirror caught my headlights and reflected them back into my face, effectively blinding me. I skidded to a stop to avoid maiming small children.

While still seeing tracers and little floating constellations, I watched my sister block Frick from exiting the door. She began her monologue before I reached the door.

"It's 11 fucking o'clock. My five-year-old is five years old. He has a bedtime."

That was news to me. I had come over so we could stay up late watching pointless movies.

"Yeah, well, when I was his age I was nine, so give me a break. I wasn't sitting by the pool popping bon-bons into my mouth. I was grading papers."

"But you were sitting by the pool . . ."

"I was sitting *near* the pool. It's December." She smells like menthol smoke and Wild Turkey, her holiday scent.

Taking one giant step per minute, Frick strode into and out of his mother's shadow while she continued to talk at me. I began eating a banana and couldn't hear a thing. Then he jerked his head in a northerly direction toward the TV room. Soon he was spelling "TV room" in the air with his finger. Repeatedly. How did so reasonable a creature live in peril of the two fools he calls parents? My only option was to join him. While no one with a dram of sense trusted his mother, I had iron-clad faith in Frick. Don't get me wrong, the kid had his quirks. If a girl infiltrated our circle, he stood stock still and repeated "go away" until they did. He called all girls "Miss Priss." He could tell tremendously tall tales, especially where his father was concerned.

So we stormed the living room with an armada of food—popcorn, chips, Cheez Whiz (anything with whiz in the title). First we tried to make up our own lyrics to "the Twelve Days of Christmas," but didn't get farther than "three wiener dogs." We picked things off the floor using our feet. We balanced popcorn on our noses.

Behind the televisions were seven Christmas trees of varying size. This would be my mother's first Christmas without my father and each of us had the same solution—buying her a tree. The first of the trees held exclusively Star Trek ornaments and blinking red and green lights. The second had Tiffany blue bows and silver balls accented by small white lights. The third was covered with tinsel and arts & crafts. Everything from linguini spray-painted gold and stuck to cardboard in the shape of a bell to paper-maiché globes. Three were strung with lights and no ornaments. Mine held garlands of cranberries and popcorn, gingerbread men in flight and candles melted to branches. Behind the trees was an elaborate tangle of plugs, wires and outlet extensions around the room's one 120-volt outlet, which serviced six trees, two lamps, the television, stereo, VCR, clock radio, air conditioner and space heater. This is who we are really.

I envied Frick's naïve admiration for the glowing trees. Not long ago he sent me something he had made at school. It was a clear baby food jar, inside which he had put water and silver and gold glitter. Inside the jar he had also placed a picture of the two of us. When you shook it, it looked like we were in the middle of a ticker-tape parade or in front of the paparazzi, lights flashing gold and silver. This was how Frick saw us, so this is how we were.

We were sitting in the brown, pleather Lazy-boy, where my dad had spent half his life. I'd brought bubblegum cigarettes. We took turns puffing all of the powdered sugar out in little white clouds; we squinted at one another through the smoke, chewing absentmindedly on the faux filters. In no time we were down to the end of the pack. Late-nights with Frick were especially great because he did this thing where once he was comfortable and sleepy he regressed a couple of years. He softened and cuddled close to me.

We went through his dinosaur flash cards; cards I hadn't seen him use in years. He knew the name of dinosaurs I had never heard of, ones that had either just been invented or discovered. He knew which ones ate "treetops" and which ones ate "dino-meat." We went through a stack of thirty or so cards, each he identified correctly from diplodocus to barosaurus. He corrected my pronunciation several times. When we were done he wanted to watch a videotape of a PBS special about dinosaurs.

Frick put the tape in, handed me the remote and clambered back into my arms. He was wearing Aquaman Underoos with webbed feet and holding one of his many stuffed creatures. This one was Popeye's friend Wimpy, famous for saying, "I'll gladly pay you Tuesday for a hamburger today." The doll's pants, jacket and tie were all too small for him and his belly. He had a brown bowler hat, a paintbrush moustache, a red nose, a round, almost bald head and a hamburger attached to his hand. As I watched Frick holding him closely, I realized Wimpy was the perfect likeness of my father.

We had watched this tape many times before. It was a tour of the dinosaur exhibits at the American Museum of Natural History conducted by long-winded men in white coats. Most of the tape showed one scientist or another clad in their white coats standing in front of a white wall blathering on. Frick hated seeing these people, each time they came on screen he would say, "No people, just bones," as a sign that I should fast-forward to the next part where the dinosaur bones were shown. During those sections, he was completely silent.

This night was different. As we scrolled passed the scientists, I wondered if we should stop and listen. They looked so knowledgeable.

When I stopped and tried to listen, Frick was emphatic, "No people, just bones!" He grew frustrated with me and the words came out of his little mouth as "no peebul, just boe-ownes." His stress on the last two syllables did not leave any room for argument.

So we looked at bones, a whole epoch's worth, and smoked fake cigarettes and held Wimpy close to our chests.

I tried one more time as we were nearing the end of the tape to listen to the scientists and this time Frick looked up at me and said simply, "Pop-pop's not gone."

It was a statement and not a question, but I still felt the need to respond, the need to share some small bit of wisdom gleaned from thirty years on this planet.

When Frick was born, I had the revelation that hope exists in a newborn child with a quality like infinity. But, even in his five short years, I'd watched this hope diminish. I watched his chocolate eyes change knowing that there was bitter chocolate in their future.

What do I say? I couldn't tell him that I didn't want to believe this. That I needed to part ways, to say goodbye, to shake that 280-pound bugbear.

Reflected back in the blue-black of the iris of his eye I saw a future greater than mine, a me greater than me.

Some dead white guy—maybe Emerson—said something about the spirit of infancy, something about the soul being privy to truths in infancy that a person only becomes distanced from as life continues.

This thought did more to explain Frick's statement than to give me something to say in response. At that point I was much more willing to trust his intuition than mine. In my own arms, Wimpy would have been shabby and vulgar, fond of drink, repose, Fruit of the Looms. In Frick's arms, Wimpy was loveable, loveable not because he loved you, but because you loved him.

I said nothing. I said nothing to Frick then, and we never would talk about it again.

Frick was ready for bed, and I knew the drill. Without a word, he rolled over on top of me, his face just below mine, his lips an exaggerated pucker. I kissed him once hard and blew air out with as much force as I could. His body went limp, and he slid down mine until his feet touched the floor. He dashed down the hallway whistling like a missile headed for a target.

Down the hall I heard the percussion of a bomb blast as Frick dove into bed, the light in his room turning on and off.

Hammer was right; I couldn't touch that.

# Never, Ever Land

It's not Christmas in my family until you unwrap a present the giver received as a free gift in exchange for coupons, box-tops or small business transactions. A plastic, desert-camouflage, Time-Life rain poncho. A Cap'N Crunch lampshade. A book of Cheerios trivia.

My goals are to sleep as much as possible and to spend the day in my pajamas, unshowered, fright-wigged, smelly. My destiny will lead me to the mall on the 24th, as it always does, with my younger brother, quietly discussing whether or not we should buy certain gifts, any gifts, whether anything we buy could possibly not end up on the shelf in the closet of my parents' bedroom. Plants? The ones we bought last year died of starvation. Books. The ones from two years ago are still unopened, although I have heard them talk several times of owning the titles. I could send my children to college with the money I had wasted on Christmas gifts over the years. But I do not plan to have children. We do not stand on ceremony. There was no pretense of making a go of it with a new item.

My parents wear jeans and sneakers to Christmas dinner. Aunts and uncles initiate conversations that are exact duplicates of former ones--high school sports, imaginary glory days, new sneakers. They reminisce about things that never happened. The wan attempts to recapture a past that we do not share. The generic gifts. I receive presents that reflect who my family wishes I was, not who I actually am. A red v-neck sweater with rhinestone Santas? A Laura Ingalls' peasant dress?

My Christmas past and present has freezer burn. Why cook a meal when you can defrost and reheat a former one? This isn't a home anymore; it's a museum. There's no living going on here. This museum, this melancholia retrospective, preserves everything in freezer bags. Bereft of life, taste, nutrition.

The misery is exquisite; I cannot look away. I am embarrassed by the mediocrity, the dearth of human emotion, the lackluster everything.

Father slouches in the middle of the hubbub staring away at the television, his own personal Lazy-boy, not even feigning interest. The patriarch. Why does anyone still try with him? I know I don't.

Sure glad I'm here; can I leave now? Three of my four presents were free gifts. A Cup O' Soup flashlight? A Long Island Credit Union alarm clock. A Head & Shoulders umbrella. None relate to my life in any way. Gladly there is so much hubbub that I can open these presents in relative obscurity and masque my horror.

*I look forward to the day when I can leave here and never return. Say goodbye for good. Adios. Sayonara. Aloha. Good riddance. I'm removing the de riguer family millstone and leaving it by the front door.*

*Flight not fight. Runnnnnnnnnnnnn.*

*Failure runs in my family. I know this. For some reason I keep coming back.*

# Fuse

For your consideration:
*The Masque*

The lights are out. She holds her breath. One hand slips inside her shirt along her side. Warm, surprising, soft fingers. Slowly, cautiously. Cooing across tremulous skin. Moving up her body. Over her hips and across her figure. She isn't wearing a bra, a discovery that causes him to pause and close his eyes. His fingers hot enough now to burn, if they stayed in one place.

These are never before touched breasts. Lightly freckled, virgin skin.

He pops one button. A pause. A second pop. Are they falling to the floor? A third, a fourth, fifth and sixth. He wets her dainty pink nipple with his tongue. He polishes it in circles. He inhales soft flesh. Pleasure in every cell.

Tell me one of your stories, she says.

A hand slides between her thighs and up. Beneath a scratchy skirt. She tries to remember what underwear she is wearing. "Monday"? "Wednesday"? "Naughty"? "Nice"? "Please, not 'Hello Kitty.'" He fingers the band of her cotton, bikini Baby Phat underwear. Expectation and guilt become need and fear. Letters cannot shape themselves into words or even sounds.

She isn't sure where to touch or how.

He tastes like snow and smells like rain. He reaches for her hand and closes it around himself. It is magic this thing in her hand. Soft, hard, hot, pulsing. As indivisible as a prime number. A hammer wrapped in velvet. A hammer with its own heartbeat. It makes both no sense and perfect sense. He gasps faster and faster and faster. She fumbles. He gasps. His breath shortens, staccatos. Is he crying? Going to sneeze?

Lips on the dome of her knee. Tongue butterflies along a writhing path. Tongue flicks. Tongue thrusts. Tongue seems to know the secret. Tongue tells her a story. He speaks to her in tongues.

His tongue pauses at the bead of flesh at the very tip of her, melts like butter in a hot pan, like foam in water, like a snowflake on naked skin.

They fuse.

Just what is that? She is a game show buzzer. A red light lighting. A chrysalis cracking open. She holds on, holds off, holds back with everything she has. For the longest time. For forever. Whatever she is holding back is a secret that she herself doesn't even know. It doesn't express itself in language. They haven't covered this in health class. Letting go feels like the biggest mistake she could ever make, separating her from an irreplaceable part of herself. She is breaking into pieces. Jigsawed like a puzzle. Cracked like china. Sharded like glass. Burst like a bubble. White-fingered waves spilling on the beach and melting into the sand. Water soaking the sand on the shore then recanting, water soaking the sand on the shore then recanting.

She is an unstrung puppet.

A kite with a broken string. Sailing off. Out of sight.

And this. This is the happiest she has ever been in her life.

Ever.

Submitted January 2002

# My Time of Day

I was torn between confiding in Pussy that I may have exaggerated my singing and acting experience and begging to be cut from the "Guys and Dolls" cast or sucking it up and muddling my way through. If I confide, she and others may see past the miasma of lies I have created. She might take away the New York apartment.

I rued telling Pussy I could sing. My high school band, "The Blow-Pops," was fictional. My feigned love for musicals was me playing along, being a good guy, sharing enthusiasm, keeping the conversation flowing. I had no idea I could end up in an actual musical. I went to austere Catholic schools in bad neighborhoods. Music education amounted to singing in church. We weren't allowed to play instruments or taught to read music. Music was for prayer, period.

Our first rehearsal entailed standing around a piano singing songs. Each person suggested a song and then we sang it together as a group, which was good because the other voices can drown my voice. I stand behind the piano reading the lyrics off the pianist's sheet music. When it was my turn to choose, I can only think of songs by Marilyn Manson and Nine Inch Nails. What song do I know that they too would know? The Star-Spangled Banner? Amazing Grace? Rainbow Connection from "The Muppet Movie?" I finally dug "Greased Lightning" out of my fourth grade memory bank. Everyone laughed at my suggestion, but then we sang it. They rejoiced over the swear words.

The play's director was recently divorced, diminutive Nan Doughty, the school's drama teacher. Nan wore Laura Ashley dresses and white, matronly, patent leather pumps every day of the year. Nan was heavily medicated. She also seemed to be tone deaf, which made me feel much better. The pianist was music teacher Geoff Wroth, renowned for a peculiar war injury that left him unable to bend the middle finger of his right hand. When he was writing on the board, it appeared as if he were giving the entire class *the finger*. The gesture fit with his angry, impertinent way. Everyone gathered around the piano was laughing and smiling except for Geoff and me. This gave me the motivation to change my ways. By the end of the first rehearsal, I was singing like a canary on its way into a coalmine.

When the technical side of the music was discussed, I made sure to nod and gesture without actually saying anything. When someone asked, "what key is this in?" I paused and nodded my head as if I was thinking the same thing until someone else answered. When Geoff said that the pitch of the first note is off in my version of "My Time of Day is the Dark Time," I agreed with him and then just tried to sing it *better*. Nan's notes left more room for interpretation. She said things like, "That was a little bland, or at least blander than it could be." Bland I understand. Later she said, "We don't want to find out later that the show could be a little more this and a little more that. Try to have more fun with things."

Rehearsals proceeded apace with Pussy and I doing our best to appear friendly but not too friendly. No one said a word about the fact that we were cast opposite one another, although Nan had to know it was Pussy's doing. I did my best to be nice to Nan. I appreciated her vague way and told her so. The other cast members spoke to me as if I were 12 which I didn't mind because it kept their expectations low. I think they thought I just graduated from college.

Pussy and I played it safe, exchanged no knowing looks, never got too far into character. My Sky Masterson was a decent, religious guy who openly respected the institution of marriage, and Pussy's Sarah Brown was a pious missionary who only cuts loose when the music played. Pussy also played one of the Hot Box Club, a savvy maneuver, which allowed her to frolic, dance and be scantily clad with the other showgirls.

Most rehearsals ended with more singing around the piano, which I originally found astonishing—all of these adults, smoking and drinking and smiling and singing! Now with the help of a book of show tune lyrics, and several hand-rolled cigarettes, I played along as if I were a Von Trapp.

Rehearsals often ran past midnight, and I was the only one who had to attend morning homeroom circa 7:45 a.m.

My classes during the month of rehearsals are blurry. First I tried assigning writing that required students to work quietly by themselves. Then I realized that method meant I would actually have to read these assignments leading to more not less work for me. I already have stacks of vocabulary quizzes from weeks past that I haven't touched. (Some found their way into the wastebasket.) Then I tried to be creative and, for instance, have the ninth grade, while we were reading *Romeo and Juliet*, create insults using lists of adjectives and nouns used by Shakespeare. We played a game I call "Thou Mother" modeled after MTV's "Yo Momma" where everyone attached their insults to the lines "Thou mother est _____" or "Thou art a _____." This was a smash. Kids stopped me in the hall to try out new insults. "Bull-pistle," "nut-hook" and "canker-blossom" were incorporated into the lexicon of the school. Students muttered the best insults to themselves as they walked down the hall. They i.m'ed me their latest concoctions. I stretched this activity to fill three class periods. Because I had no time to review the reading before each day, I pulled one idea from the text and used it to start a discussion that has no real direction but lasted a full fifty minutes. When the assignment was to read the scene at the Capulet's party where Romeo and Juliet first meet, I started one class by writing, "Romeo has madd skillz" on the board. Students called out their responses. In classes as small as twelve students, it was fairly easy to preside over a discussion that did not require raised hands. Occasionally I pulled a word from the conversation and write it on the board. Students dutifully transcribed everything I wrote into their notebooks. At the end of the class period about Romeo's skillz I have "slut, bro's, ho's, playa, fool, sympathy date, pity, mistake, pedophile, date-rape, and stalker" written on the board; this was not the direction I imagined the subject would take. The only thing the class agreed on was that the balcony scene is "stalker-ish." Still I had 9th grade boys raising their voices over Shakespeare so I felt less fraudulent. Other days I stole clothing from the costume closet and brought swords to class. We acted out Romeo and Juliet and practiced swordplay. We each took turns dying.

On the weekends I was still staying in the apartment on the Upper East Side. My social life consisted of going to clubs with Gus, going to movies by myself and grading papers. Occasionally Pussy asked me to run an errand or pick something up for her. In theory the apartment should have really improved my dating life, but getting Manhattan girls to pay attention to someone with a teacher's salary was difficult.

**"I have lost my sense of loss."**

~Elaine Equi

It was about here that my appendix burst and left me lying on the sidewalk outside of Dorian's Red Hand, which didn't make the average passer-by inclined to offer assistance. Eventually I made it to a hospital. I was given a room with a gentleman who didn't speak. In the morning, after about 12 hours of trying to engage him, a family member visited him and used sign language. At one point there were four nurses pow wowing over my penis trying to figure out why the catheter wasn't working. I wanted to disappear. I begged them to let me go home. Finally I just got up and left. I had $7 for a cab ride, which got me to within 10 blocks of Penn Station. The only consolation was the Vicodin in my pocket. The first one took me to another place in time. Not only do I feel no pain, I couldn't feel my toes; I'm not even sure if I still have toes. Toes are so over-rated. Vicodin could change the world. Life would be glorious if it all felt like this. There would be no war. I entered another dimension. Was I sleeping? What do you call this state? How can I become a permanent resident? Or governor? Damn that stuff was good. I intended to buy shares in Vicodin tomorrow.

The second Vicodin was different, providing nothing similar. Two at a time caused nausea that woke me up and left me driving the porcelain commuter train.

When I finally made it back to my apartment, I spent several horizontal days where Brickhouse and Juliet actually brought me chicken soup; I thought that only happened on TV.

Somehow Hester, AKA Loxi, found out I have been ill, and she sends me several surprisingly friendly emails. It may just be the Vicodin talking, but there was genuine concern and affection in them. I didn't expect that. She even suggested not one but two activities for the weekend: a movie night at her house and a trip to see her friend's band play CBGB's. I was skeptical. What happened to the other Hester? Are these sympathy dates? I will keep my guard up.

The only way I can make it to the Bowery for movies was by having my sister Alice drive three-hours roundtrip from Hackysack. Alice is eager to see me get married and off her back. She gave me a Smarties candy necklace to give to Hester. "Flowers?" she said, "What is this, 1950?"

The necklace was a hit. She sucked on it the whole night. She occasionally let me have a bite. We sat and watched "8-Mile." Her choice. I brought "Amelie." She initiated the touching. At one point she kissed the side of my face with feeling. I kept my distance, playing with her hair only briefly. We laughed our way through the movie, although laughing hurt my stitches. When the cab arrived, we had our first warm, mutual hug. She let herself sink into me, and she squeezed me back. Then she kissed me, slowly, three or four times, warm, wet lips slightly parted, moving from my bottom to my top lip. Our lips fuse together for a second. Those were our first real kisses. I forgot where I was, where I was going. I almost ran into the door. I heard myself using the words "oy," "golly" and "wunnerful." I heard her laugh.

I woke up the next morning in my apartment by myself.

While I rehearsed Sky Masterson, Hester rehearsed the role of Bunny Flingus the starlet in a JCC production of John Guare's "The House of Blue Leaves." Thankfully she was so caught up in preparation for her acting showcase that she did not ask to see me perform. It's also possible that I hadn't mentioned my role to her.

It was then, about the end of February, when my i.m.'s with Love became peculiar. She would write things like: what color is pain? And, if fear were a sound, what would it be like? Not long after that everyone was talking about her hair. She started out just shaving the side of her head. Then she gave herself a full Mohawk. Then she died it blue, the color of her eyes. I tried to be the one person in the school who was nonchalant about it.

# ZZ

Ren had a woodie. He was dress-slacked and wing-tipped, for Model U.N., and he had a massive erection in Twelfth Grade English. We were taking notes. My back had been turned. However, today was another effortful day, maybe I hallucinated. I was sleep-deprived and probably hung-over. Yes, that must be it; his pants bunched up. I tried not to look again.

Shit happened whenever I wasn't confident with the material. Teenagers can smell fear. I Cliff-noted through Shakespeare in college and canker-blossomed my transcript with a C from a bloviant nut-hook with a Pulitzer Prize. Consequently I stammered my way through lectures concerning the Bard. The Shakespeare Festival might just might be my Waterloo.

Dress pants don't lie. I was right; Ren definitely had wood. I could practically read the serial number on that thing. (His johnson was a commendable size for such a little guy. Maybe 1/5 his height. Nice work, Ren. He could chop wood with that thing. Signal aircraft. Measure drapes. Shave.) I could excuse the inopportune erection—penises were unpredictable—but now Ren was hitting it. With his fist. Punching it. At first it looked like he was mad at it as if it were a younger brother he wanted to go away. Then he appeared to be pummeling a speed-bag. One fist at a time. Hard. Really hard. Probably too hard. Gosh, Ren, you are going to hurt yourself. "Beat off" is just a phrase people toss around, a figure of speech, a slang term. Don't take it so literally.

What do I say? I can't say anything. He would die. The whole class would roar. If I asked him to go to the bathroom, he would have to walk across the room with a ruler in his pants. Everyone would notice. Besides he probably couldn't stand up straight right now. He'd have to transfer to another school. I would be fired. People would wonder why I noticed a teenager's erection. These are small classrooms, only 12 or 15 students per class. It was hard not to notice. I wish I hadn't. My ignorance would be blissful for both of us.

No whacking off in English class. Isn't that a given? Did I need to establish this as a rule?

Maybe I should just pretend it's not there, go on teaching, let him be. Ignore it. It will disappear. Penises are magic that way, right? Focus on the board. Turn my back. Shun it. Think: Shakespeare, the Globe Theater, the groundlings.

Teenagers are groundlings. They pay one cent to see a show; they mill about purposelessly smack in front of the action, readying rotten produce or song and dance depending on the quality of the production. If they don't get their money's worth, they extract their money's worth. Win the groundlings, and you win the war.

Ren commenced hitting his erection with both fists. Jesus. This wasn't going to end well.

Then I had the thought I wish I didn't have. The thought that complicated everything. What or who was causing this? Shakespeare? The female lead of the Scottish play?

Next to him, oblivious, twirling her hair on an absentminded finger, blowing tiny bubbles off the end of her tongue was Wendy Love. No! Not innocent little Love. Ren is a panting adolescent. He is nasty. Pubescent. There will be no whacking off over Love. I was tempted to saying something now. Then I glimpsed the other side of the octagonal table at which they sat. Palmer was exposing herself. Her breasts in full view. High beams shining straight at Ren. What the fuck! Has the world gone completely mad? (Note to self: no more turning your back for long stretches to write notes on the board.)

Okay, I must really be seeing things. Sweet, hard-working Palmer has her breasts out in English? Science maybe, but English? C'mon. Her sister might do that, but . . .

Ren, still with the pounding? You gotta stop, man. You are going to be a much less happy camper in a couple of seconds.

Maybe I was imagining this too. This can't be. Palmer and Ren? I prayed for the bell to ring, actually paused and said a little prayer. No other solutions presented themselves.

When I looked back at Palmer I realized she didn't know what was happening. She had turned her chair around and straddled it with her arms resting on the ladder-back of the chair. Unbeknownst to her the chair-back held her shirt above her breasts. Her rose pink, satin bra was as diaphanous as Ren's pants. Her skin buttery. (It *is* possible that Shakespeare caused *her* erections.)Should I say something to her? She would die too, and the boys would get a titty show. And I would be fired.

The door knocked. Or someone knocked at the door. Whichever. Just what I didn't need. Maybe it was the police. They've come to take me away for impersonating a teacher. Eliza Zable, the incorrigibly happy head of admissions, entered with two prospective parents. (SHS parents dubbed her ZZ until someone informed them that meant penis in French.) ZZ smiled her toothiest smile. Her hands, clasped admirably behind her back, said, "This ship is shipshape. It sells itself. Why don't you take a look around yourselves?" The timbre of her voice is one part campus minister, one part helium.

"This is Mr. Goodspeed. He teaches Ninth and Twelfth Grade English." Christ. The visitors' blazers boasted mismatched crests comprised primarily of complicated swirls of gold thread. Very Ralph Lauren.

"Hello." May I kill myself now?

"Mr. Goodspeed went to Harvard." And has no idea what he is doing.

"Please don't hold that against me." And pay no attention to Ren and Palmer.

"They're studying Shakespeare and preparing for the school-wide Shakespeare Festival." And getting in touch with our bodies.

"Yes, that's right. Lots of strutting and fretting going on here." The class smiled on cue. I curled my arm and showed off my bicep. Thinking: create a diversion, any diversion. The adults belly laughed. Such a phony display would normally nauseate me. (Later I would be pilloried for it.) That was the lesser of my worries. I raised my eyebrows quickly twice and turned back to the board.

"Thank you, Ben. Have a glorious day."

"Thank *you*. You too." I think? And don't let the door hit you on the ass . . . Next time phone ahead, won't you?

Disaster averted; the whole room sighed relief. They invoked "strutting and fretting" under their breath. I studied the scuffs on my shoes and sweated.

The bell went off like a mortar. I jumped. Everyone laughed. I didn't stop sweating until my room emptied. I can only guess what came of Ren's erection.

The next morning a cellphone photograph appeared on the school's website. Without thinking, I emailed Ren at his Intel e-dress.

Ren,

Remove the picture of Palmer or else.

I hate being a person.

The sky is lucent grey like the underbelly of a shark. The air is wet and cold. I balance the tripod of the telescope on the peak of the roof, which I straddle, to look at the stars. The rusted rooster weather vane creaks and turns its head away from me.

Night falls.

With one eye open, like a pirate, I view colored planets against a backdrop as black as the inside of a coal. I imagine shooting stars to be spaceships returning to dock after a night spent in another dimension. Space is astronomic, and I am not. My life is a pinprick. This is the sound of one hand not clapping. I miss the simplicity of being six-years-old when a cookie could change your day. Maybe astrophysics wasn't such a good idea. Maybe I would be better off with astrology. Or baking. Or the circus.

The boys in the physics department are reptilian; the one other girl is hermaphroditic. The sciences are strictly for the Dungeons & Dragons crowd. They wear t-shirts with slogans like " I heart Quidditch." "I'm not as think as you drunk I am." and "Orgasm Donor." They refer to one another as space monkeys. They stand with their feet pointing due east and west.

School is a black hole. I can't escape it. It sucks everything in. Looking at it is like looking at the sun; it could kill you.

My dating prospects are limited. Rensallear Wright is really the only upper classperson who talks to me. He looks like Harry Potter. He has the glasses and forehead scar. His scar looks more like a question mark than a lightning bolt. For the talent show, he played Beethovan's Fifth Symphony on piano punctuated by pauses where he turned to the audience and announced, " I like it raw!" Over and over. "I like it raw!" Pure. Genius. He spent the next two weeks in detention. He hacks into corporate computer networks and sends me funny emails from CEO's. I hope he doesn't get caught. I don't want to have to testify against him in court.

Today they cloned a sheep. Big whup. High schools have been cloning for years. My depression is an English Mastiff; it outweighs me by 75 pounds. Still I am reading and writing like a steam engine. Robert Fulton is my fucking idol.

I enter the labyrinth of cyberspace. I search for things that will make me feel. Desiring to touch something and be touched. I am the fingers of a million hands reaching out, plumbing the darkness. Virtual jazz hands. Reach out and touch someone. Let your fingers do the walking.

I do not discriminate. (Or, would not, if given the chance.) I am an equal opportunity employer. (Or would be, if given the opportunity.)

My dad's Who album crackles and pops on the rickety turntable. "See me. Feel me. Touch me. Heal me."

I enter a chat room titled "Star Whores." I use the screen name "LonelyLeia." I read and answer questions. Age/sex/location? Straight/gay/bi? Someone calling himself "Luke_Skyfucker" contacts me.

**Luke_Skyfucker:** How do you want to be fucked?
**LonelyLeia:** Like an animal.

He launches into elaborate descriptions of what he plans to do with his cock, as if it were some kind of weapon. Yuck. His messages arrive with a slashing light-saber sound effect. The conversation sounds sorta like a duel, but it's the sound of one sword clashing not two.

I watch the words pulse by. The cursor is a kind of heartbeat. I yield to my desire for conversation.

**Luke_Skyfucker:** My johnson has your name on it.
**LonelyLeia:** I like it raw.
**Luke_Skyfucker:** Are you really 18/f/L.I./bi?
**LonelyLeia:** Yes.
**Luke_Skyfucker:** righteous
**LonelyLeia:** how do you want to fuck me?
**Luke_Skyfucker:** like a dog.
**LonelyLeia:** how big is your cock?
**Luke_Skyfucker:** ginormous.
**LonelyLeia:** if it were a tree, what type of a tree would it be?
**Luke_Skyfucker:** a fucking oak tree
**LonelyLeia:** mmmnnn . . . I like sequoias.
Long pause. Oops
**LonelyLeia:** Oak trees are also a fav.
**Luke_Skyfucker:** damn straight
**LonelyLeia:** are you touching it?
**Luke_Skyfucker:** yah!

# Never, Ever Land

*Tonight I go out with "Marco" (AKA: Luke_Skyfucker) the guy I met in that chat room.*

*It is a time of lip balm, anoraks and half-truths, of coins tossed in paper coffee cups. I wear a short skirt for the occasion. We meet in East Egg. I unbutton my blouse from the neck down, revealing the swell of my breasts. He sweats like a gland.*

*When he penetrates me, his eyes are huge and black. Outer space black. Inside of a coal black. His hair sticks up straight, making him look surprised at all times.*

# Pajama Game

The winter weighed me down. All of the days were the same. The sun rises and sets and waxes behind a dressing room blind. It whirls week after week, month after month in a steady blur. Snow and ice outline the contours of the world. Wake up in darkness, go to school, argue with students, come back home in darkness, do schoolwork until incredibly late, watch some garbage on TV, then sleep fitfully.

Days go by.

I go to work.

I come home.

I go to work.

I come home.

This world was so much less exciting when it was covered in actual cloaks. We huddled in ice rinks and gymnasiums. We breathed frosty air. We passed one another in the heated confines of our cars, windows rolled up.

The knock at the door didn't wake me. Twelve people shuffling into my tiny apartment didn't wake me. The flash of a camera in my face did wake me. I woke to laughter. Twelve people staring down at me as a Polaroid camera noisily spit out a photograph. Backlit they looked like watercolors of themselves.

"Good morning, Mr. Goodspeed," they said in singsong fashion.

"Good morning?" I groaned, still too groggy to connect names with faces.

"You're coming with us." Barcley Conner stepped forward in a flowered nightgown and plaid robe and started pulling on my arm. The breath of cold air outside my covers helped me focus. Everyone was in their pajamas. The Bloomers were there guffawing. Trinka Grace. The Beckers. Jonathan Crisp's mom. Other faces I cannot place. One man was wearing a tuxedo. Everyone was wearing floppy galoshes that left waffle-shaped stains on my rug. The air was cold and redolent of cigars and flannel.

"I am? Why?" These seemed like fair questions.

"Yes. Because." Is what Trinka said trying to sound stern and official.

"Doctor's orders."

"Hurricane watch."

"Quarantine. Flu epidemic."

"Birthday surprise." Everyone was holding back laughter.

"It's not my birthday."

"No, it's mine. Surprise." Everyone but me laughed. Mrs. Conner steered me via my elbow toward the door.

Crouching in a foot of snow on the Dalrymple's lawn was a white limousine breathing smoke like a dragon. The world is a grey and black Rothko with feathery edges. We marched down the steps and climbed into the limo. Strewn on the floor was a bowling ball, a license plate, a brick, a weed eater, a can of whipped cream, a mannequin's arm and a head of lettuce. There was a stop sign propped against the opposite door, along with a series of Polaroids taped to the window: Mr. Bloomer with clothespins on his nipples. Two men kissing. Someone's rear end—I'm guessing Trinka's—in a thong. And the whole group pictured in some poor soul's bed.

There I was apprised of the master plan. They had a list of items to pick up. My name was on the list. "The photograph was just for fun." "We have to kidnap you." Jonathan Crisp's mom got behind the wheel of the limo. I wonder if I am the only one who thinks that is a bad idea. Empty bottles of varying size, shape and color rolled around our feet and clinked together as she pulled away.

"Next on the list is a speeding ticket. We fought over this one and Gloria won." The driver turned to me and raised one eyebrow. She hiccupped once.

With snowflakes falling like stars, the world blurring like a crayon drawing; and streetlights wearing soft halos, we tore past every police station in the county for the next forty-five minutes. There was nothing but snow and the things it covered. At 3:00 a.m., we were the only car on the road. We also looked to find: a parrot, a prostitute, an un-circumcised penis, an onion—which someone had to eat—and a report card with all D's or F's. According to Barcley these were "do-able." Our list was ten pages long. I read only a couple of pages. I was not yet in the mood to shave my eyebrows, fit into a Magnum condom, or deep throat a banana.

With no cops in sight, we changed our focus to acquiring a Jaguar anonymously. "Piece o' cake, but we'll have to split up afterward." We pulled into Pussy's driveway, and I thought to myself, "Oh fuck! How will I explain this one?" Barcley swung a hip into the door at the side of the garage and disappeared inside. Two minutes later the garage door opened and

Barcley drove out behind the wheel of the Domini-king's pewter XJS, wearing DK's plaid newsboy driving hat.

"If people only knew that no one on the North Shore locks their doors or takes the keys out of their cars." Trinka said wistfully as she arranged shot glasses filled with Sambuca on a silver tray. Mr. Conner leaned forward to light each glass with the blue flame of his Zippo.

> **"Have children ever been so safe in their bed . . .**
> **Here, after all were peace and safety."**
>
> ~**Phillip Roth**

"Cheers?" Trinka said to me, inflected like a question, conveying in a single word concern that, one, I was having fun, and, two, that the whole open-door-keys-in-the-car policy could lead to trouble someday. The empty bottom of her glass magnified the long lashes of her closed eyes.

"Cheers." I said.

At 4:30 we rendezvoused with the judges at the school parking lot. Parked haphazardly were five white limos, three Jaguars and about fifty pajama-ed and shivering parents. The air was fumed by exhaust and hard breathing. The wind moaned. The cars creaked under the weight of the gusting wind. It sounded as if we had just disembarked from a fleet of old wooden ships. Each team had one person tuxedoed. Finn was there in his p.j.'s, as were B-, $C^2$, Asshead and Nan. No Pussy and no Brickhouse. Interesting. Despite the cold, spirits were high. When a goat bleated inside one of the limos everyone cracked up. "Happy Rockefeller" was the only one who didn't look happy. Team captains surrendered their lists to Cole Grace. One person on each team had to swallow a goldfish. Hot toddies were circulated. Asshead mingled chuckling at people's pajamas. He wore a leopard print bra over his camouflage skivvies.

Barcley raced back to our car. "We're in third place. No one has a speeding ticket yet. The license plate only counts if it is from the police car when the speeding ticket is issued. I think we need to drink more; the other teams are getting naked left and right."

We piled back into the limo and left the Jag behind. Barcley was driving. Mr. Becker said, "Our house, pronto. Polar-bearing and naked hot-tubbing in one shot."

I am the type of guy who isn't comfortable walking around with his shirt off in the summertime, so . . . I will need more liquor to get through this part. We started passing a bottle of Chivas. I was the only one under 40. Some were over 50. Trinka and I looked worried; no one else did. The others were surprisingly competitive for 4:00 a.m.

Unbuttoning, untying and unzipping on the fly, almost before we came to a stop, everyone raced to the dock, which was strung with blinking Christmas lights. I was drunk enough not to care about getting naked, but sober enough to think others were foolish for discarding their clothes in the snow. I carried mine. Our breath rose above us as one cool, white cloud. There was something beautiful in the determination on Barcley's face. Birthday-suited and running full sprint speed between the wooden railings of the dock, her skin shined translucent in the moonlight. You could see through to who she was as a kid. Her stride was the stride of someone who hadn't run in decades but who also wasn't holding anything back. She did a textbook jackknife dive before hitting the water with her toes pointed perfectly. Jesus, who can top that? Everyone else cannonballed. Out of respect for Barcley, I did my best swan dive. The air above the water was warm, and I forgot for a second that it was winter, and I wore only boots, and the parents of my students were watching. As I descended, I remembered and tried to pull out of my dive but only made it half way. I belly-flopped into arctic water.

If the oily water weren't so goddamn cold, I would have hid under there for several hours. The others provided a polite golfer's clap for my reappearance. I bowed. Curtsied. Somebody snapped a picture of us from the dock.

We hottubbed for survival. Monroe Becker brought out our clothes hot from the dryer. We laughed. Toasted. Started to sing "For She's a Jolly-Good Fellow" before she hushed us and pointed upstairs.

We entered the limo with new life as if the night were just starting. We decided to drive to the city because the items left on the list worth the most points were all in Manhattan. The drive provided a great opportunity to pick up that speeding ticket. If not, the streets of Manhattan were usually swarming with cops.

Again Gloria Crisp drove, and Trinka served drinks. Mr. Becker bragged about how few cents a day his hot tub cost. The cold had left us ravenous. Mrs. Conner listed things she would like to eat.

"Buckwheat pancakes with real maple syrup."

"Blueberry scones and Earl Grey tea."

"Waffles."

"Eggs benedict."

She wasn't talking to anyone in particular.

The excitement over the swim, the steam of the tub and the steady hum of the motor at 85 mph made everyone sleepy.

Our commercial tags required us to take the pedestrian Long Island Expressway over the leafy parkway with its charming, low-slung stone archways. The LIE was crowded even at this hour. We shared the road with every truck in the tri-state area.

The city seen from the Queensborough Bridge was a gossamer of lights, swaying in the breeze. The city from way up high was a promise of all the crime we could ever hope for. It looks new to me every time I see it. Five a.m. appeared exactly the same as 10:00p.m. No one slept. Every building had lights on.

A rising siren provided the appropriate signifier of our arrival. I expected to see water ferries shooting streams of colored water. Zeppelins welcoming us. It took a minute to recognize that siren as a police siren from a cruiser pulled up behind us. The faces of the people across from me flashed red and white, on and off, as the light atop the police car spun silently as we pulled to a stop. Never before has a moving violation met with such loud cheering. Gloria clenched her fingers together and waved her fist above her head first to the right and then to the left.

"Yeah, my very first speeding ticket!" Trinka sang, as if we couldn't guess.

"How fast were we going?" Monroe Conner wasn't satisfied yet. We get ten points for every 10 miles an hour over the speed limit we are.

"Only about 65 in a 40; the tollbooth thingee slowed me down." Gloria was genuinely upset with herself. Her hands slapped the steering wheel at 2 and 10:00.

"Mental note everyone: if you want to get arrested, go to New York City."

"Of course, why didn't we think of it earlier?"

"It's implicit. It should say that on the welcome signs."

"Shh, here he comes." The police officer arrived with a ticket in hand.

"I'm going to have to issue you a summons for reckless driving. You went through the EzPass lane at 30 miles an hour."

"But . . . but I wasn't driving recklessly; I was speeding. I drove 85 the whole way here. I was definitely speeding."

Trinka rolled down a rear window to say, "She was, officer. She was speeding. It was wrong, and we admit it."

"Well, you're lucky then that you'll only be getting this one ticket." He looked in the back window at the mess on the floor, noted our attire, tipped his hat and rubbed his forehead. The lights of the city reflected in his glasses.

"But . . ." Gloria appealed to us for help.

"Can you make it a speeding ticket and we'll call it even?"

"Yeah, we'll trade you a reckless driving citation for a speeding ticket."

"I'm a city cop. We don't barter."

"Clearly you are the good cop," Gloria said, "where is the bad cop? Is he coming?" She looked back at the squad car.

He grimaced.

"Okay, so how about reckless driving *and* a speeding ticket?"

"Yes, we do want to pay our debt to society."

"Yes, we take traffic safety very seriously."

"Then why were you speeding?"

"Touché, officer."

"Yes, touché."

The officer chuckled to himself and walked away.

Barcley crawled back into the car with the license plate from the police car.

We punched through the skyline and entered glossy streets. We were inside the labyrinth. We walked on air down Park over the grates of the heating ducts of the spankiest apartments. When Trinka stopped to feel the warm air blowing up her nightgown everyone else kept walking. When I looked back her gown floated above her waist. She held her arms out as if she were flying. Her bare bottom and cleanly shaven front were as naked as Italian marble. No 1950's coquetry for her.

In short order, we: stole teacups from the Russian Tea Room, jumped in the fountain in front of the Met; bought hot pretzels from a street vendor, took a horse-drawn carriage ride in Central Park, and climbed to the penthouse of Trump Tower in the service elevator.

A white stretch limousine dropped me off in time for homeroom wearing a sweatshirt and sweatpants. I headed straight for the "lost and found" for a shirt and tie. The sweatpants will have to do for today. I'll tell everyone I sprained my ankle. I hope I don't forget to limp.

# April Fools

If you want to remember that your students really are just children or if you want to understand exactly how young they are, call them on the phone. Regardless of what kind of talk they talked in your presence or within earshot, or regardless of how close you are or how much time you spend together, or how long you have known them, or how recently you spoke, on the phone they will be bashful in direct proportion to their chronological age. The scale runs from very bashful at 18 to damn near baby-talk at age ten. The telephone is the great de-equalizer. Call to talk to a student's parents, and I assure you that you will not recognize that student's voice over the phone; you will assume it is a younger sibling or a child they are babysitting for or a random toddler who happened to be there when the phone rang. I have tested this theory over many months, through too many phone calls. The initial moment of recognition over the phone is startling for both parties.

At 11:30 on a Sunday night the phone rang. The caller i.d. said, "private." When I picked up the receiver a voice called out from the bottom of a well.

"Mr. Goodspeed?" A tiny voice, a deep well.

"Yes."

"Hi." Rising ever so slightly in the well.

"It's me, Love."

"Hi, Love."

"I'm sorry to bother you so late."

"That's okay. What's wrong? You sound like you have seen a ghost." Actually you sound like you are a ghost.

"I've never heard your voice over the phone before."

"Ditto."

"It's funny. You sound different."

"So do you."

"I have a question."

"K, shoot?"

"You have to promise you won't share this with anyone."

"Okay."

"How was your weekend?"

"That's your question?"

"No, it's small-talk: a noun, meaning casual or light conversation, chit chat. Synonyms: banter, chatter, gossip."

"Thank you, Merriam Webster. I like chit chat best. And Mmmmmm . . . synonym is my favorite flavor. Mmmmmmn."

"I prefer banter."

"It's a toss-up really."

"Love, you're not a small-talker, what's wrong?"

"I could be a small-talker, if I wanted to."

"Yes, you could. But I hope you don't."

"Hypothetically speaking, how does a doctor know if someone is pregnant?"

"Woah, Love, please tell me you are kidding."

"You are kidding."

"C'mon, this isn't something to joke about. You're 13."

"14."

"Whatev."

"Well, they do some tests."

"Of course, what kinda tests?"

I don't know. I faintly recollected a test that puts a rabbit's life in jeopardy.

"Are you writing a report?"

Love sneezes twice rapidly.

"Uh . . . no, I am not writing a report."

"Jesus, Love, we shouldn't be having this conversation."

"Why?"

"Because you are too young."

"Too young to talk about being pregnant?"

"No, too young to be worried about being pregnant."

"Who said I was that?"

"Why else would you be asking?"

"Intellectual curiosity? Civic duty?"

"Ha ha."

"I'm asking for a friend."

Right, the "friend defense," we've all used that one. I am more embarrassed by her lie than offended. Embarrassed because for her in this moment she *is* asking for a friend.

"Well, let's hope this is a false alarm. How late is this friend?"

"Ten days."

"Is that a lot?"

"That's what I wanna know."

"Sounds like a lot. It is almost two weeks."

"So, what should this friend do?"

"See a doctor."

"What if this friend can't afford a doctor?"

"There must be free clinics."

"There aren't. I checked."

"Well, then, maybe a home pregnancy test would be a good starting point."

"How would I get one of those?" I let this pass.

"You can buy them at the drugstore."

"No, I mean how would I get one of those. I don't drive. The closest drugstore is several miles away. It's 11:30."

There was a pause that would be considered, in almost any other situation, pregnant. It stretched out and lied down. I conversed with myself. Walking was out of the question in her part of Long Island. It's too cold for biking. Should I call her a cab?

> **"How do you know what you are going to do till you do it?**
> **The answer is, you don't."**
>
> ~**J.D. Salinger**

"You still there?"

"Yes.

"Can you go tomorrow after school?"

"I doubt my bus driver would be willing to stop and wait for me at the drugstore."

"You're probably right."

"Welcome to my life."

"It's normally a fairly compelling saga."

"Oh, right. My life had *ABC After-School Special* written all over it until now. Now it will go straight to video."

"Or Cinemax."

"You're not helping."

"Sorry."

"This is serious. My dad will kill me if I am pregnant."

"He won't actually kill you."

"You don't know my dad."

"But I do."

"Not really. He wears the mask at school. You have no idea. He'll take me out of Sag Hill for sure. Hello Hicksville High. They use metal detectors there. They'll make me be a seventh grader."

"Yikes."

"Yep."

"What about your mom?" That's a bad idea. Her mother is a stern woman, a public school teacher, most often sighted standing by herself at parent meetings, arms crossed, one toe tapping.

"What about her?"

"She could take you."

"But . . ."

"But, what?"

"But then I would have to tell her."

"And then she would know."

"Oh."

"I see."

"Well."

"Maybe. Maybe that is what you gotta do."

"Have I mentioned . . . That I am 13? . . ."

"14"

"The age of consent in this state . . ."

"Christ, the age of consent? Fuck."

"I've never heard you swear before. It's funny."

"What about the father? Possible father. *Alleged* father. Can you ask him?"

"Uh . . . well . . . er . . . uh <<cough>>"

"That's a good question."

"I'm *asking* you."

"Oh."

"Yeah."

"I see."

"So."

"But, what about . . . one of the seniors . . . ?"

"Right, my buds, happen to have any of their phone numbers?"

"Hi, I am in your English class. We've sat next to each other for 8 months and never talked once, but I thought I would call and ask for a little favor . . ."

"You don't talk to any of them?"

"Not for a lack of trying."

"Not even Palmer?"

"You were in high school once, right?"

"Yeah."

"So, then, do we need to really pursue this line of questioning?"

"I went to an all-boys school?"

"And that is relevant, why?"

"It was different."

"Boys at your school were especially communicative?"

"Uh."

"Yeah?"

"I'll shut up now."

"Be my BFFN, pick me up and take me to the pharmacy." I could hear the tears in her throat.

"BFFN?"

"Best friend for now."

"It's 11:30."

"I know. What time is better for you? For you and me to be driving around together that is?"

"Again, shutting up."

The next thing I remember is the hiccup of the phone hanging up.

In retrospect I could have said no. In theory no is such an easy word to say. Just say *no*. But Love and I both have heard no many more times than yes in our lifetimes. No-es define us. No is who we are. Two no-es in the land of yeses.

If you want an explanation for why I was at CVS with a thirteen-year-old at 11:30 on a school-night in my thirty-first year on this planet, I don't have one. Love asked. I have recounted the conversation here. What I presented is what I remember of the conversation, and what I remember I remember verbatim. It was at least twice as long. I could have said no. Could have said a lot of things. None occurred to me then. Many occur to me now.

My first reaction was repulsion and retreat. I went to my room and ruminated, rumpled my hair, slapped my face, modeled a variety of hooded sweatshirts and moaned through clenched teeth. I came out of my daze and found myself in the car. Then, with all possible caution, on mental tiptoe so to speak, I drove. How Love was going to get out of her house without some mishap was not clear.

Our car ride was solemn. We had a job to do. We did it. No one saw us. The only thing worth recounting was on the way home, a song by Staind came on the radio. Love turned it up. When the chorus arrived we both sang along,

> But I'm on the outside, the outside
> And I'm looking in
> I can see through you
> See your true colors
> 'Cause inside you're ugly
> You're ugly like me
> I can see through you
> See to the real you.

When I dropped Love off it was 1:15. She made it out of and back into her house without getting caught. I made it home without seeing a soul.

John Charles Lawrence

For Your Consideration

## I am Not

I am not the girl you keep.
You know this
from the beginning, or soon after.
But I am the girl you remember and go on
remembering after all the others have faded
to photographs,
names,
snatches
of music.

I wear fall colors in spring
guzzle the last of the Rice Dream and
demand that you fuck me at three am when you have work at six.

I whistle back at construction workers
On the highway I cut
in front of trucks
and you cover your eyes.

I am not the girl you marry
though I will flirt shamelessly
with your wife.

Later
lying beneath her
you will superimpose my face over hers.

I am the one who haunts you.

~ Anon E. Muss 2002

# Brute Neighbors.edu

I am not a fan of photographs. I don't wish to see myself frozen in time. It is like listening to my voice on tape. Could I sound that dull? That monotone? Like I am going to cry? Do I actually travel through the world all day sounding that way? The horror. Photographs document what I don't want documented. If I look at myself through the foggy glass of a post-shower bathroom mirror, I feel like I can make it through the day. The basic lines are okay. I would never look at a mirror in regular daylight or "God no" fluorescent light. I prefer the fuzzy, amber lens of nostalgia. I never look at my pictures in the yearbook. I never have. I don't keep pictures of myself around the house. I have a vague sense of what I hope I look like. Photographs disrupt this vision. I have never even looked closely at my driver's license to know what the photograph looks like. I trust that it is a picture of me. I was there when it was taken. It would be okay if it wasn't me.

However, when a photograph of me and Love in my car outside CVS appeared on the school's website, I looked long and hard at it. What was I thinking? I was pictured rubbing my eyes in frustration as Love appeals to me about something. When you clicked on the photograph a short videotape played of me and Love talking, Love getting out of the car, walking in front of the CVS sign, going inside and then coming out with something in a brown paper bag. The time was etched in red digits in the upper right hand corner of the shot. It was 12:15 a.m. I looked at least ten years older than I am. My posture was horrible; I was hunching. My hair was a freak-show. Love didn't look a day over twelve. I don't remember her wearing pigtails. The angle of one frame made my face disappear behind the back of Love's head as if we were kissing. We don't ever touch, but there was an intimacy like touching in our exchanges. The final frame showed Love revealing a box emblazoned with a daisy and the letters EPT writ large. Do I just know that is what it said or can everyone see that? I can't be sure. Am I dreaming this? I returned to my computer, punched the keys "is this a dream?" The screen said back, "is this a dream?" I looked outside. The air was still. Round balls of charcoal clouds rolled across the sky. Or was that smoke? From a fire? I was afraid to look. My career up in smoke? That fuse I lit each morning;

had it finally hit its mark? There was no sound. At 7:30 a.m. I had more caffeine in my bloodstream than blood. My steps were the steps of a person hip deep in murky water. My heart was running; my blood beating. The light was clouding; my mind casting shadows. The ground was blinking; my eyes turning. The air was quick-ticking; the clock stagnating. I left my body and viewed myself from a distance as if it were not me at all. As if this were a dream.

> **"No one can be more wise than destiny**
> **Many drew swords and died**
> **Wherever I came, I brought calamity."**
>
> ~A.L. Tennyson

Whereas some photographs set the school talking, this one cast a silence. No students teased you about it. No faculty referred to it. On the surface it was as if it wasn't even there. In case you failed to notice that it was there, you received a copy of it in your mailbox in the teachers' lounge. A black and white copy was in every mailbox, like the morning paper, cold with news.

The world became a Jacob Lawrence pictorial, all simple forms and flat color, all faces blank faces in a crowd.

Today was an exam day, so classes did not meet. Students took a morning and an afternoon exam. Your exam was given yesterday. English always goes first so English teachers have time to read all of the essays and grade their exams. Other teachers can give exams that are all multiple choice if they want. That was frowned upon in English.

It was Tuesday; you must grade 85 exams and calculate final marking period, second semester and year-end grades and write 85 grade reports by Friday morning at 9:00 a.m. Graduation is at 4:00 p.m. Before then you will also proctor four exams.

The wavy June heat blew in your face like the breath of a solicitous dog.

You have also been chosen by the seniors to be the graduation speaker. Somewhere along the way you have to write a speech. You have no idea what to say. The headmaster wants a copy of the speech in his office Thursday so he can proofread it, which is perfectly fair. Otherwise you could get up there and say pretty much anything you want. Even if you were not about to be fired, he should be wary concerning such a public event. The students didn't choose you because you were a safe choice. They expect you to make things interesting, and you originally did not intend to let them down.

The week happened. You get up and go to school and spend every free minute grading exams. At the breakfast, lunch and dinner tables. During final chambers meetings. While you are on the phone, the treadmill, the toilet. In bed, in the car at stoplights. You eat cereal for breakfast and dinner. Lunch was provided at school. The essays melt into one long essay. Your comments became more and more concise. Finally you were writing only "good" or "huh?" You have developed ways to fix exams where students have underperformed. Essays and short answer questions gave you the leeway to do this. You desperately wanted to fix the grades of asinine students who over-perform. When you finished you went back to make sure all of the grades were "right." You made some adjustments. You checked your comments to make sure that in your delirium you haven't insulted anyone's mother or said anything too harsh. You whited-out several "are you kidding me?"'s, a couple "I'm not as think as you stupid I am"'s, one "we spent three weeks on this and you can only come up with one sentence on the subject?" You tried to spin everything positively. Next to an identification question for Thoreau an 12th grader wrote, "the guy who lived by that lake. He sorta went crazy." You wrote, "It was a pond. What else did he do?" Another said, "On page 1 Holden Caufield talks about some madman, which is exciting. But the madman never shows up, which is disappointing." You responded, "Interesting interpretation."

When you finished grading exams and calculating averages, you had to write 85 half-page narratives concerning each individual student's progress. You've spent the semester jotting notes to yourself that you intended to use in this process. You read your notes again. You had notes for a grand total of 11 students. The notes are: "mature," "a step behind," "potential," "silly," "okay," "often disengaged," "super quiet," "temper tantrums," "nice girl, on task," "in & out," "spacey," "a talker," "solid" and "Asian." These notes will not prove helpful.

To break the ice you wrote some first impressions and quick thoughts about each student that you intended to go back and translate into teacher-ease. One student was "insanely good." For another you write, "look ma no hands—confidence good, overconfidence bad." For another, "his handwriting is difficult for me to decipher, it must also be hard for him to read, too."

In October you waxed. You crowed. You preened. You grandstanded, showboated, showed off. You thesaurused. You disported. You used words you had to look up in a dictionary. You consulted educational theory. You paraded examples. You quoted students' essays verbatim. It was a rare opportunity to showcase for parents what you, the teacher, are made of. Every student was a glorious individual. Every student's report was scrupulously original.

In June you euphemized. You spun. You twisted and contorted. You whitewashed. You shoveled. You used passive voice to soften sharp edges, to allow for alternative interpretations, to sidestep the thorny issue of blame. You copied, cut and pasted. These were somebody's babies you were talking about. Instead of saying that a student never did any homework, you said, "Two areas where Billy could focus more time and effort are preparation and follow-through. At Dartmouth his professors are less likely to monitor his homework on a daily basis." For a student who was probably sociopathic, you said, "Martin often struggles maintaining focus. His struggles can lead to verbalized frustration. More self-control will be expected from Martin in the future." For a slutty, goth, ninth-grade cutter who never wore long sleeves or slacks, whose creative writing was all about Wicca, whose grades ranged from zero to 86, you said, "Tabitha's best efforts produce commendable results."

You went to bed at 2:00 and woke up at 5:00. Wednesday you slept in a chair. You woke to a hissing radiator and the looming, inexorable dread of another job lost and a career ended. Thursday you deterred sleep with Ritalin and No-Doze and, at 4:00a.m., began stringing together ideas for your graduation speech. You could not help running your fingers up and down the keyboard of that year.

Friday you took the red pill.

On Friday you spent the day proofreading the reports of other teachers and they yours. Yours were riddled with typos, fragments, misused homonyms, verbs that disagree with subjects, split infinitives, contractions and "colloquious" language. All week you have tried to look everyone in the eye to communicate innocence. No one returned your gaze. Today your eyes never left the floor. Guilt slowed the movement of everything. You were sinking slowly to the bottom of the ocean.

The rest of the day was filled with harsh conflicting lines, shadows and refracted light.

At lunchtime teachers ate on the veranda overlooking the water where graduation was to be held. The tables around you filled up, you remained seated alone. This was the fifth turkey sandwich you have had for lunch this week or maybe you have been eating one long sandwich all week. The sandwich, like the essay, had no end to it. The band and chorus were practicing on the right-hand side of what will become the stage for graduation. This was the first time since the photographs that you have seen Love. She had one knee up; she was tying her shoe. The cicadas whirred. From fifty paces, through the shade of our beloved birch trees, past scornful colleagues, you and she will hold a gaze as if time gelled.

Time jerked forward at the sound of Asshead's voice, "Rookie, here are s'more corrections." He handed you a mess of papers, no two facing the same way, presented like a pizza. "Due in my office at 3:00. Good luck this afternoon. If nothing else, you will have a captive audience." His tone was no longer avuncular. Inside your head, that radiator from this morning was still hissing.

All of the tables and chairs around you were empty. The music has stopped. Ilse Fortune was standing stage left, sobbing into a bouquet of flowers. She was retiring after 35 years. Today is her last day.

You finished correcting your grade reports at 2:30. You had 30 minutes to shower, shave, dress, and practice your speech. You have not taken your suit, your one and only suit from this era, which you bought at Syms, to the dry cleaners. You found it on the floor of your closet. It was wrinkled and covered with the fur of the Dalrymple's dogs. The only clean dark socks you have did not reach much higher than your ankles. You will be seated on the stage with the headmaster and Pussy who is the president of the board of directors. You duct-taped over the holes in the soles of the tasseled loafers you have owned since freshman year of college. You used magic markers to make the tape blend in; it didn't really work. The bottoms of your shoes look like they are made of steel.

Sleep deprivation and the running shower kept making you think the phone was ringing. You stopped the shower three times to listen for the phone. You did not have time to practice your speech.

*Please Consider:*

## It didn't take much

It was spring and we were caught in it for the moment,
Forgetful of our separate designs
I didn't reason any of this out
It was there as instinct

We did so in a resolutely innocent way, never admitting
To ourselves what the real objective was:

I lived in a place where everybody knew me,
I couldn't help but try to introduce new versions of myself
As my interests changed, and other visions failed to persuade.

The absence of light became oppressive to me.
It took on the weight of other absences I could not admit to
Or even define but still felt sharply, on my own in this place.

For the rest of the day
He kept looking over at me, brushing back my hair.

I was subject to fits of feeling myself unworthy,
Somehow deeply at fault. It didn't take much
To bring this sensation to life, along with the certainty
That everybody but my friend saw through me.

But he didn't. He walked along in his
Crisp military stride, shoulders braced, head erect,
And never looked back.
He was going to make up for lost time
And I was going to help him.

# Never, Ever Land

We had dreams
dreams of freedom and dominion and taciturn
Self-sufficiency,
Dreams of transformation.

It was a good night to sing
And we sang for all we were worth
As if we'd been saved.

Memory has its own story to tell, but I have done my best
to make it tell a truthful story.

I had my own dreams of transformation.[6]

Anon E. Mous

---

[6] This is a "found" or collage poem utilizing lines and phrases from Tobias Wolff's *This Boy's Life*.

# Extinguish

### SUBMITTED to *THE MASQUE*

There is something staring at me. Although lonely, I am not alone. An echo of the door clicking shut behind me recurs in my mind. There is no other egress, save the air vent in the upper corner of the farthest wall. Four tiled walls. Each white, separated by a plastic curtain, once clear, sparkling, and see-through, displaying a colorful map of the world; a map that is now cracked and faded, its lines barely visible. I have this feeling. This odd feeling. I've had it before. It's like, like the opposite of déjà vu; I'm not experiencing anything again, but I am seeing, feeling, sensing, what happens next. The cold touch of the porcelain on my bare hip. Goose flesh spreads in pink ripples down my thigh.

"Naked." I pronounce aloud, as if words would provide some kind of company or cover. "Nek-id," I say again, one of my favorite words and least favorite feelings, as if someone is watching the minute I take off the last piece of clothing. (A thousand celluloid images flash through my mind; each an arched woman's foot, the final piece of clothing slipping free of it. It doesn't occur to me that each of these films is a horror film, and that each of these women would soon die.)

I forget the mirror and focus on the vent. Dust, cobwebs, some sort of filth clings like Spanish moss to slats of the vent and sways in and out with barely perceptible inhalations and exhalations of cool air. More goose pimples. My hand lingers on the shower curtain as I focus on the rhythm of each breath. I-n and o-u-t. I-n and o-u-t. S-l-o-w-l-y. Just as I am about to pull back the curtain, the vent pauses its movement for just a second, before coughing to life stronger than before. This movement, this cough, this time a *warm* breath launches three moths into the otherwise still air.

Their sudden appearance is both peculiar and predictable. When you are lonely for years at a time, you get to where you can sense the presence of others. I have stayed up entire nights listening to the mice race back and forth on my kitchen floor. I have tracked the flight of a single mosquito in my living room for hours at a time. The buzz of a bee could wake me from my deepest slumber. The moths enter as quietly as a chainsaw, although they make no sound.

These are city moths. Country moths are twice the size, hairy and flat-out gross. Caterpillars with wings. City moths are thin, comparably beautiful, almost fairy-like. Their wings are nearly transparent, not so much a particular color, but more a glossy, fractured reflection of the colors around them. As they flitter haphazardly in front of the curtain, the colors of their wings change in waves – first aquamarine out over the Indian Ocean, then magenta over Africa and then silver as they approach Antarctica. It is as if they change shape and color at will. I am envious. The light catches their outlines and tiny membranes and shines through.

Their presence reminds me that I am naked causing me to pull a towel up to cover my front, while swinging my arm to keep them from flying behind me. Both their sudden appearance and their presence scare me. Their existences are miraculous, but fleeting. Where did they come from, where do they go? What is the point? Why here? Why now?

A shower suddenly sounds even more like a bad idea than it did before. I do not want to be in the bathroom at all, but I do not want them to escape either. Who knows what would happen? I know that they must go away, but I am not about to go near them, much less touch them.

I have an idea. I quietly step out of the bathroom and get a candle. I light it, put it on the closed toilet seat and turn off the light. I am nervous that I am doing something wrong, or that the moths will escape and hurt me. I shut the door. The click of the latch on the doorknob resounds again. This time making me feel safer; I am on the right side of the door.

Still draped in a towel. I slide down the wall opposite the door to sit on the floor and wait. I wonder how the moths manage to scare me. That is what I am thinking about while I wait for the moths to be drawn into the flame. I hate the idea of killing anything, but a moth being drawn to a light, only to be singed and burned by that light seems normal to me. It is their fate, right? It's like one of those awful things in life that happen so often it becomes normal, commonplace, like the way everyone seems to have some form of cancer these days. I hear that type of news so often, it is as common as a cold. What? Cancer? Oh phfew, I thought you had been in an accident. You scared me. Yes, of course, that's too bad, but everything will work out. (During every one of these conversations, I am silently praying that the next call from this particular friend will come only after the chemotherapy is complete. I like to hear the word remission, other prognoses make me anxious. More anxious that is. Anxiety is my m.o.).

I am not sadistic in any way. I do not want to kill these moths, I just want them dead. Maybe not even dead, but just gone. All I was trying to do was take a shower like Dr.

Mullen said I should. Baby steps just like he said. Just like I promised. If I could pretend they weren't there, I would skip the shower and go straight to bed. Tomorrow will be a better day for baby steps.

Although I know she will be furious with me, I call my mother's cellphone. I cry into her voicemail that she has to please come and help me. I am careful not to sound hysterical. I neglect to tell her exactly what is so terrifying. I ask her to please come home as soon as possible. I know she is going to be mad, but there's no one else left to call.

I return to my watch on the floor outside the bathroom. Again I can see, feel and sense what will happen next. I picture the fitful blue flame atop the candle. I picture its flickering and flashes. Its red-hot center. I picture the flight of the moths across the map of the world. From afar I admire their flight, the beauty of their wings, their evanescence. They fly boldly. They traverse whole continents, sail seas, scale mountain ranges in the dark as they ride their jumpy, circuitous orbits to and from the flame. Like Icarus, they fly toward the sun. Like a Siren, the flame beckons their return. Like Anne Sexton, this is how I want to die.

~ Anon E. Muss 2002

# Mountains

Your high school graduation signified nothing. You were going to college, most of your friends were going to jail. You drank beer and pierced one another's ears before the ceremony. You arrived with blood on your gowns; no one seemed to notice. The ceremony was a tremendously long list of names. No one in your family was there. When you got up to speak, your friends thought you were fucking with everyone, that you weren't actually supposed to give a speech. You never really told them about your grades, and they never asked. They didn't seem to recognize or care that you went off to different classes every day. They hadn't connected the dots, and you weren't about to help them. When they asked you about your plans you always said, "yawn, college." You never used the name of that school in Boston.

The Sagamore Hill graduation was a grand affair. The boys wore chalk white pants with matching suede bucks and blue sky seersucker with boutonnieres and white straw boaters. The girls all wore Caucasian gowns and carried blood red roses. The band was tuxedoed in black, and the chorus robed in crimson and dishwater grey. Bunting and flowers and ribbons and plants and trees decorated the school. From the stage you saw fifty rows of white chairs in front of the smiling face of the sea. White chairs arranged in perfect rows throughout the courtyard reminded you of the tombstones in Arlington cemetery.

Similar to the ritual of a wedding, you, Finn, and Pussy sequestered yourselves in the headmaster's office before the ceremony began making for twenty of the most awkward minutes of your awkward lifetime. A week ago you could have wiled away hours together. Today you didn't speak until Finn asked you to "pick your poison" revealing a small bar hidden inside the Victorian dollhouse he had in the corner of his office. The crystal glasses actually had the names of poisons etched on them. Yours was hemlock; Pussy's was arsenic. A drink helped ease your tension. Pussy required several more. By her third, she was ready to talk. She started somewhere in the middle of a conversation she must have been having with herself.

"So you're sleeping with her?" She rasped, inflected somewhere between a question and a statement, loudly enough for Finn to have understood every word. You did your best to avoid looking at him and still discern his reaction. He looked down and stirred his ice with his finger.

"*Sleeping with* who?"

"It's 'whom,' by the by." Finn said partially to himself.

"Fine. *Fucking*. Are you fucking her? Is that better?" She thought you were questioning her terminology.

"I meant, to whom are you referring?"

"Puh-lease. You and that seventh grader. Are there others?"

There was no real answer to these questions. None that would save you. No way to fix this. Appearance is reality here, which is a quality you used to enjoy.

"She has a name. And technically she was a twelfth grader. And no, I'm not. And no, there are no others." Other than you.

"She's still 12."

"14."

"Are these important distinctions? She's a child for fuck's sake. So do you wish you were? Or you just aren't anymore."

You had never heard Pussy swear before. It would have been funny if the situation weren't so sad.

When you first heard knuckles rapping on the door, you assumed they were a sign we should lower our voices. When Asshead poked his head in to say, "Chief, we are ready for you," it took you a minute to understand what he meant. The opening strains of "Pomp and Circumstance" helped. It was time to lead the graduates up the center aisle.

They were arranged three abreast in order of their height, casting long shadows in black ink. We trailed behind a series of velvet banners decorated with a variety of dead languages and abstruse symbolism. You are in no mood for hermeneutics. The final banner is one word: Meliora, which means "better."

The program is embossed with the official school title for the ceremony: The Centennial Closing Exercises, along with a black silhouette of Teddy Roosevelt. You tried to maintain the attitude of someone who was both a participant in and a spectator of a great event.

> **It is impossible for someone to lie,**
> **unless he thinks he knows the truth.**
>
> ~**Harry Frankfurt**

The ceremony was a trip through the past. Adults read Latin from scrolls. Teachers wore black robes and the colors of their university. The graduates responded to pronouncements with phrases like "so be it" and "it is done." A Chinese gong would have provided a nice finishing touch. The program slated your speech at the very end of a long list of activities allowing your anxieties to grow ever larger. The Lord's Prayer was recited. Songs like "Morning has Broken," "Go Forth with a Song" and "America the Beautiful" were sung. Boys and girls were moving back and forth, up and down, sitting, standing and singing in the orderly bustle that is graduation. Although there were only 28 students in the graduating class, their parents, siblings, grandparents, aunts and uncles, along with the rest of the upper school and their parents and the founders and their families and faculty and their spouses and recent graduates and their friends amounted to an audience of around 500 people. Inside your head, that radiator from this morning was still hissing.

The "Presentation of Prizes" seemed to be what everyone was waiting for. Almost all of the awards had long fancy names or were named after founders or former headmasters, all except two: best boy and best girl. These titles seemed left over from a different era when the general public was more inclined to consider people in terms of "best" and "brightest" and even "boy." All of the awards had unofficial names as well. Although best boy and best girl hardly needed a nickname, they were referred to as "the golden child awards" because they went to people who usually did not have the highest grades and were not the best athletes, but they were people who did everything well and easily, including simply walking the earth with grace and good humor.

"The biggest pussy award" earned its title back when it was called "Beaver of the Year." It was the only award for which the students had a say, therefore the faculty dubbed it the BP Award because it always went to one of the school's beautiful people. Still the faculty was often surprised by the choices. This year's winner, Montgomery Burke, probably won because his three older brothers had won. His brothers had illustrious athletic careers that led them to play hockey and lacrosse for MIT, Annapolis and West Point, college choices that further solidified the family reputation as people who stood out from the crowd. Monty himself was nothing special. It was hard to say whether or not the jagged scars on both of his wrists influenced the voting. The "biggest weenie award" went to the student with the highest four-year grade-point average. The "Carrot Top award" usually went to the biggest character. The academic department awards were most often given to the favorite student of each respective department chair. In English we weren't even allowed to nominate candidates much less vote. The "Uncle Tom award" went to the student who worked the hardest and contributed the most to the school. The alumni award, named after a founder with the unfortunate last name Gay, became the "homo award."

The awards were followed by more singing, "We May Never Pass this Way Again" (Seals & Croft) and "I Will" (Lennon and McCartney). By this time your lips are stuck to your teeth, and you can't crack a smile.

For the "Presentation of Diplomas," seniors were seated by height in the front rows. One by one their names were called out, and each student disassociated him or herself from the group and marched forward alone down the center aisle. The call was alphabetical. As each student passed down the aisle, there was applause, perfunctory for some, pronounced for others. Pussy then shook hands with each student, while conferring the diploma with her left hand. After the diplomas were awarded, each student paused by the headmaster's side. Dr Fenstermacher, sweeping the assembly with his all-embracing, sharp, haughty gaze, like a beam from a lighthouse, spoke about each individual student. Sometimes he referenced memories from primary school. Some were heartfelt and touching. Some made you wonder why he didn't ask teachers for ideas. Having a family spend several hundred thousand dollars on over a decade of education and the only memory the headmaster can recall is a vague reference to a memorable smile or a pair of sunglasses or the way you would put your arms above your head signaling a touchdown whenever something went your way were such superficial contributions that they had the opposite of the intended effect. Each year people left graduation fuming.

You were as surprised as everyone else when Pussy arrived at the L's in the alphabet and called out, "Wendy Love." Love, wearing red and seated with the chorus, stood and approached the stage. You knew Love intended to go to college full-time next year, but you did not know that she wanted to leave Sagamore Hill or that the school was going to let her graduate with the twelfth graders. The audience seemed just as surprised; the applause for Love was so perfunctory that it was inaudible above all of the whispering and head wagging. You tried to maintain the same attitude toward applause and eye contact for Love as you had for the others. While most faculty children have their faculty parent hand them their diploma, Love received hers from Pussy like the others. Pussy chose not to smile for Love, and Finn took pains not to mention the fact that Love was the only 14-year-old graduate in the 100-year history of the school or that she had been in sixth grade just last year. He didn't mention her college courses. Her little vignette was the clearest goodbye of any of the others. He didn't mention her hair either. For the occasion she has spiked her Mohawk straight up, stretching a foot above her head. She was pale, her skin flawless except for one pimple artfully flourishing beneath her plump lower lip. Clearly he had conceded about the diploma and its public conferral, but wanted as few people as possible to notice, which was a ridiculous goal at this point. You think, am I the only one wondering if she has a child growing inside of her?

Your introduction as graduation speaker occurred so soon after Love's diploma that the two events appeared to be linked.

Slowly, very slowly, you trod to the podium, looking neither to the left nor the right, but straight ahead, fixedly, your chin up, carefully, not faltering, steady. You were pleased to have the podium to rest your hands and hide how much they were shaking. As you stood at the podium your legs began to shake too. If you had coughed, the air would have filled with butterflies. You begin by beginning.

"I've had one particular recurring dream since coming to Sagamore Hill. It begins with me standing in front of a class of fifteen students. When I look down at my schedule it is blank, and my notebook is empty. I have no notes anywhere. I am immediately frantic. What do I do? What do I say? What subject is this? What class? Which period?

"Experience tells me something: stall for time. Something will come to me. I rely on the tried and true method of erasing the board as a stall tactic. Something will come to me. I turn repeatedly to clean the chalkboard, while occasionally turning back to my notes imagining that something might appear. Yet, each time I turn back toward the class, it doubles in size before my eyes. This fascinates me, and I begin just turning back and forth and fixating on watching the class grow in size. Finally I am left standing in front of hundreds of people, unsure of what to say, unsure of just how to begin.

"I've had one particular recurring dream since coming to Sagamore Hill. It . . . begins . . . with me . . . standing in front of a class of fifteen students . . ."

You paused for effect, looking confused, unsure of yourself.

"So I guess you could say I am living a dream being up here today. Rest assured, I'm *pretty sure* this is not a dream; because in the real version of the dream I am bald and in my underwear."

You stepped out from behind the podium and touched your head and your coat and tie. You breathed a heavy sigh of relief, hunched over for effect, took big gulps of air.

"You have no idea just how lucky you are.

"Students, Parents, Faculty, and Alumni, I come before you, to stand behind you, to tell you something I know nothing about: life.

"William Faulkner said, 'It the writer's privilege to help man endure, by reminding him of the courage and honor and hope and pride and compassion and pity and sacrifice which have been the glory of his past.' Today it is my privilege to attempt to do the same thing. Today, Eich bin Sagamore Hill.

"If only I could have started my education at a school where the headmaster greets *everyone, every morning* with a handshake and a smile. My principal used to greet me at the door every morning, but she was never smiling and her hands were not extended for a *friendly* greeting. It didn't take long for me to figure out I was not the only one she greeted this way, but I was the only one she referred to as "Mr. Smarty-pants." This is a more vital and loving place than I remember my school ever being.

"Sagamore Hill is a sanctuary. We preserve children here. We have given you a place to live and grow, safe from the mediocrity and violence of our surrounding world. For me the most moving part about being up here today is not the fact that so many of my students are graduating, but that so many of their parents are Sagamore Hill graduates. I am humbled to think that I have been asked to talk about Sagamore Hill in front of Robin Señor, Cole Grace, Barcley Conner and Carolyn Periwinkle . . . among many others . . . all people who not only graduated from Sagamore Hill but who returned to entrust their children to us. To me that act is filled with more profundity than I could ever offer here. To me, this school can receive no higher praise and no stronger vote of confidence. To me this picturesque setting is symbolic. This building, this day, the trees, the blue sky above us, the rows of shining faces are all symbolic of what goes on in this building on a daily basis, that is to say, something beautiful, something extraordinary.

"You see, my dream was not so far-fetched. The good news is we have provided you with survival skills—reading, writing, reckoning and reasoning, the bad news is that we will not do so without exacting a price. Reading and writing—those were minimum requirements. There are many greater lessons we have taught. Having been shaped by history and tradition, each of you owes a debt to it. Having been formed in this community, you have the obligation to become its emissaries to the world. The world requires certain things of us, but the tradition of Sagamore Hill requires more. In case you want to plan ahead, this is what you will be required to know:

- The world needs people who take injustice personally.
- We need people who are willing to be unpopular.
- We need people who will admit when they are wrong.
- We need people who share.

- We need people whose loyalty is primarily to the world, not the nation, for we have reached a point where we must see the welfare of all human beings as inextricably linked.
- We need people who are concerned with the world of the spirit, the world of non-physical things – love, humor, intellect, sweetness, friendship, loyalty, talk, ideals and ideas—all things that you can't hold in your hand.
- We need people who understand that the more we know the more we are in touch with what we don't know.
- We need people, like Jefferson, Emerson, Thoreau, Lincoln, Dickinson, Angelou, Kennedy and King, who believe that singular, even quietly spoken words can change the world.
- Who we are is who we were. No amount of talk after the fact changes the fact. Who you are is who you have been all of these years. You are Roosevelts and Graces and Loves. You are artists and poets and athletes.
- When one has put away all of the books, and all the words, when one is alone with oneself, when one is alone with God, what is left in one's heart? Just this: we live and we die. Life is finite. Things come to an end. Endings make beginnings and middles so very important.

"How will you know you have succeeded? How will you know if you have repaid your debt? The Book of Timothy provides a simple test. Ask yourself two questions:

* Have I pursued justice, truth, faith, love, charity and patience?
* Have I fought the good fight?

"Before I go I would like to say this to Sagamore Hill parents: In his book *The Prophet*, Khalil Gabran describes the parent as an archer's bow that launches the arrow of the child into the world. I contend that the two of us together, you and Sagamore Hill, make for a strong bow and your young arrows should fly far.

"To the ladies and gentlemen of the Twelfth Grade, I leave you with a Tibetan proverb. An ambitious young man is said to have set out to visit the mountaintop where the greatest wise man lived. Although he could not reach the peak where the wise man resided, he called out to him from below. He asked the wise man to tell him what he sees from his exalted place on top of the mountain. After looking forward calmly first to the right and then to the left, the wise man called back to the young man, "MORE MOUNTAINS!"

"I congratulate you for climbing the Sagamore Hill mountain. You could have gone to another school where the workloads were lighter and the teachers were less demanding. And you are better for having remained here. However, there are more and higher mountains ahead that will need to be climbed. Because you began here, I have faith that you will have the confidence and strength to scale any peak.

"T.S. Eliot said, 'Home is where one starts from.' Sagamore Hill is where you started. Therefore, Sagamore Hill is home. Please return to visit. This is a place–like home–where you are always welcome.

"I've been to a lot of fancy schools, read a lot of thick books, and climbed my share of mountains, but until last year I had never been to Sagamore Hill. And I have never known young people as talented and as fortunate as you.

"I thank you for sharing this place with me. It has been an honor and a pleasure."

You paused before stepping away from the podium, not for dramatic effect but because you couldn't trust your legs to move. Your muscles felt like wood.

The applause began and then rose. The applause became a storm. It rose and soared and banged and thundered. The whole audience rocked now with release from tension and was still wildly applauding.

You had not expected this response. You had not expected any response other than relief that it was over, and that you had not told everyone to fuck themselves.

You walked to your seat. People were standing now. What were you supposed to do? Bow? You have never had to bow for anything in your entire life. You are philosophically opposed to bowing. You looked out at the audience and tried to smile. You quickly pantomimed a curtsy. You looked at Asshead, and he nodded his head and thinned his lips to say, "not bad, rookie." (So, it wasn't he who had been the cinematographer of your demise.) You sought out Mincemeat, the Latin teacher, your other suspect; he was the only one in the entire audience who was not standing. He had a silver pairs of scissors out and was clipping his nails. His eyes as black as 8-balls. You should have known. Your doppelganger. A bitter pill from a bitter man.

For the final song the chorus shuffled onstage stiffly in their stiff robes. They sang "Seasons of Love" from *Rent* without the interference of the band. You could pick Love's silvery tenor from the other voices. It chimed like a bell. While hers sounded the sweetest, all the voices soared that night. The notes were crystalline. The song floated across the lawn and echoed back, floated across and out to sea.

Words seemed superfluous to music in that moment. The chorus asked the question, "How do you measure a year in the life? In daylights, in sunsets, in midnights, in cups of coffee. In inches, in miles, in laughter, in strife." And repeated the phrase, "525,600 minutes," over and over in response.

The harmonies were so pure and exact your eyes filled with tears. The notes rolled and swelled like the ocean. And you lost yourself in this surf. If lifted everyone up and set them down, lifted them up and carried them off.

Love had the only solo. She was the girl with the blue Mohawk and the perfect pimple, and she touched it once or twice as she sang. She sang:

"525,600 minutes!
525,000 journeys to plan.
525,600 minutes
how can you measure
the life of a woman or man?

In truths that she learned,
or in times that he cried.
In bridges he burned, or
the way that she died."

She finished by imploring the audience to measure the year in love. As she sang she lightly stamped her left heel.

You were close enough to touch Love, close enough to reach out and take her hand.

And that is what you did. Right there on stage in front of 500 people. You reached out and laced your fingers through hers, and she took them without looking and squeezed, and you both closed you eyes. Her hand was so light. And soft.

You distinctly remember begging God for a thirteen-year-old girl, sixteen years ago you begged God for a thirteen-year-old girl, and here she was.

In front of 500 people. You did this. And a chorus sang a song about love, just as your season, your 525, 600-ish minutes, your year in the life commenced.

# The Rest is Silence

It occurs to me now; I knew the people of the Sagamore Hill School intimately and not at all.

On Monday I met with Fensterfucker. He was tanned, rested and relaxed in curt white tennis shorts and a carnation pink shirt. He gestured toward his couch with the head of a tennis racket. About graduation he said, "nice words," while pantomiming a backhand volley. I took that as his version of a compliment. I said, "thanks."

Raising the racket high above his head, he said, "This is what Henry James generally referred to as 'the windup.' Today I distribute the last of the prizes, pensions, husbands, wives, babies, millions, appended paragraphs and cheerful remarks." He was quoting from somewhere.

Gee, what then would he have for me? He tossed three cans of tennis balls and his racket into a madras plaid gym bag. He unzipped the cover on a second racket, tested its weight, grip and balance. His windup did not fit the occasion for which I had dressed.

With his racket as a service tray, he provided me with my prize—a prefabricated letter of resignation on school stationery. I looked at him dumbly. For a fleeting moment I could picture the strange glamour that had once invested this room. Above his mantle the school crest hung proudly with its open book, its anchor, and its beaver. Its Latin motto had been replaced with the phrase "Go Forth With a Song." The Victorian dollhouse that doubled as a bar twinkled brightly in the corner. It occurred to me then that he was not a teacher and that was what made him so reticent with teachers. He didn't know what to say, my world was not his, and he didn't want me or anyone else to know either of those things. He had been on the other team all along. Reared in Manhattan and Montauk, golfed at Crooked Stick and Shinnecock, he knew how to tack and jibe. He knew how to keep this ship afloat. That was his raison d'être. We didn't talk specifically about Pussy or Love. All I had to do was sign the letter. I did. With a flourish he scripted his initials at the bottom of the page, which was inexplicably irritating to me. He asked that I look back at my year at the Sagamore Hill

School with fondness. He assured me that he would; I assured him I would. The meeting was as iffish and offhand as our first, except we didn't hit any golf balls this time.

Still I love this place for what I wanted it to be as much as for what it unashamedly is. With that thought I shrugged. The camera stopped. Freezing him in mid-gesture.

> **"The Clan was like a lizard, if it lost its tail it soon grew another."**
> ~Chinua Achebe

Finn was the lesser of my worries. Brickhouse caught me when I pulled in the driveway. She was trimming the hedges wearing sweatpants and a sun visor. She waved me over with the 15-inch blades of her garden sheers and then went immediately back to stabbing her shrubbery. Her face was red. I had never seen her sweat.

More than anything else, I did not want to lose her, too. I stooped a little in order not to look disrespectfully tall.

In the glaring midday sun, our world grew as quiet as a theater with dimming house lights. She continued to cut and slice, the silver blades glinting and gleaming.

She said that she had learned to put up with a lot having two teenagers, but she had to draw the line somewhere.

I tried to assure her that line drawing was not necessary, that I had not crossed any lines.

She said she felt strongly about the institution of marriage.

It took me a second to figure out what she meant.

I assured her I felt equally strong about marriage. I spoke with seriousness and care, particularly about husbands.

Her laughter held the bitterness of disbelief. It occurred to me then for the very first time that if I wanted to convince her I should have spent the last week convincing others. Like Finn. And my colleagues. Even today, as recently as now, I wince when I remember that. Only a teacher would understand how little fight is left in you each June.

When I was finished, she asked, if I wanted her to forgive me.

I said yes.

She said no.

She said, "Something about this, I don't know, it just feels wrong to me."

"Funny, if you had asked me two weeks ago, I would have said that I have never felt anything that feels so right." I replied.

"That's your problem. Wrong is right to you."

"And up is down."

"Don't make lite. Now is *really* not the time." She held her shears up and snapped the blades shut for emphasis.

"I was agreeing with you."

"There is a difference between alright and all right."

"Are we still talking about me and Mrs. Señor?"

"You mean *Pussy*, don't you?"

"I try to avoid using that word."

"Interesting . . ."

'Why? You call her Robin."

"I'm not her lover."

"Well, that makes two of us."

"I'm not interested in arguing with you."

"Why not? If it will save us."

"Us? There is no us. Even if there were, you are the only one who needs saving."

"It's too late for that."

"Why?"

"I signed my letter of resignation today."

"Why?"

"Finn asked me to."

"You could have said no."

"That didn't occur to me."

"So right is wrong too?"

"It's not always so easy to tell the two apart, you know."

"Especially if you are not trying."

Over her shoulder the front door was wide open; from this angle on the front stoop it looked like her home was the sunshiny sea. It was noon, the water was money green. E Unum Pluribus. The doorways of the North Shore. The elastic bob of the surf was both incongruously cheerful and too much to bear.

"It was an accident."

"What was?"

"All of it, I guess. We live in a world of accidents."

"Well, I don't. Maybe you do."

"Stuff happens."

"No, stuff doesn't. One thing leads to another. People make decisions. Responsible people take responsibility."

I was dredging my mind for things to say and bringing up empty buckets.

"I hope to be a grand example of the fundamental irrationality of man."

"Mission accomplished, professor. Maybe you should write a book about it."

"Any book I write would end up being about you."

Brickhouse squinted through the sunlight at me to see if I was kidding. Another fact is obvious in a similarly tardy fashion—what passed between Pussy and me or me and Love is a liquid and what existed between Brickhouse and me was a solid, as solid as a brick house. I would spend the rest of my adult life searching unsuccessfully for a similar friendship.

"Make me taller in your version."

"Will do."

"And give me a charming accent or something."

"You'll be from Parish, Fransh. You'll wear hoopskirts and petticoats."

"Yesh, exshellent. How will it end?"

"Shwordplay. A duel. The usual. I'll get the girl this time."

"Which girl?"

"You had to ask? I guess you will need to buy the book."

"How do they say goodbye?"

"They don't."

"Nice idea."

"I have only so many goodbyes left in me. Every relationship I've ever had ended with one."

"You need a goodbye thesaurus."

"The Goodbye Thesaurus. Maybe that's what I will call my book."

"Sounds like a plan."

The sun cast a spotlight down on us. Our shadows touched in ways that we couldn't.

"The movie version of me will be stronger; he'll make better decisions."

"Casting should begin immediately."

"I guess 'thank you' doesn't really say what needs to be said."

"It seldom does."

"So 'I'm sorry' is out of the question."

"Especially if you don't mean it."

It ends with a dolly shot. Very Spike Lee. You stay where you are, framed by the loving embrace of the sun. The camera and I roll away, until it is so far away that we can't tell whether you are waving goodbye or hello.

# The Age of Consent

When the police officers came by the boathouse that next morning, the only sound was the creaking leather of their belts and shoes. They stood in the hall, their hats in their hands.

There were two of them, both male. The tilt of their heads, the shuffle of their feet said something less than officious, something like, we regret to inform you, or we really don't enjoy this part of our job.

At high tide in the gauze of morning sunlight, there was nothing left of the world but a great sheet of water with one wooden dinghy bobbing on its surface.

The first one stiffened, then tried not to stiffen, forced a smile but rethought that too.

The second one whistled through his teeth at the view. "Like being inside a postcard" was all he said.

Finally the first one said, "you know why we are here?" as if he didn't want to say so himself. If you've spent your life committing petty crime, one, you are never surprised by the arrival of the police, and two, you learn not to volunteer information.

"I'm hoping you will get to that part."

"Are you Benjamin Goodspeed?"

"Yes."

"Are you aware that the age of consent in this state is 17?"

"What does that have to do with me?"

"Enough apparently."

"Enough what?"

"Enough that you will need to bring shoes and identification with you."

"Am I being arrested?"

"Yes."

"Would you care to elaborate?"

"You are under arrest."

"What are the charges?"

"Don't make this harder than it already is."

"Forgive me for being concerned."

"Will we need these?" The second one said to the first, holding up his handcuffs.

"Will we need these?" The first one said.

"I doubt we will." I said.

"I doubt we will." The first one said.

It was an Abbott and Costello routine without the funny parts.

The back of a police car is an unpleasant place. The doors and windows don't open from the inside. The blue vinyl smelled like my people, the great unwashed, liked crushed dreams and sweat.

> **"Don't let us be sad. Life is so short—and the world is so beautiful. Just to breathe is delicious."**
>
> ~John Wilkes Booth

The police station was a comedy of errors. I stated my name about a hundred times, was finger-printed twice, had my picture taken five or six times by two photographers who were not sure how to operate the camera.

A jail cell makes the back of a police car look like the beach. I couldn't break out of there with a jackhammer and a construction crew.

The whole North Shore was desolate. The wine-dark sea was still. All the cars had their left wheels painted black as mourning wreaths. Swizzle sticks were set at half-mast. As was the moon. Phones were left off the hook; people shuffled about to a chorus of dial tones.

At school virgins set down their bows. Ripe fruit refused to fall. Real toads stopped leaping high. The Italian gardens burned. Weeping willows wept.

A fog horn wailed all night along the water.

"This afternoon marks the beginning of composition. Word composition. Writing. The first wall between one liver and another. Putting thoughts in writing for the other instead of the direct route of speech or touch. I'm both gratified and sad. Talkers and touchers are never lonely but writers are. Here is the beginning of loneliness . . .

**. . . One twinnie is writing on the blackboard:**

**'The fish is jumped.**
**The fish is swimming.**
**The little fish in the sea.**
**The fish he have no leg.'"**

~**Sylvia Ashton-Warner,** *Teacher*

# Writer

### By Wendy Love

The coffee scalds my throat, but I do not notice until the next sip, so intent am I on reading his face, the fine lines, a story of what has happened between Then and Now. A nondescript coffee shop on route 25A, where I have stopped to grab a scone on the way to work. I work at Nikon, writing camera manuals, and I hate going to the office on weekends. Today is Saturday. I was standing in line behind that brown coat as it swished around and its occupant exclaimed, Kay! Is That You? I remember his pallor; now his skin is sandy brown: proof of his time off. Would You Stay For A Cup of Coffee With Me? he asks, and I agree, thinking, fuck work, because he is my hero, lost until this moment in this coffee shop on 25A.

I remember him perched like an elf on the hexagonal table, long legs drawn up to his cleft chin as he talked about the importance of Writing every day. I could hear the capitalization in his voice when he said that: Writing. Writing was not important before he became my teacher. You All Have Something to Say, he insisted, looking out at my twelfth grade class. Write It Down.

Are You Writing? he asks as we sit on wobbly chairs and I pick at my scone. His coat is draped over the back of his chair, and he is wearing a green velvet shirt. I write every day, pages upon pages in my journals. I write on the pad on my dashboard when I am stopped at red lights. I write my name in henna on my girlfriend's back. I write camera manuals, checks, letters, phone messages. No one has ever paid me for my writing; no one is requesting that I do it. Am I writing? A Little, I say. I tell him about part-time college and my pet finch named Atticus and how everyone from my class has moved away or gone to rehab or college.

You're A Fantastic Writer, he told me once, You're Going Places. Don't Let Anyone Ever Tell You Otherwise. I blushed and nodded vigorously. I wanted to go wherever he was going. His articulate hands, chicory eyes, his suede vests and silk shirts with mandarin collars, hailed from somewhere beautiful and far away. A waterfall of glistening hair tumbled down the ionic column of his neck in the picture I kept on my desk.

Are You Still Living In Arizona? I ask.

I remember when he moved to Arizona to become a novelist. My parents had been to Arizona once. They told me about eating fry bread and riding horses through Canyon de Chelly. He would have wonderful adventures, I knew.

No, he said, glancing behind him as if checking to make sure Arizona has not followed him here. He stares into his coffee cup, pushes his hair back behind his ears. I Could Never Picture You in Arizona, I say.

I could picture him performing in the Rose Theatre. I could picture him fighting Tybalt or wooing Rosalind or riding into battle against Henry V. He was a writer and thinker; he belonged somewhere where he could recite poetry in the rain. Arizona Was Beautiful, he tells me; I Learned a Lot. I ask him if he wrote his novel. I always Look for It, You Know. Nearly Every Time I Go Into a Book Store, I Walk Through New Fiction and look up 'Goodspeed, Benjamin.' I Hardly Ever Read Fiction Anymore, But I Go Look for You. He chews thoughtfully on a wooden stir-stick. I Wrote a Novel, he tells me, One Was All I Needed to Write. I'm Working as a Geologist Now. You Look Terribly Shocked, But It's Not That Drastic A Change. I've Created My Own Art, and Now I'm Stepping Back, Looking at the Natural Art That Is the Foundation of This Earth. Rehearsed, but poetic.

I remember how his blue eyes twinkled as he insisted: That story you are dying to tell? Tell it, or it will destroy you." If You Have Something To Write, Nothing Will Be Able To Stand In Your Way. My classmates dozed and passed notes, but I hung on every word.

I Am Kind of Shocked, I admit. It Really Seemed Like Writing Was Your Life. It Was My Life, he tells me, And It Still Is, In A Way. But I Was Not Writing To Become Famous, Or Even To Be Published. I Wrote Because There Was Something Inside of Me That Needed To Be Expressed. Now I Have Done That. Listening to him, I thought: Maybe there are writers and some people who just write. I write camera manuals; that does not make me a writer. But when I commit my dreams to paper, when I write to purge or share or develop my thoughts, and not because I have been told to, not because I'm getting paid, then I am a writer. I wonder if Mr. Goodspeed talks about this in his book. So Where Can I Get That Novel? I ask. He shakes his head. You Don't Need My Novel, My Hand-Me-Down Thoughts, he tells me, his eyes meeting mine and holding them.

I remember how he told us about Shakespeare, his blue writing uncoiling across the whiteboard in curlicue letters. I wanted to learn everything he knew, that wealth of knowledge he poured forth without notes or warning.

It's Benjamin by the way, I said. What is? He replies. His name, I answer.

He stammers over the beginnings of several sentences and finally decides on one. He says, there's a lovely line from Albee's "Tea and Sympathy" that fits here somewhere, Years from now, when you talk about this, and you will, please be kind. He stutters through it as if it were a sentence that had taken him several years to compose.

You Don't Need Me To Be a Writer, he says. It's Time For You To Write Your Own Book. He pats me on the shoulder. I Have To Go Now; It Was Lovely Having Coffee With You. Slipping his coat onto his thin frame, he walks to the door. A brief wave of the hand, and he is gone.

A pen lies on the table. It is too late to motion him back inside and return it. I pick it up. I unfold my napkin, uncap the pen. After all, I am a writer.

"Every place will be a place without her."

~ Michael Ryan

# No Frigate Like a Book

I do not intend to confirm or deny anything.

I live in Harlem. I teach sixth grade language arts at a public school in the Bronx. The walls of my school are covered with wanted posters like at the post office. Police officers patrol the hallways. In every hallway you can hear their radios clicking on and off, listen to the day's crimes unfold. I arrive at school at 8:20 and leave at 2:17 sharp, no exceptions. Union members police the hallways after 3:00, making sure all of the teachers have gone home. We do not read novels because the school does not own any novels. We read from "Readers" which are designed to prepare students for the state-wide language arts exams. Today we read an enchanting and richly human story about a family of impetuous cats and their relationship with a similarly impetuous family of mice. Eighty-five percent of our fourth graders failed the exam last year. I do not write narrative reports; I give grades. E, S+, S, S-, or U. I don't know any of the parents of my students. Teachers here are referred to as Mister or Miss, no last names are used. It's hard getting used to having students call out, "Hey, mister" when you see them everyday. Students have nicknamed me Professor Utonium from the Powder Puff Girls, probably because we are both tall and white and wear ties.

Outside my apartment, minivan mutations with 24-inch chrome spinners and air-brushed dreamscapes blare Salsa music so loudly sometimes it is hard to hear the sirens and the screams. I remember a vicar, whose home I found myself in for reasons I cannot recall, saying that before the race riots in the 60's, he remembered hearing "the music of the Congo" playing day and night in Harlem. The music told him that the riots would happen. He was not surprised when they did.

I do not know what the music of the Congo is, but that is not what I hear. The music I hear tells me that the people here are homesick, that they fear losing themselves by coming here. I can sympathize. I am sick for a home and have always been. Hackysack isn't home. Nor that school in Boston. Nor the north shore of Long Island. I fear losing myself even though I admit I am not sure exactly who I am.

Some people take snapshots—"clicks" the English would call them. They save them. Hang them up. Carry them around. Return to them. Pictures which remind them of that day, or those days, of then or now. I see why they do that finally, for the same reason the Salsa plays all night. People are afraid of losing themselves. My photo albums are empty except for the postcards from lovers I have long since forgotten. (I do love those cards, their dog-eared edges, their line drawings and longing, their hyperbolic speech and clumsy poetry, simple reminders of place and time.) I see things through my mind's eye, colored by years of loss and regret. Focus softens with time, forgetting the awkwardness, the misunderstanding, the bitter, the heartache, the pain—the necessary denial for slumber and survival. My mind's recollection leaves me with vague notions of a life lived, clicks that are more impressionistic than literal.

I can't live this way forever. It seems silly that I spend my days cajoling children to write and then do not heed my own advice. So I have taken to writing myself. Each morning I wake at 5:00 and write until 8:00. Like Maya Angelou, I pour myself a glass of sherry and write. I write for two more hours each evening. I have written a novel. Who hasn't, right? I have to admit; it was my lawyer's idea—that crafty bastard.

> **"Between my finger and my thumb, the squat pen rests; snug as a gun."**
> ~Seamus Heaney

My case was thrown out of court after the charges were dropped by the DA due to a lack of evidence.

After I created the first chapter, I showed it to an old professor. He said it was the best thing he had read in years, and he asked my permission to show it to his agent. His agent loved the chapter and wanted to know what would happen to the characters next. I couldn't tell him that nothing happens next, that chapter two didn't yet exist, that would have ruined my chances. I had to create what happens next. That involved actually writing a chapter two and three and four.

I have never liked hearing authors say that a book wrote itself. Whatever!!! That it just poured out on the page. If that were so, wouldn't novelists be much happier people? Wouldn't they write more novels? But now I know what they are talking about. Please accept my apologies for saying so, but this book wrote itself. It came to me as I typed it out. I knew exactly where each character was headed. I knew what they looked like, how they talked, who loved who and why and where they would all end up. It is exactly as if it had all just happened this way, as if I had actually known these people.

A writer friend of mine said, "Sometimes if the truth is hard, typing it can hurt again." He is right. It did hurt. Again.

Sometimes I feel like I am trying to tell you a dream I had, trying to convey that dream-sensation—the absurdity and surprise and joy and bewilderment—that whispery feeling of being captured by something incredible.

Another funny thing is: I thought novelists were paupers and that they had to support themselves by teaching or editing or subcontracting or driving a taxi. I guess novels are big business these days, especially if your story is set in New York or Los Angeles. Most of the country's book buyers live in NY and LA. I'm serious. Yes, LA. You can look it up. No, not screenplays, actual books. Of course it would be untoward of me to come right out and tell you how much I was paid for my novel, but let's just say, strictly between the two of us, I am going shopping this week. In Manhattan. Below 96th Street. For an apartment. To buy. My perky broker with her half-moon glasses and Chanel Number 5 keeps leaving flirty messages where she refers to me as Mr. Fitzgerald. That kills me. She's a crafty bastard too. I'm considering asking her out.

I hope the picture is becoming clearer for you. You know it now too, don't you? I have an ember in the reed at my side. I am whistling a merry tune. I am walking the walk. The Promethean pimp-walk. The walk that will change me and mine forever. If forever is an awfully long time, and failure has run in my family for an awfully long time, then forever is failure. Or forever was failure. Forever used to bum me out. If this new feeling lasts forever, I'm good with that.

My book is my emancipation proclamation. It will set my people free. No more manual labor. No more hourly wage. No more union. No more second hand. Leftover. Left out. Let go. No more un-invited. No courtrooms and jailhouses. No pink slips. No behind bars and closed doors. No public defenders and no pity.

So, at my lawyer's behest, I am telling my tale. I have been advised not to answer questions and not to provide further clarification. So please don't ask: can I go see the dust cloud? Or, what did you get on your SAT's? Or, do those people really exist?

I told tales. I tattletaled. I created fiction. Fictions. Whole genres concerning me, my, mine. I have always had a hard time separating my facts from my fictions.

The answers are all in my book.

I admit exactly two things: this is a love story, and I am liar.

Edwards Brothers, Inc.
Thorofare, NJ USA
September 2, 2011